The Brazilian

Rosie Millard

Legend Press Ltd, 107-111 Fleet Street, London, EC4A 2AB
info@legend-paperbooks.co.uk | www.legendpress.co.uk

Contents © Rosie Millard 2017
The right of the above author to be identified as the author of this work has
been asserted in accordance with the Copyright, Designs and Patents Act
1988. British Library Cataloguing in Publication Data available.

Print ISBN 978-1-7871998-7-3
Ebook ISBN 978-1-7871998-6-6
Set in Times. Printed in Poland by Opolgraf SA.
Cover design by Gudrun Jobst www.yotedesign.com

Rosie Millard is a journalist, writer and broadcaster. She is currently Chair of Hull UK City of Culture 2017.

Rosie's career includes working as BBC Arts Correspondent for ten years, profile writer at *The Sunday Times*, columnist for *The Independent*, arts editor of *The New Statesman*, theatre critic and feature writer. She makes TV and radio documentaries and appears as a regular commentator for a number of national TV and radio shows.

The Brazilian is a sequel to her first novel, *The Square*, described by Jonathan Maitland as 'A waspish portrait shot through with wit, insight and buckets of glorious bonking.'

Visit Rosie at
rosiemillard1.wordpress.com
or on Twitter
@Rosiemillard

To Phoebe "Miss Brush" Florence.
Keep on being amazing.

Chapter One
Jane

Jane is lying on her back. The beautician in Love Your Body asks her to make a number four shape with her right leg. She is naked from the waist down, save for a pair of paper knickers. Soft pipe music plays hauntingly around the tiny room. There is a bowl of hot wax bubbling in the corner. The beautician looks at her enquiringly, her raised eyebrows suggesting, briefly, that Jane needs to make her mind up. Should it be a Hollywood? Totally hairless? She's got a new swimsuit. She envisages the horror of looking down and seeing a single corkscrewed hair jutting up at her. However, the thought of a completely naked pubic triangle makes her feel queasy. No, it must be the usual. "Yeah, a Brazilian, please," says Jane.

"Going on holiday are we?" says the beautician, as she smooths the wax over Jane's groin with a large wooden spatula and pats the brown viscous gloop down. Jane tenses herself for the moment. Thinking about it is always far worse than the actual experience, but she can't help seizing up. "Yes, yes I am, I mean, we are, huoooo…" she says, half-squeaking and sighing as the beautician swiftly rips off a wide strip of cooled wax with an expert hand. The hairs rip out of the skin, each pulled out from its root. "Ibiza," she manages to tell her white-coated torturer. The beautician puts her hand over the red, naked area.

"It's in the Med, you know, just below Spain. One of the Balearics. Next to Majorca and Menorca." The beautician pastes more hot wax onto this most soft, tender skin. She smooths it down and then once again, scorchingly rips it from the tender flesh, putting her hand down on the angry area. "Oh, I know where Ibiza is," says the beautician. "Now, put your other knee across, love."

One side of Jane's groin is now bright red, speckled with small raised spots. She thinks about the beautician. Smearing wax all over the pubic region of other women and then ripping it away. All in a day's work. Jane doesn't know how she can bear it. Yet it is addictive. Once you start, you can't stop. Furthermore, she loves the complicity of the room, its quiet intimacy untroubled by text messages or Wi-Fi. She wonders how many women come in here a day.

The beautician knows there is a particular person who gets waxing done. This is the fourteenth client she has waxed this morning. She sometimes looks at women on the bus and wonders which of them voluntarily undergoes it. What style they go for. She can usually tell.

"My oldest son is going there too this summer, what a coincidence," she continues nonchalantly. Jane isn't very interested in where the beautician's son is going on holiday. She wants her time here to be wholly about her. She focuses on her holiday. Ibiza. Hot. Delicious. Always sunny, no mosquitos, still fashionable, yet, not too trendy. So no need to bother about all those silly nightclubs and digitally streamed music by bands and singers of whom she has never heard.

"Did ya want your bottom done?" says the beautician. "Roll over then and hold your cheeks open." She lies face down on the bed and obeys the instructions. The paper knickers have a G-string at the back. Why bother, thinks Jane.

Life is rather tiresome at the moment. Jane is living out of suitcases, away from her large London house where she and her husband Patrick have lived for, oh, ages. She can't even remember when they moved in. Feels like years. It's being redecorated from top to bottom after a burst tank connected to the water main drilled down through each of the four storeys. They had to move out into a rented flat in a much less smarter area, around the corner.

Jane dislikes the arrangement. So much so that she has started to deliberately keep herself busy. She peppers each day with a series of treats. Coffee with friends, lunch with better friends, cinema trips. Self-improving appointments. Chiropodist, hair, waxing, mani/pedi, GP, opticians (even though she doesn't need glasses). Shopping. Anything to get out of the flat. There's so many opportunities to make life nicer, thinks Jane.

"Right, that's it. I'll leave you to get dressed. Here's some cream to put on if you like. I'll see you by the reception outside," says the beautician. She goes out of the room and shuts the door quietly. The music continues to tinkle. Jane eases off the bed, swings her legs round, forces herself to inspect the poor, erased skin. Once it has calmed down, turned into an approximation of marble with a single strip of hair, she'll appreciate it. Even if Patrick doesn't. She's been doing this for so long she can't even remember when she started, or even why. She just knows it is something women of her age and class should do.

Forty minutes and a flat white later, she is back in the flat. She wonders when her son will appear. George goes to a private prep school. He is eight. George wears a cap and a striped blazer every day and studies Mandarin, Latin and French. He is also learning to play the piano. Back at their proper home, that is. Jane is not happy here. She does not care for the shame she feels when she gives her address to taxi drivers. Definition by postcode, even a temporary one, is affecting her mood.

By contrast, George is happy. For the first time in his life he has friends next door, two small boys called Jack and Sam. Previously his friends emanated from a giant privately educated diaspora of privilege. Now he has local mates. Jack and Sam do not have to labour over musical instruments, they don't have to do Latin or Mandarin, and they don't seem to have much homework. There is always a reason for George to pop over to Jack and Sam's house and see what's going on, because something good usually is. At the very least, a PlayStation and always lots of snacks. He likes it.

Jane's husband Patrick doesn't mind having a bit of a break either. He's glad to have a change of scene. Things locally had come to a bit of an embarrassing pass for him with a nanny of their neighbour back in the old house. Very good looking. But to be found kissing her, well that was embarrassing. Sometimes he allows himself to think of her. The Polish nanny. Played the piano like a genius. Beautiful fingers. He sighs when he thinks of those fingers and what they did to him. Once, they had actually made love on the kitchen table. That was something. Nobody knew about that, of course. But to be caught kissing her was not clever. He had had to make it up to Jane. In a grand way. Weekends at spa hotels, trips to the opera, that sort of thing. Now the nanny is back in Poland and they are all in this flat. He thinks about how she had lain back on the table pulling up her skirt, unabashed and not wincing about the wooden table top. It was one of the most erotic moments of his life, and he uses it as a mental indulgence in which to revel during dull moments in board meetings.

Jane sways around her room, looking at her face in the mirror. She peers at her features. At the moment, she's happy with Botox, but you never know. She pulls off her top and removes her bra. Is she too old to go topless? Well, in front of George of course, impossible, but privately? She jumps up and down, jiggles them a bit. Then she reaches for a pencil. If you can hold a pencil under your boob that is a sign that they have dropped and you are on the way to menopause and a sexual Gobi desert. That's what she has been told. Although frankly, thinks Jane, what's new about that? She picks up the pencil, puts the cool cylinder beneath one breast, and takes her hand away. The pencil drops to the floor immediately. Good. Still aloft. She flops onto the bed. Who cares? "Oh God I am so BORED," says Jane aloud. Her house is under dust sheets. So is her sex life.

It has been that way since her neighbour moved. Jay. The man next door. Jay and she had – what should she call it – a fling? An affair? Jay and she had an arrangement. The arrangement was basically to have sex. Everywhere. In his house, in her house, in hotels. Once even in the grass in the middle of the square, at midnight. She hadn't been too taken with that occasion, since this was not only dangerous behaviour, but it had been slightly dirty, too. In a real, muddy way, not an erotic one.

Anyway, after that, just after their house was flooded, and just after that silly thing with the Polish nanny, imagine, kissing her husband, Jay had sold up. He actually had the nerve to move away from this great flood of sex with Jane. She occasionally gets the odd risqué text from him. She always deletes them immediately with a fierce, jabbing finger. She'll show him. Who was the winner in their affair? Her for remaining or him for leaving? She imagines him with his wife Harriet, who was large and anxious. Jane stretches out on the bed and thinks about how she is basically superior to Harriet in every way, but particularly the sexual one. He'll be missing that, Jane thought, with burning envy. Well, he should have worked that out before moving, and leaving her.

She lies very still. She wonders if she will go to sleep. Sometimes she does, just from the action of not moving. Her groin still burns from the waxing. She raises her hands above her head and thinks about sunbathing in Ibiza. She can't wait to feel the heat on her body. She's looking forward to paying herself some proper attention, giving herself some proper downtime. She'll have quite a lot of that, she thinks happily. She'll be able to relax. She doesn't need to bother about anyone or anything else. Even George, because of course she is bringing childcare.

Belle is her childcare. How old is she? Jane's not sure. Grown up, but still young enough to be bossed around. She's the daughter of a neighbour. Actually, daughter of the neighbour who employed that awful Polish nanny. But Jane has got over that now. The Polish nanny was sent home, or was sacked, and must never be spoken of. Too old for nannies now, Belle does a bit of babysitting. This year, she's coming on holiday with Jane and Patrick. To look after George. Jane considers Belle has been handed a great deal on a plate. Jolly lucky to be coming on holiday with them. A free trip! And with only one child to look after. And not all day, either. She hears the door slam. George. Off the school bus and home. Jane puts a robe around her shoulders and pads down the corridor.

"Why is she coming, Maman?" says George. "*Pourquoi*?"

"Very good George," says Jane, coming into the kitchen where she encounters her small son playing on her iPad. "*Très bien*." She likes it when he tries out his French on her. "Please turn that off."

"But why?"

"Bad for you."

"What, Belle? Belle is bad for me."

She sighs. "Oh, sorry. Sorry. I meant you and that dreadful iPad. Do you mean why is Belle coming? Because…" she tries to think about what truth will be most palatable to her small son. "Because you'll have fun," she says lamely. "Oh I don't know, darling. It seemed a nice idea at the time. You don't want to spend lots of time with me and Daddy, do you?"

"Yes."

There is a pause. George regards his mother steadily.

"I don't want to go on holiday. Why don't we stay here for the summer? Can't we stay here, please? Jack and Sam from next door aren't going away. Well, I think they might be going caravanning. Can we go caravanning?"

"No we can't. We've got a lovely big villa in Ibiza with a lovely pool, you'll have such fun in that with Belle."

"But why can't I swim there with you? In the pool, why?"

"Well, because, George," says Jane, exasperated. "You'd get bored."

"I wouldn't. You'd get bored, you mean."

George stares into the middle distance. What is Ibiza? Why does it sound like something strange, with that 'th' sound? He tries to imagine having fun in a strange pool with a girl who is twice his age and whom he knows is only looking after him because she wants to go to The Reading Festival. The mental exercise fatigues him. He turns away, trying not to think about the caravanning trip that Jack and Sam are taking. When are they going? He has no idea.

"When does summer begin?" he asks his mother.

Jane sighs. "Well, for you it will be at the end of term, poppet."

"I shall mark it on my Lego calendar," he says, formally. He walks away towards the fantasy world of the Lego Nexo Knights, where nobody is left behind or has to move or is given a chaperone for a fortnight. Maybe I'll build a caravan for my Knights, he thinks.

Jane watches him leave the room. She examines her hands. Decides against a manicure. In a week, she'll be away. Last night, she had asked Patrick what he thought about inviting some friends over to stay in the Ibiza villa. He had looked actually quite angry about it.

"Like who? I thought that we were meant to be having time together. On holiday. As a family. It's bad enough bringing Belle, to be honest. Why on earth do you want to bring people from over here out there, when we can see them here any time?"

But we don't, thinks Jane. We don't see them. I wouldn't want to see them, or entertain them here. Not in this scummy flat.

"Anyway," continued Patrick, "we will have Belle looking after George during the day, and I understand you've arranged her to cover for most evenings as far as I can see. If we have a whole gang of people over we will hardly see him at all.

What about the idea that we focus on the notion of a Family Holiday, with Family Time?"

"Oh, of course," she had said, kissing him.

Now, on her own, she thinks about this vision. Family Time. It is always best when firmly in the future, Jane muses. It starts with wonderful plans involving notions of picnic baskets and rugs, and ends with a row, rain, and a mercy dash to a restaurant. Or someone being sick in a car. Why does Patrick go on about it so much, when he can't see how nice it would be to have some adults over to stay with them? On the other hand, she considers, examining her nails again, maybe he's right. She knows friends on holiday ought to be a time for hilarity, shared experiences, long tables draped simply and crisply in white linen, groaning with perfect food while people drink and whoop with laughter and indulge in perceptive and witty conversation. The reality is more like a weekend of misery with bad mattresses. Three rain-swept days of sniping, fatigue, chaos over meal choices, subtle analysis of body fat, and competition surrounding salaries, children, schools, husbands and basement extensions. All overlaid by the crushing weight of hangover.

Anyway, having friends visit would mean she would have to look after them. Whereas on this trip, she can relax all day long if she chooses. Belle will be doing all the heavy lifting, while she, Jane, will be luxuriating in bed. Would Patrick be luxuriating with her? Probably not. He is not in her mental picture of the bedroom. He is in the kitchen, washing up. Or playing with George. Or working. Or driving. Doing many, many things. Just not in bed with her. She tries to imagine Patrick covering her body with cream and then licking it off, as Jay once did. She thinks longingly of Jay making love to her, the way they used to sneak out for afternoons in hotels. She thinks of how he used to pull all her clothes off, desperate, practically before the door closed. Or when they had no hotel reservation and instead made love in the spare bedroom of his house. That was weirdly compelling.

She used to want to leave her underwear beneath the bed, for Harriet to find, her fat fingers pulling on the lacy, flimsy pants and wondering whose they were. She had fantasies of confronting Harriet, of forcing her to leave Jay. These had never happened, of course. Jane knew she was too cowardly to face her.

Thinking about Jay makes her think of home, of her home. She forgets about sex. She remembers, suddenly, that she has an unpleasant fact to process. Her insides clench with the recollection.

Yesterday she had had a text from Tracey, Belle's mother. *Jane! So funny! I must tell you that not one but I think TWO of our neighbours are also on their way to Ibiza – in a TV programme! It looks like the dreaded Alan Makin, you know, the TV finance guy who lives in Jay's old house, and that very strange artist Philip Burrell are BOTH doing some TV reality show. Can you believe it? You might bump into them! Amazing! Tracey xxxx*

Jane had looked at this missive for a long, long time before deleting it crossly. Why have these two people been chosen for television glory and fame? Alan Makin she could understand, she supposed. After all, he is a television presenter, or at least he has been. But Philip Burrell, that crazy artist? She always particularly disliked him. Apparently he keeps pornographic pictures of his wife on the kitchen walls. As for his art! Emperor's new clothes, she calls it. She can't believe that people pay thousands of pounds for it. In her view, it is about as artistic as a Scalextric track. Tiny models of marathon courses and golf courses, rendered on boards which you then hang on the wall. You call that art? thinks Jane. She doesn't. And now they are on a big TV show and everyone will watch it and think they are achievers.

Jane was once quite keen on appearing on television herself. Someone once said to her that she had 'a natural face for the screen', and when she gave up working in the

City, she had actually signed up for a £3,000 television presenting course and learned to read off an autocue. She hired an agent, who charged her £850 for a showreel and never sent her to one audition. After a while, she had buried the dream. Occasionally, like now, it chose to resurface. It had been her ambition. She had wanted to be famous. Had wanted? Still wanted.

It was just so unfair. Act like an arse and a show-off, like Philip Burrell does and that silly Alan Makin, who bought his way into the Square without so much as an invitation, just slapped his money down, and what happens? You get on television. Quietly get on with being sophisticated and stylish, like her, and what happens? You get ignored.

Fame and sex, thinks Jane. These things are important to her. She wants to have both of them. She has neither of them. And she's in her forties. In a few years, she won't be able to have either of them. Pack your stuff, she thinks. Pack for the holiday. That will push the pain away from her chest. She actually has a pain in her body from envy. She throws the empty case on the bed, pulls armfuls of clothes from her wardrobe, presses them all down into the rigid box, amassing outfit after outfit which she imagines might delight the locals in the village where she will wander, flip-flops slapping on the sunny pavement, for her morning espresso.

"Maman?"

She spins round, sees her child in the doorway.

"What, George? Can't you see I'm packing? Have you packed?"

"Yes, and yes." He plumps onto the bed. "Belle packed for me."

"Belle? When did she come here?"

"Oh," airily, "she came over when she dropped her case off earlier today. It's in the hall. Didn't you see it? Can I take my Lego?"

She hugs him tightly, inhaling the fragrance of his soft hair. Maybe it doesn't matter. Philip and Alan, they will be famous but they are childless. So. She has that over them. They don't have the loyalty of a George. Her son will love her regardless of her dalliances, and misdemeanours, and regardless of the fact she has hired a nanny to look after him during their family holiday.

Chapter Two
Simon

Stansted Airport, 0730 hrs. The team stands, wearing large anoraks and baseball caps, waiting for something known as the 'Carnet'. The Carnet is a customs document allowing the admission of television equipment into a foreign country without the need to pay duty. "Have we got the Carnet yet, chaps?" shouts Simon to two men in the middle distance. He chews gum anxiously. "Come on, come on." Simon is the director. It's his job to get the crew to Ibiza.

His production manager, Kate, walks up to him. A woman wearing a roll-neck jumper, carrying a large file and whose only gesture to grooming is a sleek blonde bun of hair, she rubs his shoulder affectionately. "IIWII," she whispers. "It Is What It Is." Simon smiles, as if her touch is painful. Two weeks of 24/7 filming in and around a beachside villa in Ibiza putting a bunch of nobodies through a series of ridiculous tasks. Particularly as they are all trying to be somebodies. Plus one massive celebrity to arrive later. He sighs, thinks of the money, all that overtime. It must be worth it. He'd far rather be working on *Panorama*. "Come on, guys," he mutters beneath his breath.

While the crew fiddle around with a stack of bright, hard, shiny, ridged cases, the nobodies sit at a table drinking tea and, in one case, whisky. They are the cast for the latest series of the well-known daytime ITV reality show called

Ibiza (or Bust). Each of them has signed up to go on holiday with nine other unnamed, vaguely notorious people. In Ibiza. For at least a week, possibly more. The hitch? They each vote each other off. Everyone gets a £3,000 fee for turning up and taking part. The final person on the show gets £20,000. They have all just performed the first task, namely the staged 'Meet'.

Simon told them each what to do and they obeyed him to the letter, like children. Everyone was brought out one by one. They were each obliged to kiss everyone else, twice, on the cheek and gush with unbridled and spontaneous happiness. As if they knew each other. As if they were friends. Famous friends. They must enthuse that they are all going on holiday together to Ibiza. The show promotes togetherness, but is of course designed to highlight separation, confusion and confrontation. They greet each other but inside, their heads are whirring with alarm and confusion as they struggle to identify each other. They are strangers but must seem as friends, individuals pretending to be a gang.

They have been selected by Simon. They include Philip Burrell, a contemporary artist with as yet unfulfilled ambitions on winning the Turner Prize and a TV financial adviser called Alan Makin. Both of these characters live on a notoriously prestigious square in North London. They do not like each other. Then there is Gemma, a 'celebrity estate agent', who Simon rather suspects will go out first, and an ageing man known as Jasper The Wizard, who once had a magic show a long time ago on ITV. Then there is a married couple, Nigel and Jocelyn, presenters of *Families Ahoy!*, a travel show on a distant satellite channel for 'adventurous parents and their offspring', a 'celebrity farmer' known as Moo, whose fame largely lies in the feat of feeding a baby lamb with human breast milk on Breakfast TV, and his partner, Cresta, an obviously sexy It Girl who may or may not have provided the breast milk. Finally, thinks Simon, the chap he keeps forgetting. A contemporary hippie and environmental protester called Fish.

This bunch is going to be joined on the island by a tenth, as yet unknown celebrity. It is this person's availability that is responsible for not only the time, but also the place of the filming. This is someone who is properly famous, thinks Simon. He's told the other contestants, the nonentities, about the arrival of a tenth celebrity and was gratified to see the effect it provoked. There is a distinct sense of tension about the group, aided by the faint aroma of body odour.

"Well," says one of the Adventurous Parents, stretching her hands high above her head and in the process, revealing two dark patches that have already started to form underneath her arms. "Hope getting away has been easy for everyone. It's been a piece of cake so far for us. We haven't even had to worry about clearing it with the kids' schools." She looks around, hoping someone will challenge her on this. "Because they are all homeschooled, of course," she continues.

"How many children have you got?" asks Gemma the celebrity estate agent, who has a strong sense of conversational duty.

"Eight," says the Adventurous Parent.

Gemma widens her eyes, and can't think of anything to say.

"My pelvic floor is just fine, if that's what you are wondering," says the Adventurous Parent, "isn't it, Nigel?"

Her husband giggles inanely.

Gemma, who has no children, is lost for words.

"You've moved into the Square?" says Philip to Alan Makin, the TV financial adviser, with scant enthusiasm. Philip is not sure he is very pleased about this. Finding a neighbour on this show was not part of his plan. Indeed, he had hoped that he might achieve this daytime televisual challenge wholly undetected. Philip is a snob about most things, but particularly about daytime television.

"Indeed I have!" says Alan loudly, looking around at

20

the other candidates. "Hey everyone, Philip here and I are neighbours! I judged a talent show there earlier this year. Fell in love with the Square. Wonderful Georgian rigour. Marvellous use of light in the main rooms. Do you know it, Gemma? Part of your catchment area? Great heritage. Very, very well refurbished, if I may say so. Didn't, er, didn't you take part in it, Philip? The talent show, I mean. I remember you were there, weren't you? Great fun."

"I may have done, dear boy," says Philip, who remembers the event quite well. "So many things going on at the moment." He stares off into the distance. He is already regretting signing up for this nonsense, regretting leaving his wife Gilda behind, regretting leaving all his work just sitting idle in the studio. His assistant, Jas, is going away too. There'll be lot of work when he gets home. He's damned if he'll be voted off first, however. Let that idiot Alan Makin go for the fall.

A silence descends as everyone muses separately on the forthcoming challenge. "Well, here we all are," says Gemma unnecessarily, touching her hair. "I was really amazed to see who else would turn up on this!" She examines a manicured hand. "I mean, it's going to be great fun. I really have no idea what to expect! Who do you think is going to win? Although of course I don't think it's about winning, of course. It's just about making some great telly, isn't it! You guys. We are all going to have a hoot! It's just about fun!"

"No," says Philip drily. "It's about winning."

There is a silence. Jasper The Wizard drains his whisky rather loudly and stands up, barely concealing a burp. "Sorry, chaps. Right. Anyone for Departures?"

"Are we all getting on?" asks Simon, bustling over to the table. "Have we all got our boarding passes, hand luggage, everything? Has everyone been to the loo?"

"We are not children," says Philip acidly, quickly smiling in Simon's direction to let him know that he didn't really mean it. "Arse," he mutters under his breath.

The group is herded by Simon beside the Body Shop while a camera sets up the shot, and then on instruction from Simon, moves together, talking and wildly laughing, towards Customs. Cresta, the It Girl, leads the charge. Gemma notices that Cresta always makes sure she is surrounded by a herd of men, swinging her hair back and giggling whenever the camera focuses on her.

"And… cut!" shouts Simon. "Brilliant! You are all naturals!" Kate walks up to him and peers over his shoulder at the group. "How on earth are we going to cope with this gang?" she murmurs.

"I have absolutely no idea," replies Simon. "But that is the magic of television."

At the gate, Alan Makin cheers up immensely because he has been recognised by a member of the public. "Did you see that?" he says, laughing loudly as he wanders back from WH Smith. "Lady over there when I was buying a copy of the *Mail*. Noticed me. Comes rushing over, oh she was so happy to see me. Loves the shows! Think I probably made her day. Of course, I had to have the obligatory selfie with her." He looks quickly across the group.

"That's nice," says Gemma. "I bet that happens to you a lot."

"Well, from time to time," says Alan modestly. "I still have the old fan base."

The others remain silent. Alan's fame and their comparative lack of it, a lack that might prove fatal on this show, hangs quivering in the air.

"I was once recognised on the Great Wall of China, funnily enough," says Jasper, presently.

Nobody says anything.

"Come on, then!" shouts Simon, making herding motions with his hands.

Chapter Three
Belle

"So this is the deal, again," says Belle to Jas. "Because it's you, I'll go through it for the fourteenth time! As I said. It goes like this. I have to look after George every morning, get him up, AND give him breakfast. So they, his mum and dad, can sleep in. Right?"

She smiles at Jas. He rolls his eyes.

"These people."

"I know. What the hell. Then we, that is George and me, we hang out by the pool or go and build sandcastles or something. Fun stuff. After lunch, I think I have some time off. Who knows? In the evenings, his mum and dad will be out. They've told me this already. They like eating out. So... looks like I'll be babysitting until about ten. And that's not going to be difficult. Put him to bed, simples. Oldies get back and THEN the fun begins. I sneak out, yes, sneak out, and meet up with you somewhere."

"Really?"

"Honestly, it will be cool. Probably somewhere quite nearby, well definitely quite nearby because I can't afford a taxi. Then we just have fun in the night. All of it. As long as I'm back in my room by about 7.00 in the morning. Don't you think that will be fun?" Belle looks up into his face.

"Honestly, Jas. It will work. It will be great. Like a free holiday."

He stretches, falls back on the bed.

"Suppose so. You seem to be doing all the hours though," he says at the ceiling.

Belle laughs. "It's cool with me. You know how these sort are during the school holidays. They worry if they have their kids hanging around all day. These people need help with their children. If there isn't a Kids' Club or some sort of 'improving' course," she says, miming quotation marks, "or someone to look after their child, they panic. I honestly think some of them only have kids for the Christmas card photograph. I honestly do. Anyway, I'm getting £500 for the fortnight, plus flights. And we'll have a laugh."

"Yeah, only you're forgetting about the sneaking out bit, aren't you? What if you can't manage to? What if there is an alarm? A guard dog? Security lights? What if they find out?"

She pauses for a second.

"It will be fine. I mean, I'm not working all the time. And I could say I wanted to go for a night time jog or something."

"Night time jogging? Sounds a bit unlikely to me."

"Come on, Jas." She wants the plan to work out, to be believable and acceptable.

"Yeah, well in the meantime, I'm going to be hanging with some right geeks. I'll have to get some walking boots."

After extensive online searching, Jas has found that the most economic way of staying in Ibiza is to join a group of vegetarian walkers, known as Club Windswept. Club Windswept booked an entire hostel in the Old Town for a fortnight. Since they booked it however, one of their party cancelled, leaving one available room, which they have offered to Jas at a discount.

"Do they know that you aren't exactly an experienced hiker?" asks Belle.

"Yes. I don't have to go walking with them, of course. They just want to get some money back for the room. I told them the truth. Or at least, a variation on it. I said that I was an assistant to the famous artist Philip Burrell, which I am. And that he is thinking about doing a series of art works inspired by the Balearic Islands. Which he is. Or at least he might be. He's away somewhere at the moment. At least, he's definitely gone away."

"But you have no idea where?"

"No, I think he is in the Med. Well, he could be in the Med. Or St Petersburg. Or Venice. Who knows? He's away. Shut up the studio. Gone somewhere Top Secret. So secret that he's even left batty old Gilda behind."

"Oh, what a shame." Belle considers Philip Burrell a pompous charlatan, but she rather likes Gilda, a woman in her sixties whose glamour is resolutely undimmed. Gilda enjoys wandering around in fairy dresses and tiaras and doesn't give a damn about what people say.

"I think it's a publicity stunt or something. Something for television. 'Possibly a week, possibly a fortnight dear boy' was all he said to me. So, no worries." He stretches again. "As you say, it means we can have a summer holiday, baby. Of sorts. If, and it's a big if, IF you manage to sneak out successfully."

She strokes his cheek. She loves Jas. They have known each other from primary school, but seem to have only just met. They both grew up in the same block of social housing behind the Square. Everything changed when Belle's mother Tracey won a lump sum from the Lottery. This windfall meant that Belle, her younger sister Grace and their parents were able to vault into a different universe comprising of a house actually on the Square, private education, BUPA membership, gym membership, a smart car, music lessons and even a Polish au pair. The one who kissed Jane's husband, who was sent back to Łódź in disgrace.

Belle had only met up with Jas again last year when she managed to get a fortnight's internship working for Philip. His studio was a place so strange and alien, so disengaged with the real world, that it made concerns such as social housing and private education look like irrelevancies. It changed her, or at least it felt like it changed her from a person formerly who only understood things in two dimensions, to one who operated in three dimensions. What was once a flat progression of stages, her childhood life, is now a rounded, wholly formed thing, with her and Jas at the centre of it.

Since she met him, Belle simply doesn't care about the things she used to obsess over such as her position in the peer group, her younger sister, her weight. She is always checking her phone, waiting for a message from him. She keeps every single text message he has ever sent her. She takes photograph after photograph of his long, thoughtful face. She goes to sleep every night envisaging kissing that face.

Through him, she has learned about art, and about artists and the art world. She is no longer the spoilt child of happenstance and fortune, who used to throw clothes on the floor and expect her au pair to pick them up again. The same au pair who left in a cloud of scandal after kissing the neighbour. Now she has no au pair, doesn't need one. She is seventeen.

Ah, what a stroke of luck that Jane, (whose husband had been the snogger of the au pair, which Belle of course knows all about, but pretends she doesn't), has offered her the job of looking after George in Ibiza. There is no way Belle is going to go away for a fortnight without Jas. Particularly somewhere like Ibiza! So she had come up with the idea of bringing him along too, and because Philip was away at the same time on some mission, he took her up on the offer. Naturally she knew she would have to keep this arrangement secret from Jane and Patrick.

Now the time has come. Belle cannot believe she has managed to combine a job abroad with the prospect of two weeks clubbing with her boyfriend. What skill, she thought to herself. No matter that she didn't much like Jane. Her son George she hardly knew. But how difficult could a child of eight be? How difficult could it be to sneak out of a holiday villa once he was in bed?

"If all goes well, we'll go clubbing all night baby," she says. "Ibiza's famous nightlife. We'll do the whole thing."

"Hope you won't be too tired every morning."

She laughs. "I'm seventeen, babes! Of course I won't be. I'll be relaxing by the pool all day, won't I? George won't be any trouble. He's eight! I'll make sure he brings lots of toys. It'll be easy."

"We'll see." He checks his phone, stands up in the same movement.

"Gotta go, babe. Gotta get my stuff ready."

Later that morning she leaves her house and walks through the Square. It surrounds her like a set from a Georgian TV show; each house white, each front door black, immaculate façades featuring serried ranks of crystal clear windows beneath pointed pediments and above perfect window sills. She thinks she would love it if the matching fronts could all swing open at the same time, like an advent calendar, the prizes a revelation of the myriad lives continuing behind each door. The Square is like a homogenous community from the outside, but behind the prim front doors, wild differences range.

She turns the corner and bumps into Gilda. Gilda is tottering along the road in a pair of platform boots, a Vivienne Westwood mini-crinoline skirt from the 1980s and a boob tube. The entire ensemble is topped off by a flower crown sitting on her peroxide hair.

"Oh hi Gilda!" Belle is genuinely pleased to see her.

They embrace in the street, Belle thinking about what Jas had just told her.

"I'm lonely," says Gilda. "Come round and see me this week, please. You know Philip is away don't you?"

"Yes I did. Jas just told me. I'm going to be away too, unfortunately but yes, Jas did mention Philip was off. Where is he going?"

Gilda tosses her head back.

"Gone. He's gone already. He's gone to Ibiza, of all places. He is working. On a TV show. Can you believe it? Television! At his age. At last he will be on television."

Belle knows that Philip has long wanted to be the centre of a serious arts programme, the sort of thing that might be commissioned for BBC4.

"Is it a big retrospective?"

"Chance would be a fine thing, darling. It's a reality show. On daytime telly!"

"Oh, Gilda that is fantastic."

"Is it? I don't think so."

"Well, where is it being shot? Somewhere exciting?"

"I told you just now. It's in Ibiza!"

"What?" A sense of dread washes over Belle.

"Are you sure?"

"My dear, of course I'm sure," says Gilda, sounding like an English teacher and not an artistic muse with a crazed fashion sense and a former life as a porn star.

"My husband has agreed, for a sum of money, to go to Ibiza along with a bunch of strangers in order to be on television." She shrugs. "I know. Quite mad. And he's left me here." She pouts.

"Oh Gilda," Belle manages to say. "Never mind. You'll have a nice time here for a week or so."

She snorts. "Are you joking? I'm not staying here while my husband gets famous on TV. I want to be on that show too! I'm going to go and visit him."

"What, you are going to be in Ibiza as well?"

"Yep. I'm on my way to the travel agent now. Can't be doing with all that booking it all online. I want to get the ticket actually in my hand."

"Does Philip know about your, er, plan?"

"Of course not." She looks at Belle with a studiedly neutral gaze.

"I want to surprise him. I suspect he's hoping to charm

some of the other contestants on the show, you see. You know, come and see my etchings, I am a serious artist. Well, I will be there to make sure that does not happen. You've got to rule them with a strict hand, my dear."

"Wow. Gilda. That is certainly a... er, a plan. Well, good luck."

She might as well come clean.

"Actually, can you believe it, I am going to be in Ibiza myself, I'm working for Jane and Patrick, you know, looking after George. Maybe see you there." Belle edges away.

"Really? You're going to Ibiza too?"

"Yes, I am. With Jane and Patrick. You know little George?"

"Look, Belle, can you do me a favour?"

Oh God, thinks Belle. She knows Jane cannot bear Gilda.

"What?" says Belle cautiously.

"Well, darling, the thing is this. I don't actually know where Philip will be on the island. It's fine, I've got irons in the fire to find out, but of course he is incommunicado. Could I just have your mobile number, in case I need some help?"

"Of course. But I don't think I will be able to find out where the house is, and anyway I won't have my phone on too much."

"Oh," says Gilda, clearly disappointed.

"Look, Gilda let me text it to you. Give me your number."

She takes two seconds, tapping in the numbers with the speed of the teenager.

Gilda waves a hand as she walks unsteadily away.

"Thank you, darling. Of course, I don't know when I will be travelling. Maybe not for a few days, maybe a week. Who knows?"

Belle watches her hooped lilac skirt swaying down the road. Then she texts Jas.

Fucking hell! Just bumped into Gilda. You were right. It IS Ibiza. And nothing to do with researching anything. He's on a bloody daytime TV show. Can you believe it? And now

Gilda is going to be there as well. She wants to be on the show too! Awks.

Her phone buzzes back.

Ha! Crafty old bugger. Don't worry. Philip is 68. He's not going clubbing is he? Chill out.

Chapter Four
Simon

At that exact moment, Philip Burrell is anything but chilled out. He is not thinking about his wife, en route to the travel agent in London, he is only thinking about the fact that his baggage does not seem to have arrived. It is 25 degrees outside. It is eleven in the morning, Spanish time. Philip has a cracking headache and is missing his morning cup of coffee quite badly.

"Philip!"

"Eh?" he says, turning round crossly, squinting over the carousel.

"You're at the wrong carousel! Everyone's bags have arrived at this one!"

He marches across, putting a testy hand up to a cameraman who is backing away from him, recording as he goes.

"No pictures now, dammit? Can't you see? I'm just searching for my fucking bag."

"Cut! Cut!" shouts Simon, the director, to Rupert the cameraman. "Thanks, Rupe. Philip, come over here."

"No, I am collecting my effects," says Philip as he reaches the correct carousel and, to his relief, identifies his bags.

"No, Philip, you don't understand," says Simon, hurrying across. "This is filming 24/7. Rupert and the second cameraman, Alex, in fact Kate and the whole team, we really must have access to you at all times. It's just no good putting your hand up and swearing. This is daytime television! We can't have our main characters swearing."

"I know," says Philip. "That's why I did it. I mean, who the hell is interested in seeing a middle-aged man, actually rather an elderly man, collecting bags from a fucking carousel, tell me? Eh?" He squints up at Simon.

Simon sighs, briefly, flickeringly remembering a time when he thought working in television would be a wonderful thing to do, a noble thing to do, a profession which promised a career full of public service and important communications. Education, Information, Entertainment, he thinks. Not making programmes that focused on greedy, vain, pompous... Oh it doesn't matter. What does Kate always say? It is what it is.

Simon knows that he possesses a tough side for moments like this. Well, here goes.

"Sorry, Philip. Look, you have to be amenable to the cameras at all times. That means available for filming. At all times. Without the language either. If you don't believe me, read through your contract. It's all down there. And not in small print, either. If the contract isn't adhered to, you will be sent home, sued for malpractice and jeopardising the production, and obviously you won't get paid." There is a pause. Philip is staring, open-mouthed.

"Now, team?" says Simon, turning round to check everyone is present. He refuses to look at Philip again. "Where is the hippy... I mean... where is Fish?"

"Praying to the sun outside," shouts the Adventurous Mother.

"Well, he can't. We need to go out into the airport as one. But if he's gone through Arrivals already, he won't be able to come back airside, in other words, where the planes are. Where we are now." Simon sighs. "Oh bugger it. He'll just have to be out of the shot. Kate," says Simon, "could you go and scoop up Fish?" Kate giggles and runs out towards Arrivals, waving and calling, "Fish! Fishy!"

"The cameras will be ahead of you," continues Simon. "Be

aware of them. Out in Arrivals you will meet your guide, who will take you to the van. And then to the villa. Here we go!" he ends, with a sort of weedy hand flourish. Get them whipped up. He notices Gemma is applying some bright red lipstick, having brushed her hair for the twelfth time. That's more like it, he thinks. "Ibiza or Bust, folks!" he shouts.

Philip realises Simon is not going to pay him any more attention, and quietly curses as he bends down to put his errant bags on a trolley. These mad people, he thinks. He recalls his studio, where he is king and emperor and can boss around his young assistant Jas and has lunch made for him every day by his wife Gilda. He wishes he was back there. But he is competitive at heart, and now he has entered this show, and taken the shilling, as it were, he is going to win it.

They issue out in a huddle into the Arrivals concourse where a large sweaty man in a straw hat and a clipboard is standing. The clipboard helpfully reads *Ibiza (or Bust) Channel M*. The sweaty man holds out a sticky-looking hand. "Hello. I'm Robin," he announces. "I'm taking you to the villa."

"What sort of a bloody name is that?" mutters Philip to Alan Makin, the TV financial adviser. "Robin? At least give us someone local."

"I couldn't care less where he's from," says Alan. "All I care about is getting to the villa and sitting down for a moment."

After a journey of about twenty minutes, they arrive at the villa, which is very large and airy and full of high legged stools, bowls of ceramic fruit and giant vases of dried grasses. In each room, a fan with wickerwork blades spins rapidly, making a breeze in the high, wooden beamed ceilings.

"No air conditioning?" murmurs Alan.

"Don't you care about the environment?" says Gemma. "Air conditioning is destroying the ecosystem."

"Well said, Gemma," says Simon, speaking loudly to the entire group. "This is a Green Villa, everyone. Everything is recyclable, everything is organic. There is hardly any wastage of energy, which means, obviously, no air conditioning.

Chemicals are at a zero." He can't help glancing at Fish, who gives him a thumbs-up.

"What about the swimming pool?" says Alan. "There's bound to be a chlorinated pool, isn't there?"

Simon smiles. He's been looking forward to this moment. "Guys?" he says, beckoning to the crew, motioning them to attend behind his back. "Better get this. Alright, chaps, listen up. Robin, can you just edge out of shot, thanks mate."

"Hey, I'm not a chap," comments Gemma. She is startled by her outburst, but quite proud of it at the same time.

"Of course you aren't, darling. Sorry."

"I'm not a darling either."

Simon sighs. "Of course not. Sorry. Anyway. As I was saying. The pool. Do you all want to come out? Drop your stuff, we can find your rooms later. Let's go and see the pool. Turn over, guys," he says to the crew. Well, at least they are all male, he thinks.

The cast of *Ibiza (or Bust)* walk out of the villa as a group, in what has now, to them, become almost a familiar manner. They pass half a dozen recliners on some wooden decking and find themselves standing on an area of grass looking down at a large expanse of greenish water. Part-submerged reeds and bull rushes wave gently in the breeze. A stone heron looks down into the liquid, which is murky. The television crew arranges itself around the specially curved edges of the pool.

"This isn't a pool," comments Alan loudly. "This is a POND."

"It's an eco-novelty," says Philip loftily. "And by the look of it, inspired by, but quite inferior to the Men's Pool at Hampstead Heath."

"Ooh, I know that pond," says Alan. "I used to live beside the Heath, did I tell you?"

"I think you did," murmurs Philip.

"It looks so lovely," smiles Gemma, regaining her good mood. "Freshwater pools are the latest thing, did you know? I've sold a couple of houses with them. I hate swimming up and down lanes anyway. How delicious. Is that a waterlily?"

Simon nods. He doesn't want to speak while the crew is filming.

Jasper The Wizard walks up to Simon anxiously. "How deep is it? Do you know I can't swim very well?"

Simon, who didn't know, sighs deeply again. He silently curses the researchers. Someone will have to watch the pool at all times. Can't have a death on the show, even if it is out of shot. "Yes, of course we knew," he whispers. "You'll be fine, mate. Fine. It's not very deep. And the bottom is just mud. With a layer of plastic beneath it."

Nobody quite knows how it happened. Even afterwards, when he is telling Gilda, Philip can't be sure. He always suspected Alan was the culprit, but he supposed it could have been the Adventurous Mother, or indeed one of the television crew, because the event, when it was broadcast on the show, was suspiciously well framed.

Whatever the actual truth, as the candidates were inspecting the freshwater, reed-filled pond, someone pushes Philip into it. Or he slipped on the grassy ledges. Either way, Philip falls into the pond, fully clothed, with a shout and a large splash. The water level is deep enough to wholly cover him. Choking and spluttering, he resurfaces immediately, swearing volubly, his hair plastered to his face.

Cresta, the It Girl, screams. Gemma screams too, and immediately holds both hands to her mouth as if she isn't quite sure if she is allowed to make such a noise. "OhmyGod he has fallen in! The artist! OhmyGod are you OKAY?"

Simon, careful not to be in shot, but not wanting to seem either negligent or enjoying the moment too much, lopes alongside Philip who is attempting vigorous strokes of crawl across the pond. Streaks of green pond weed appear on the white linen of his suit. He is gasping with cold and shock as he navigates waterlilies and bullrushes.

"Philip! Are you alright, man? I am so sorry," calls Simon. "This has never happened before, I mean, obviously this was not planned. You are managing very, very well. Very well. Kate! Kate! Can we have a hand here?"

To everyone's surprise it is Jasper who hauls him out. "Come on matey," he says, portly legs astride the grass, hand straight out to the tall, lanky artist who is covering some distance in what appears a pretty decent swimming style. Philip grabs Jasper's hand, struggles to get some traction on the muddy sides of the pond and eventually manages to clamber out in a wholly undignified fashion. The TV crew runs over to get a close-up of the two men.

"There are actual steps over here you know," calls Alan from the other side.

Philip, now standing on the grass, soaking wet, looks back at him with undisguised venom.

"Yes, well thank you for that observation, Alan. Very good of you. If I hadn't been somewhat surprised to find myself in a fucking fake pond full to the brim of icy water and choking on pond weed, I suppose I would have discovered a fucking diving board, too. Alongside the steps. And the waterlilies. Fucking Monet." He pauses, coughs, removes his filthy jacket, undoes his shoes and pours water out of them.

"Only trying to help, mate," calls Alan, blithely. "Wanker." he continues under his breath. "Wish I had bloody well pushed him in."

"Thanks Jasper, anyway," Philip manages to say. The crew carries on filming. "Who the hell did that? And thought it was funny? I'm going to bill you lot for a new suit, no question. And shoes. And a new iPhone. Get me a towel. Oh, what a surprise, there is a pile of them right here. Maybe I have just unwittingly provided the first scoop of the show. Gold dust. You lot should be thanking me."

"Of course, of course," says Simon, wiping his eyes. "I mean of course NOT. God, Philip I am so sorry. You must have slipped. I don't think anyone pushed you, heavens above. And it certainly wasn't planned. I speak with total confidence here. I'll get the IT department to get you a new phone.

Although phones aren't allowed on the show, but, oh, look, anything we can do to make this up to you. Anything. Come on, here's a towel, I'll take you to your room. I think we ought to give you the best room, after all you have gone through. I was going to give it to, er... Gemma, or, er..." he points to the It Girl, who smiles beatifically at him

"Cresta, love," she says helpfully.

"Yeah, to Gemma or Cresta, but I think you deserve it."

"Oh completely," chimes in Gemma, nodding her head. "He not only deserves it, he MUST have it."

"Yeah," chirps Cresta.

"Good," says Philip in his shirt sleeves. "Where is it?"

After a busy ten minutes, in which Philip is ceremonially given the master suite and claims he is already seeing the funny side of the morning as long as his suit is replaced, and his shoes replaced, and his phone upgraded, everyone else goes to their rooms.

Gemma lies back on her bed, looking at the fan spinning high above her. She mentally goes through all her clothes, neatly packed and ironed in her cases. Much of the stuff is brand new.

She has been on a diet for a month. She worries about how she will look. First impressions are one thing but this show will film her all day long and all night. It will film her without make-up on, she knows it. How will she manage to look calm, thin and beautiful all the time? Plus, how will she manage to get her views across without sounding like a fool? She was a bit worried about snapping at Simon back then.

She uneasily feels that she is not so well versed in public speaking or television presentation, or indeed, ideas as the others are. Particularly that awful Adventurous Mother, and the It Girl. And who is the new person, the Big Celebrity arriving? It's bound to be a film star, someone better looking and thinner than she is. She closes her eyes and falls into a deep sleep.

Chapter Five
Belle

They push their trolleys through the main concourse at Stansted in a small trail. Patrick first, then Jane, then Belle. George is sitting, thrilled, atop Belle's pile of luggage. Jane stops first to scan the screens.

"Zone B. That's where we should go. Zone B"

"I'm just going to get some stuff at Boots," announces Patrick.

"What stuff? I have packed everything, you know. Enough pharmaceuticals to kit out a small hospital. Enough toiletries for a month. What is it you need?"

Jane prides herself on being an expert packer, and a forgotten item is a personal failing.

"Oh, just shaving foam," says Patrick meekly.

She rolls her eyes, as if the demands of men are just too painful for her to fathom.

"Can I come with you, can I, please?" says George.

"Of course, of course, George. Hop off and come with me. See you at Zone B, you two."

Jane huffs slightly, picks up a magazine from her bag.

Belle looks up from her phone. She is in the middle of sending a text.

Sure. She taps into the sleek device and presses Send.

Patrick and George disappear into the neon lit congregation of Departures. Jane and Belle stand by the trolley, uncertain about how it should be, their holiday relationship. Cast adrift from the ties of home and work, they need to have some sort of mutual arrangement in this break which is a holiday for one woman, but a paid working trip for the other. After a moment or two, Jane breaks the silence.

"Blimey, look at that lot," she says, mirthlessly smiling. "They don't look like they're off for a relaxing spell, do they?" She points to some people at the next meeting point.

A large group is standing nearby. The group is clad almost uniformly in shorts, walking boots, hats and waxed jackets. They all have ribbed, knitted socks up to their knees. Some carry ski poles in gloved hands. They all have bulky backpacks. Some of them have hipster beards. A flag waves from one of them. It reads *Club Windswept*, and carries the image of a compass and a feather. Jane notices the same logo on patches affixed to some of the backpacks.

"What?" says Belle absent-mindedly, glancing at them hurriedly. She seems so disinterested in them Jane fears Belle might have thought she meant something else, but how could she? They're only a group of boring walkers.

"Oh, them. Yeah. I don't know. They're probably going up Mount Kilimanjaro or something."

"I don't think so," says Jane. "Not from the labels on their luggage. Look, they're off to Ibiza too."

"I've got to go to the toilet," says Belle quickly, pushing her trolley away at speed. "See you at Zone, what was it, Zone B?" she says, calling back to Jane over her shoulder.

"Yeah," says Jane, to an empty space. What was it she said? For God's sake. Isn't the girl interested in where they are going? Didn't she find the walkers figures of fun, like she did? Maybe this was a mistake. She had planned that she and Belle would have chummy moments. Girly chats. Small confidences shared. In the times that Belle isn't looking after, feeding and playing with her son. She checks her phone for the time.

Belle reaches the Disabled toilet beside Thomas Cook Money Exchange, and opens the door. She pulls her trolley inside, closes the door and locks it. Inside, she exhales a long sigh of relief.

"God," she says under her breath, sitting on the handrail and pulling out her phone.

I'm here, she texts.

About twenty seconds later, there is a quiet knock on the door. She unlocks it and opens it minimally. Jas edges past her and in. She immediately locks the door behind him.

"What the hell?" says Belle as he kisses her on the mouth. "That was bloody close. I mean I don't know if Jane knows what you look like, but still. Did you all have to congregate right beside where we were? In your hats and bloody boots? Bearing your fucking Ibiza stickers?! You might have just brought out a map of the island and wrapped yourselves up in it! Stansted is quite a big place, you know. You could have gone somewhere else! I had to invent an immediate loo break and I've only just been! She probably thinks I've got a condition."

"I couldn't help it. We were there, and then suddenly, there you all were. Do you think anyone saw, do you think she saw?" He kisses her again. Despite her anxiety, Belle smiles at him. She loves to be kissed by him.

"She certainly saw most of your group. I don't think she spotted you though. I didn't, but I didn't look for more than about a second, I was too nervous. Christ, what a bunch! You weren't exactly inconspicuous. Ski poles? Who the hell takes ski poles to Ibiza in the summer?"

"Ardent walkers do," says Jas, chuckling, tucking her hair behind her ears and pulling it so the skin is stretched around her temples.

"They're actually alright, my lot. I mean, so I've only met them here but they seem pretty friendly. One even said he was going to take me out on their escorted 10K stroll on the first night. Teach me how to map read." He looks at her, smiles. "Now let me just find my way around a place I am far more familiar with…"

"What are you doing?" she says, smiling at him. "Here, in

40

a disabled toilet? Are you mad, Jas? I've got to get back to the family, I've already been away for five minutes. I have to look after George…"

Afterwards, she pats down her hair, rebuttons her skirt and opens the door a fraction. A man in a wheelchair is waiting by the door.

"Oh… er, sorry," she says, as she dashes away, scanning the walls for a sign to Zone B. "There's someone else behind me."

On the flight she sits next to George the whole way, and plays endless games of Boxes with him, most of which he wins. At one point however she stands up to let someone in the window seat go past her, and she looks back down the length of the airplane. She catches Jas' eye. He is sitting next to two walkers who are earnestly unfolding and refolding a series of giant maps. He smiles over the headrests at her. She blushes and smiles back. How lovely that they are here together, secret lovers on their way to the Balearics.

Jane has also been looking around at her fellow passengers. She does not like what she sees.

"I can see those dreadful people who live in our block," hisses Jane to Patrick. He has fallen asleep and is lying, head back and mouth open, beside her. She digs him in the ribs with her elbow.

"What, what?" he says, frustrated at being woken up.

"Those people with their children," says Jane.

"That could mean any number of individuals, actually most of the passengers on this plane. What are you talking about darling?"

Jane leans over to him. "Those. People." She says, slowly and loudly right into his ear. "Who live underneath us and whose two children, boys actually, are friends with George. You know. The state school lot. Jack and Sam Something. Mother goes by the name of Michelle."

"Oh," says Patrick. "Well isn't that a good thing? Maybe George could go and play with them."

"Patch," says Jane. "We are paying Belle to play with George to the tune of £500 and a flight. Anyway what about your bloody Family Time? Remember that?"

She is almost gleeful to have caught him out. "Let's hope George doesn't see them, or we'll never hear the end of it. Funny that they are on the same flight, do you know I am amazed they could afford such a trip..." She trails off. She's slightly piqued, to be honest, that a family such as Michelle's is having, in effect, the same holiday as she and her family are about to enjoy.

Patrick raises his eyebrows and closes his eyes almost in the same moment.

Of course George spots his friends. Not on the flight, but after they have been through Passport Control, and as they are walking towards the baggage carousel.

"Mother, mother!" he squawks, running up, clutching her coat.

"I've just seen Jack and Sam! And their Mum! Mother!"

"Come on George," says Jane firmly. "Will you stop pulling at me? We have to get our bags."

"But it's Jack and Sam!"

He appeals to Belle, who is herself trying to spot Jas with his walking crew.

"Belle, those are my best friends, and they are coming to Ibiza with us and I thought they were going on a caravan holiday."

He turns back to the boys, small bobbing heads behind a dozen other holiday makers.

"Sam! Jack! It's me!"

Small hands go up in recognition. George can't bear it any longer. He sees that Belle is distracted, pulls away from her and his mother, and darts back past the weary line of people all determined to have fun in the sun for a fortnight. Eventually he reaches them. Jack and Sam are wearing identical Superhero t-shirts, shorts and pale blue Croc shoes.

"I thought you were in a caravan!" he says to them, almost accusingly.

"We are," they chime. "It's a caravan here, here in Ibiza."

"Oh!"

Michelle, their mother, smiles at George.

"What a lovely surprise! You must come and play. I'll tell your mother our address."

George doubts very much that Jane will want to know the address of a caravan park in Ibiza, and even more that he will be allowed to go over and play with his friends. He brushes aside that small hurdle. There is no question that he will locate it, and find them, regardless.

"Tell me, tell me the address. I'll just come over."

"Well, I'm sure it's not next door to you, George. Tell your mother and she can bring you over."

They are still walking towards the baggage area.

George can vaguely hear Belle calling his name, "Geor-gge, Geor-gge," above the chiming tannoy.

"Just tell me now."

"We are in Camping Cala Amante. Can you remember that? Cala Amante. When you arrive, just let the main reception know."

"Camping Cala Amante. But when, when can I come and play?" says George with urgency. "How about Wednesday?"

"I don't know. What are your family doing on holiday?"

"George!" He hears Belle calling his name again, sees her head coming closer.

"Don't know. Swimming. I'll come and see you on Wednesday," he says, naming his favourite day in the week. "Is that okay?"

Wednesday is his favourite day because it is the day after his piano lesson, or rather it was before they moved house and ended up next door to Jack and Sam. Michelle waves to him as she moves off to collect their own baggage, turning her back on him.

"George!" Belle descends, grabs his hand, trots off with him.

"Bye, boys," she says to his small friends.

"Their mum says I can go over and play."

"We'll see about that."

"On Wednesday," says George, flushed with success. "Camping Cala Amante," he murmurs to himself as he sees his mother spotting their matching luggage, and pointing at it, and his father obligingly bending over to haul it off the carousel.

Chapter Six
Gemma

Gemma tentatively comes out of her room. Rupert is outside, his camera on his shoulder. "Just be normal," he says, squinting into the eyepiece. "Ha ha ha."

Gemma's stomach turns over. I am on television, I am on television, she thinks. Or at least, I will be. This is the good time, too, before any of us gets chucked off. This is the happy time. She concentrates on breathing slowly and calmly. Rupert walks backwards in front of her as she moves to the terraced dining room.

"Hey everyone," she says. Rupert slowly edges away from her so she's framed perfectly beside the ceramic fruit and the vase of rushes. She's in her new yellow tiered dress, with thin straps and matching yellow and white striped wedged espadrilles. It was an outfit lent to her by Topshop. Well, given.

The fans whir high in the ceilings. It is already very hot. She turns to survey the side console which is set with tall glass jugs brimming with pink and green juice, baskets of pastries and bowls of thick yoghurt, one peach and one cream, so stiff that silver spoons stand almost vertically in them. Fruit and the petals of flowers have been casually scattered on the immaculate white cloth between piles of white crockery. The whole look is of careless plenitude. She turns her back on everyone and begins to slowly spoon the paler yoghurt into a small bowl. She will avoid the pastries from Day One, she decides. Avoid them this morning and then you can't break the spell for the rest of the week. Or fortnight. Depending on whether she lasts or not. She's fixated with the horror of going out first.

"Whoo-hoo," says Jasper The Wizard, who is peeling an apple. "Don't you look the pretty one?"

She turns and smiles, briefly. Being chummy to people she doesn't care for. The whole thing is a fake, and she's quite sure that the eventual winner of this farce has already been picked. Not that it makes anything easier.

Alan Makin saunters towards the buffet. He is wearing an ensemble comprising of a cream linen shirt with perfectly ironed taupe shorts. He has blow-dried hair and his nails are perfectly shaped. On his pedicured and buffed feet are soft leather sandals, the sort that chic businessmen in Paris might wear. It's clear Alan has given a lot of thought to his outfit.

"Good morning," he says to Gemma, casually picking up a pain au chocolat and breaking it with pale fingers.

"We've all decided that Jasper is going to win."

It's as if he's read her mind.

"Have you seen his trick with a lemon?"

Jasper beams. "I have been brushing up on my tricks, I confess. I said to Sue when I left, 'Well, if they don't care for my magic, there's nothing else I have to show.' And it's true!"

"I'm sure that's not the case," says Gemma nicely. "I'm sure you'll be great anyway." Then she remembers that this is not a holiday, and that Jasper is not a potential friend but a rival whom she has to beat, and sits down with a glass of juice and her yoghurt.

"What about the new person who is going to join us, then?" she asks Alan. "The Huge Celebrity? Don't forget about him, or her. Them."

"Hmm," says Alan, who had actually forgotten about this

extra element of surprise to the show. "I suspect that's going to be a non-event."

"Just say that again will you," Simon says, motioning Rupert to come and film the comment. Rupert charges over with his camera.

"And... cue."

"I suspect the celebrity who is going to join us will be a non-event," says Alan obligingly.

"I bet they won't," says Gemma.

Philip is nowhere to be seen. Nigel, the Adventurous Parent and Cresta the It Girl are swimming in the organic pond, and being filmed by the other cameraman. Cresta is laughing very loudly, getting out and leaping back into the clear water. Gemma notices she is wearing a very small bikini. Just behind the bullrushes she can see Fish performing what looks like a series of Tai Chi moves.

"Morning everyone," says Simon by way of an announcement to the group at large. Past the decking, the green, rushy ecopond glitters invitingly.

"Anyone had a swim yet? I mean, on purpose? No? Ah, I see two have braved the water." He waves his clipboard. "Right, for everyone here shall we go through the events for the morning? Ahem. Today, we are holding a Beachside Olympiad. Why are there only three of you here? Where is Philip? He knew the call was for 0800 hours. Didn't he? Where are the rest of you?"

"The Parents have been and gone. Well, Jocelyn the mother has. Said she needed to Skype their children. You can see Nigel outside with Cresta. As for Philip, our artiste, well, sulking in his tent no doubt," says Alan. "Maybe someone should go and get him." Everyone turns to look at Gemma.

"Why me?"

"Because you are the only girl here," says Jasper patiently.

Gemma stands up, her hands feeling sweaty with anxiety.

"Can we get this straight? Please? I am a thirty-one-year-old woman. I am an estate agent who has had a bit of publicity

47

selling flash apartments in central London, which is why I assume I am on this show. I am not a girl. Neither am I some sort of nursemaid."

"Rupe, are you getting this?" hisses Simon. "It's all good stuff."

Rupert crouches down in order to get a commanding shot of Gemma in her yellow dress.

"Girls are females aged between three and twelve," continues Gemma. "I am not aged between three and twelve."

She sits down again and drinks some orange juice. Her cheeks are flushed. Rupert continues filming. Jasper sniggers loudly. She gives him a death stare. "I'm not anyone's darling, either," she says with a final flourish. "At least, not on this holid... this trip."

"Great, great," says Simon. "Some contemporary feminist commentary. Gemma, anything else to say on the matter? No? Gents, anything you'd like to add?"

Alan Makin stands up, brushes offending crumbs from the linen shorts. "No," he says. "But I will go and raise our artist. I don't mind, at least." He raises an amused eyebrow. "Beachside Olympiad, eh?"

He pads along the corridor towards Philip Burrell's master suite, and knocks tentatively.

"Enter!" comes a commanding voice.

Alan pushes the door open and finds Philip standing in the middle of the room. The door to the garden is wide open. The blinds are all up. Philip is standing with his legs apart as if he were a da Vinci man, only a bit pot-bellied, which modernises the look a bit, Alan feels. He is totally naked. Alan can't help noticing that he is magnificently well-endowed. He is very relieved that Gemma wasn't forced to do this job. Alan glances quickly over his shoulder to check that Rupert and his camera aren't following him, and then looks at the floor.

"Er, morning Philip," says Alan, his gaze resting on the parquet, "sorry to disturb you. It's just that breakfast is ready and, er, Simon wants to go through the day. We're all on the, ahem, terrace. Having breakfast. Before a Beachside Olympiad, whatever that may be."

"Have you ever made a woman beg for you?" asks Philip, tossing his head and shrugging on a robe. Last night he decided that he was going to talk formally for the entire week, in a sort of Noel Coward manner. Well, for a day or two. See how long it lasts. It might take off, on TV. He also is rather proud of the pool incident last night. Sets him apart from the rest, he feels.

Alan laughs. "Philip, old thing, it is eight in the morning. We are on a reality programme for daytime television in Ibiza. We are not about to share anecdotes on sexual conquests. Get dressed and come and have breakfast. What are you on about?"

"Well, it seems to me that we each have something to vaunt in this competition. Don't you?"

Alan laughs, and turns away. He's not going to lower himself into some sort of antler-locking contest with Philip, at least not yet. "Somehow I don't think sex is going to be part of the Beachside Olympiad. It's daytime television, not after-hours cable. See you by the terrace."

"*À bientôt*," calls Philip from behind his bedroom door.

As Alan walks along the corridor to the terrace he sees Jasper bowling towards him.

"Well, that was interesting," whispers Jasper.

"What? What was interesting?" says Alan, still seeing Philip's pendulous penis in his mind's eye. "I've just had an encounter with our artist, you know."

Jasper thumbs energetically back towards the terrace.

"Her. Whatshername. Yellow dress."

"Gemma?"

"Yeah. That feminist outburst. Silly girl. It won't come out well with the audience. I reckon she'll be the first to go."

Alan sighs.

"Can we talk about something else?"

"Well, how is Philip the artist?"

Alan laughs. Despite himself, he is quite enjoying this so-called 'community' of nonentities.

"Stark bollock naked. In the true and only sense of the word."

Chapter Seven
Belle

It's not such fun, now they are off the plane, thinks Belle, and her secret boyfriend has vanished. She had watched Jas go off with the fifteen people on his walking group, everyone laughing and joshing with their ski poles, while Patrick and Jane had remained, fussing at the car hire place, demanding that the booked car be upgraded to a soft-top. As she held George's small hand and saw the taillights of the walkers' official van disappear, she felt almost tearful.

Belle realises she hasn't actually thought very much about this part of her trip. The official part. The part that involves looking after George, and being a member of Jane's entourage. She'd have to be on her best behaviour. Never let her hair down. Never sit around farting, or swearing. Belle groans inwardly. Suddenly two weeks, even in a hot country, seems like a long time. She climbs into the back of the newly upgraded car and smiles wanly at George.

"Are you okay? Put your seat belt on."

"Put YOURS on, Belle my dear," says George merrily.

When they eventually arrive at the villa, she discovers it is very grand. A steel, glass and terracotta-roofed construction, it is precariously perched on a steep hilltop festooned with jasmine and bougainvillea, in an exclusive gated community. Except there is not much hope of ever seeing the neighbours.

Every one of the villas shelters itself behind a high brick wall and security gates, through which one can get a glimpse of tennis courts, swimming pools, the accoutrements of privileged relaxation.

The feel of it is not all that different from the Square, thinks Belle, as she helps Patrick bring the cases in. Why do people want to visit exactly the same sort of places on holiday as they do back at home, she wonders.

She watches a tiny green lizard basking on a low wall in the heat, and thinks about Jas. She envisages his frugal accoutrements in the walkers' hostel. She suspects his room will be furnished with a cold water shower and a rollmat. She sneaks her phone out of her back pocket to text him with the news of her new habitat.

Hey babes. It's not half posh here. Miss you.

George hops about. He is wearing a special baseball cap with a flap at the back to protect his neck, like something from the French Foreign Legion, and bright green open-toed sandals. His skin looks worryingly pale. He sees the round pool and rushes over to it.

"Can I use the pool, can I, can I ? Is there a sauna? Is there a hot tub? Maman. You said there might be a hot tub. Might there be? Or a sauna. Can we swim? Are we near Camping Calla Armante? That's where Jack and Sam are, is it near?"

Jane stands in the doorway of the villa and looks at her small son. Her back aches from all the travelling. She would like a lie down, and a glass of rosé, frankly. Where is Belle? With a flash of irritation, she sees her out in the white heat, standing by the pool, texting.

"Belle, could you come in, please?"

Doesn't she know what work is?

"I want you to unpack for George, please, and get him into his swimming stuff. Make sure he wears that new rash vest. He's going to burn to a crisp in this heat. Don't forget the Factor 30. Or 50, even."

She stalks off to her room, relishing having someone to

order around, enjoying the size of the villa, thinking of her horrible rented flat.

Belle puts her iPhone away. She takes George to what she assumes is their area of the villa, away from the direction in which Jane and Patrick have taken their cases. It comprises of two small bedrooms and a shared bathroom. She takes the bedroom with the balcony, although it is slightly smaller. She swings George's small bag easily onto his bed, and unpacks a few clothes in order to find his swimming stuff. She knows where everything is, because she packed it all.

"Here, George. Slip these on, and put your shirt on too. Your mum doesn't want you to get burned on your first day."

When George is ready and in his trunks with their amusingly formal string tie at the waist, she suddenly is overcome by a desire to hug him. She puts her arms around his smooth, lithe, child's body, so slim she could almost wrap him twice in her embrace, and almost laughs into his warm neck.

"Can we go into the pool now Belle?" says George, peering over her shoulder, muffled but not abashed by her holding him so tightly.

"Wait a minute George," says Belle into his nape. "I have to get into my stuff as well, don't forget. Don't move. You are not to go beside the pool on your own, remember. Ever. "

She opens her arms, lets him wriggle away, slips into her room next door and pulls out her swimsuit from her backpack. The bedrooms both have doors straight onto the terrace, which is where the pool is. Water constantly laps over the edge of the pool, giving the illusion of limitless water. The hillside on which the villa is built falls away behind it with views of the azure sea, giving the illusion that you could swim right out to oblivion. Belle stands beside the side of the pool, stretching in the sun. If only Jas were here with her, putting suntan lotion on her back. If only this was an actual holiday.

George runs towards the water, leaps into the air, bunches his small body up and hits the surface of the pool with considerable force. A giant spray launches into the air, drenching Belle. He seems to surface almost as soon as he touches the water, shouting with joy. She smiles back at him.

"Oh my days! Belle, it's so cold, come in, you've got to jump in! Do a bomb, like I did, do it, do it!" She dips a toe into the water. It is freezing. She takes a step back and suddenly, so as not to give herself any time to argue against the plan, gulps the warm air and launches herself up, out into the middle of the pool. The shock of the cold almost slams every breath out of her body. She breaches the surface, gasping, swimming to keep warm.

"Blimey George, that is cold. Oh my God!" She delicately paddles across the pool, not willing to put her head back into the icy water.

He is hopping up and down on the side, arms wrapped around his body, laughing. "Oh my days!" he says again. It's a phrase he has picked up from Jack and Sam and he likes it.

Jane watches them from her room. Was this such a good idea, giving George a playmate? She hadn't thought about this, how she would feel about Belle messing around with him. She had more envisaged Belle's role as one where she would give him something to get on with, and then start emptying the dishwasher. Or cooking lunch. She turns sourly away. Well, at least this room is enormous, she thinks, sitting on the bed and watching as Patrick fiddles around, unpacking for them both. What is she going to do here for the next two weeks?

She thinks of all the clothes she has packed, preparation for various social situations she has no assurance will happen: the cocktail dress, the sundress for a family picnic. The tennis skirt. The swimsuit. The gym kit. Oh, she's sure she will swim, of course. With George. But would it be as fun for him as with this girl? She only does frenzied laps of freestyle, with tumble turns of course and racing dives. She knows George will tire of this regime after about ten minutes, and then what? Handstands? Better to let him jump in and out of the pool with Belle, she supposes. So maybe she won't actually get to swim, but that is fine. No problem. She can work on her tan, and there's all the books she has brought to read, so she can tell everyone back at home that she just 'lay by the pool and read', an aspirational phrase which she loves to deploy, since it always sounds so exactingly intellectual.

Belle and George both jump in and out of the pool for about another twenty minutes, until Belle remembers about Jas. She ought to text him again. Show him some shots of the pool this time. Telling him about it won't really cut it. That's the trouble with experiences these days, she thinks. You have to have it backed up by bloody photographic evidence. She considers staying in the water with her charge, but her loyalty to her lover gets the better of her. She gets out, dripping, and wraps herself in a voluminous velvety towel.

"Oh Belle, please carry on, don't stop," cries George from the middle of the pool. She looks at him, a small bobbing head surrounded by the bright blue pool and then further off, the equally vivid sea. He is totally encompassed by blue.

"Hang on," says Belle. "Just sending a text to my Mum. To say we have arrived."

This place is lush she texts Jas.

Good. When can I see it? he responds, too quickly.

It's as if he's been waiting for her to contact him.

God knows. Possibly never, sorry. It's difficult.

Well alright, whoops, sorry for asking! So anyway. When are we meeting up tonight? And where? No free Wi-Fi here.

She hadn't yet thought with any care or concentration about that element of the trip, but of course, it was going to have to be factored in. Meeting Jas every night. Clubbing. Being away from George. With all the detailed schedule that she had been attending to, she had forgotten about the extra element, this element of the holiday. Where they were going to meet. She had no idea. She felt a bit nervous about her ability to fulfil her promise. But she had to. It was the only reason she was here, after all. It was only fair. Particularly as she was in the lap of luxury here. Think of the cold water showers. The rollmat.

Of course, of course babes. Let me just work it out.

She worries about it all morning. At lunchtime, she leaves the table and hides in the shared ensuite bathroom in order to fumble with her phone, get online, swiftly find a nightclub, check out the map, send the details to Jas and wait for a reply. She had to achieve all of this, she knew, with a very slow online connection. The subterfuge makes her sweaty, her fingertips sliding all over the touchscreen.

She looks at the list of clubs in Ibiza. Which club should they go to? Amnesia? Boom? Cocoon? There seemed to be a limitless amount. They all looked amazing. They were all open until six in the morning. Promotional photographs showed giant halls full of thousands of people, swirling lights, works of art, tattooed DJs, just the thing. Jas would love it. She would love it. She will love it.

She looks out of the tiny bathroom window at the fronds of waving hibiscus. This was what she had come to Ibiza for, she reminds herself. Clubbing and fun. Not sitting around the pool with a child. Well, there was that too, but which was more important? She sends some of the pictures of the nightclubs to Jas and returns to the table. He could choose.

Fortunately, she finds that George is totally worn out with the early start from London followed by hours of jumping in and out of the water. By nine o'clock, he is tucked up and in bed. Belle made sure of that. Even better, Jane and Patrick had also announced their fatigue after the evening meal.

"We're just going to have some wine by the pool," says Jane. "And then turn in early. No babysitting tonight. You're welcome to join us of course… but… " Her words trail off, as if she didn't really mean them.

"Stay up and have some vino," says Patrick genially. He had caught the sun and is gradually turning pinker as the evening progresses. He smiles at Belle, in her mind for perhaps slightly too long. She remembers the au pair episode. Her Polish au pair, who was elegant and played the piano beautifully. Kissing this man. How could she? He was so old. Must be at least 40.

"No, that's fine, thank you," says Belle quickly. "I'm tired too. I'll just be in my room, doing a bit of work. I might send some emails, that sort of thing. And, er, tomorrow?"

"Well, we will probably have a lie-in. But George will need to be got up at about eight, and given breakfast, you know."

The club closes at 6 am. She'd be back in time.

"I know, no problem."

She turns into her room and lies down on the bed, just for a minute. After what seems like seconds later, her phone bleeps. It's eleven o'clock. Fortunately she had taken the precaution of putting the alarm on, just in case she were to nod off. Right. She wipes her face, properly waking herself up and flashes up the little screen on which she has downloaded the map to Cocoon, the Monday night club. Right. She says it out loud. "Right." Makes her feel a bit less nervous. God. What is she going to wear? Oh, that doesn't matter. Does it? She pulls on a pair of leggings under her red dress and slips into her trainers. It would be unthinkable to do this in heels, even if she had them. She reckons it's about a 3k walk. But that's the easy bit.

She goes softly to the door, opens it a sliver, then opens George's door. He is breathing quietly, fast asleep. Safely tucked up. She had made sure to put AfterSun on his skin, so he wouldn't wake up in pain. He smells of it. She closes his door gently and goes back to her room. She's ready. It's okay. It would be like going for a night time jog, and Jane didn't say that wasn't allowed, did she? She slides open the balcony door, estimates the drop to the ground outside. It doesn't look too far. How will she get back in? Oh, come on, worry about that later. Her phone buzzes.

Are you on your way?

Oh shut up, shut up.

Yes babes. Twenty minutes.

She climbs over the balcony, rests for a minute with her hands gripping the iron railing, then drops down onto the coarse grass beneath the window. Her ankle twists a bit, but that was all. It's easy. It's only a couple of metres. She lopes towards the high security door, presses the domed green button that she had noticed earlier. The door swings open silently, and with a great surge of confidence and optimism, Belle runs out on the tarmac leading down the hill towards town. The rest of the night would be easy, surely. This was going to be great. What a fucking great idea. This was going to work brilliantly.

She brushes past festoons of pink and orange bougainvillea bracts, illuminated by streetlights and the sliver of a new moon. Everything looks different in the dark, wider, bigger, longer. Occasionally, a dog barks from a nearby compound. That makes her jump. Apart from that, there is complete silence. The stars hang overhead. Beside her, the villas are quiet. She presumes they are holding sleeping occupants, sunburned and full of wine. Everything is silent. She only hears her feet, running towards town, and her breath, panting.

She reaches the outskirts of the town after about fifteen minutes, sweating, gasping even. She realises she is thinking with longing of her quiet, air conditioned bedroom. Then she thinks about George in his room next to hers. What if he needs her in the night? She hadn't thought about that. How on earth was she going to explain herself to her employers if her absence is discovered? Night time jogging? Really?

Patrick is probably quite a soft touch, no definitely. The way he'd been grinning at her over the dinner table. But Jane… She realised that she hadn't double-checked the door from George's bedroom which leads to the terrace, and the pool. She hadn't confirmed it was locked. God. What if he gets up to go to the bathroom and gets the wrong door, and opens the outside one instead, and falls into the pool? Should she go back now? She looks behind her at the hill that she has just run down and pulls herself together. No. Don't be crazy. She thinks of kissing Jas. She thinks of George sleeping soundly. Why would he wake up?

Hey babes! Where are you?

Just walking into town. Do you know that big Mobil gas station? I'll meet you there.

Yup. Can't wait.

Chapter Eight
Gemma

"We have to do what?"

"Beachside Olympics!" says Simon gleefully. "You'll love it, Alan. If you could please explain what we are up to in a piece to camera now, just face Rupert, there you go."

Alan sighs and reapplies Factor 50 to his legs, spreading the lotion over his freckled skin. He never tans. He looks up, barely flinches when he sees the lens of Rupert's camera poking towards his face. He knows what is required.

"Hello. This morning we are doing something called Beachside Olympics, which sounds jolly exciting, as long as I don't get the Gold in sunburn," he says wearily to camera. Alan has decided to assume the persona of the sceptical urbanite, and is quite enjoying it. Well, if his neighbour is doing Noel Coward, he can join in, surely.

Philip is in a robe, standing by the rushes of the organic pond. He waves Rupert over to him. "Of course, you see I should be awarded Gold Medal for swimming in here, after my duck was broken pretty early into this experience," he pronounces, "but I understand the Powers That Be have better things in store for us today." He goes very close to the lens. "What Oh What will that be?" He cackles and walks away dramatically.

Simon is obliged to turn away, wiping his eyes. This man is such a bloody pompous twit. It's not often Simon gets emotionally engaged with the 'turns' as the crew insists on calling the talent, but he really has got it in for this dreadful artist. And as he, Simon, is in the driving seat, he knows he can make him suffer. And he will, oh yes. Unless Philip gets kicked off the show too early. He'll have to think about a way for that not to happen. He must keep Philip Burrell on the show.

"Simon?" It's Gemma, anxiously walking over to him. Simon stops thinking about making Philip suffer and attends to her. He rather likes this woman within whom he perceives an internal battle between nonchalance and vanity. He fears that *Ibiza (or Bust)* might not be a particularly good career move for her.

"Yes?"

"This... Olympics. Do we have to be in teams?"

"Pairs, yes. I thought you'd like to be with... er Rupert, can you come over here?"

The cameraman rushes over.

"Gemma, I'd like you to be with Alan for the Olympics."

To his surprise, she beams.

"Oh, that's fine. Good, in fact. No problem."

"Why, is there anyone who you actively didn't want to be with?"

Gemma looks at him knowingly.

"Of course not. I'll just go and get changed."

After half an hour and a short bus ride, they are all in beach gear and branded t-shirts, standing on Benirras Beach. It is eleven in the morning. The beach, half sand, half pebbles, is very beautiful, isolated and natural. The only thing to indicate the day's activities are four tin trays lined up on the sand and a pile of lilos by the water's edge.

"Celebrities!" calls Simon. "Today's challenge is the famous *Ibiza (or Bust)* Fun-lympic Games! You will have to achieve excellence in sports which you have probably never tried before. At the end, we will all toast your brilliance. There are no losers on Ibiza!"

"Not too sure about that," murmurs Jasper anxiously. "I can't swim and I absolutely hate being out of control. I dread to think what we are going to have to do with those trays."

He looks nervously at the sand dunes behind him.

About fifteen minutes later Jasper, wearing a too-small t-shirt reading *Ibiza (or Bust)* stretched too tightly over his paunch, is sitting on a tin tray behind the imperious figure of Philip, who is stopping the tray from speeding off by digging his heels into the sand and grasping a rope. "When shall I push off?" he shouts in a commanding voice across the beach to Simon.

"Now! Now!" yells Simon, Rupert the cameraman crouching next to him.

Philip pushes his legs off the side of the dune and leans forward. Jasper bunches his short legs up onto the tray and assumes a crash position. The tray slowly starts sliding down the dune, gathering momentum.

As Jasper's legs are not on either side of it, it is only a matter of seconds before he emits a short sharp cry and falls off altogether, leaving the tray, with its lighter burden, to speed off down the dune at twice the speed.

Philip leans back, pulling the rope as the tray bumps down the last few hillocks and cruises onto the beach, slowing down as it reaches the shingle. "Yes, well I have always had a zen for speed," he announces to anyone who is listening. He is jolly pleased he has done so well on the challenge, and pretends to squint back up the dune towards his fallen co-rider, picking his way gingerly down the slope.

"Oh, God. Do we all have to do this?" murmurs Gemma as she sees the Adventurous Parents toil up the dune, tea tray aloft, ready for their descent.

"No, you and Alan are doing something far more amusing. You are doing the Lilo Challenge."

"Really, why? Ought we not to all be doing the same thing?"

"Oh, you know, editing reasons," says Simon lightly. "We

need to show a huge variety of events. The implication is of course that you have each done everything, but in reality that would take us all day, and we haven't got all day."

"Isn't that a bit of an untrue reflection of the Beach Fun-lympics, though?" says Gemma.

Simon looks at her kindly. "This is daytime television. Don't worry about it. At least one of this party can't actually swim, so let's leave verisimilitude to *Panorama*, alright?"

"Not quite the Rio Olympics is it?" says Gemma rudely.

"No. We are not in Brazil, Gemma, and this is not the actual Olympics," answers Simon.

And so Gemma does not have to slide down the dune. Instead, she finds herself wading out, sporting an *Ibiza (or Bust)* t-shirt, a lilo underneath her arm, alongside Alan Makin. The idea, as Simon explains it, seemed quite simple. Walk out to a buoy, and after the blow of a whistle, you have to leap onto the lilo, lie down on it and paddle to a pontoon. She can see the pontoon. It's out there, bobbing in the water. Once you reach it, you have to climb onto it, gulp down ten ice cubes, and leap back off the pontoon onto your lilo. Paddle back to the buoy and the challenge is completed. That's it.

Put it like that, thinks Gemma, and it sounds a pretty reasonable, even fun thing to do. In reality it is anything but. Wading out through the shallows to the buoy, the water is choppy and chilly. The pontoon looks quite a long way off. Her lilo is alarmingly stiff. She knows Alan will beat her. She straightens up and thinks of the money she will earn after a week on this programme. Only a week.

"Alright you two!" yells Simon. "Let the Lilo Challenge begin!"

Gemma and Alan stand beside the buoy. Water laps around their waists. Simon blows the whistle and Gemma positions the lilo in front of her and launches her body onto it. It immediately sinks and is borne aloft by the waves at the same time, giving her a feeling of nausea and intense instability. She starts paddling furiously towards the pontoon, looking ahead all the time. In seconds, the water is lapping over her entire body. She is sinking on the lilo. She paddles faster. It is freezing and she doesn't feel she is even moving. No wonder they didn't want the bloody magician to do it, she thinks. She spots Alan Makin ahead of her. He is also half submerged, half swimming, half paddling. He doesn't look like he is having much fun. She vaguely hears shouting from the beach.

Suddenly, the pontoon rears up in front of her. She's made it. She grabs the ladder, heaves herself up it with the lilo under her arm, climbing onto the reassuring wooden mass of the bobbing pontoon. She is streaming with water. There is a bucket on the pontoon in which are jammed not nice small ice cubs, but two giant lumps of ice. She picks one up and gamely shoves it into her mouth. How on earth is she going to manage to eat this monster? It is ridiculous. Alan looks at her and simply throws his lump of ice into the sea. She spits the ice cube out.

"Come on," he says.

Oh no. Back in the water.

She walks to the edge of the pontoon. From this position, there is quite a drop to reach the water. Say, about three feet. Oh, just do it. You'll be on telly, she thinks. Imagine her friends, her parents, her boss, seeing her unable to jump off a silly pontoon onto a silly lilo. It will be on YouTube for ever. She'll be a laughing stock if she doesn't do it.

Without further consideration, she places the lilo down, and then throws herself towards the water on the lilo, thinking as she does it, that she ought to have used the steps. The inflatable is not equipped to handle the height of the drop, the suddenness of her weight, or the swell of the waves, which are now considerable. When she resurfaces, Gemma finds herself swimming, with her t-shirt ballooning out around her. The lilo has floated away, far out of reach. Out of her depth, the sea is cold, dark and seems terrifyingly deep, yawning beneath her, full of untold dangers. She desperately starts paddling, looking around her for Alan, the beach, the pontoon, any sign of help or rescue. She worries she might have a heart attack, or be grabbed by the ankle by something that will pull her down. What happens if she were to suddenly stop moving? She is gripped by fear. After a minute or two, she is somewhat relieved to see that Alan has also lost his lilo, and is also swimming frantically towards the beach. She follows in his direction. Breathe, she thinks. Slowly. Stretch out your legs. Calm down. Breathe. She carries on, breathing evenly. She is at least moving. After a few minutes, but what seems like hours, she senses the colour of the sea changing, she is in control, she is in shallow waters. She puts a foot down, feels the sand beneath her toes, carries on swimming. She ignores the buoy. Just get back onto dry land.

Soon she is walking unsteadily up the sand towards Rupert and his ever-present camera.

"Well done, you were amazing, amazing!" shout the Adventurous Parents.

"How was it? Gemma?" says Simon anxiously.

She pushes past him and carries on walking. She finds she is actually crying.

"Cover Alan coming onto the beach," Simon says to Rupert. He doesn't want to show the participants as victims, before they have even been voted off. He hurries up to Gemma, puts his arm around her.

"Sorry."

"Get off me. I could have drowned."

"No, no, we had the whole thing covered."

"Oh, really?"

"Yes," he lies. "We had a lifeguard and everything. Of course we did."

"Didn't feel like it out there," she sniffs. "It was terrifying."

"Look, cheer up. You did brilliantly. We are having a barbeque on the beach, and Tequila Slammers and then afterwards, there's a surprise. Your last teammate is arriving."

"What, the properly famous one? Oh, great. One more thing to make me feel a million dollars."

"Gemma."

"What?"

"You're doing great."

A trestle table has been erected and festooned with a Union Jack tablecloth. There is a bottle of Tequila and some tonic water on the table, alongside a few bowls of crisps and some plastic cups.

"Hardly Saint-Tropez," says Gemma to Alan. She is still badly shaken after her swim from the pontoon.

"Cheer up. At least we made it."

"I have never experienced anything so awful. Imagine if there had been a rip tide. Imagine drowning while doing a reality programme."

Alan makes a funny face at her.

Despite herself, she realises she is laughing, slamming a cupful of Tequila on the already sodden table and chucking it back into her mouth, gratefully receiving the numbing liquid.

"I've done lots of things for television but that has got to be the worst," confesses Alan. "It's the way the industry is going."

"What is?" says Simon, coming up behind them and putting his arm around them both.

"Doing stupid and dangerous things like that," says Alan. "We are just your performing animals. We know our place."

"Come on Alan," says Simon, laughing nervously. "You know how the game goes."

Alan doesn't say anything.

"As long as our friend the artist gets a similar experience, is all I am saying."

Simon laughs and walks away. He goes to a large rock on the beach and stands on it.

"Right, Celebrities. At the beginning of the week, I said you were to be joined by a tenth person, a Mystery Guest.

Well, the moment for unveiling has arrived. Your mystery guest is about to arrive. By helicopter. In two minutes time."

Gemma notices that the beach has been cleared in a certain spot. Someone from the TV crew is already standing on it, waving two paddles above his head. High in the sky she can see a tiny speck that comes closer and closer. Soon it is so near that conversation is impossible under the clattering and buzzing of the helicopter, which tilts down onto the beach and arrives with a bump, rocking forward and back on its landing gear. Gradually the blades slow down and at last, stop altogether. Rupert is crouching near the door of the chopper, camera poised.

Simon gathers the other contestants around the door. Someone unrolls a red carpet, causing Philip to raise his eyebrows. There is stillness around the helicopter, and an awesome sense of anticipation.

Eventually, slowly, the door opens. Standing in the doorway is a small, grey, furry donkey, wearing a straw hat. It has a blue harness, which is held by a young, tanned man in a very small pair of ripped denim shorts, a red t-shirt and is also wearing a complementary straw hat. He looks like a farmer. The donkey twitches its left ear and slowly clip-clops down the stairs and onto the red carpet.

All that can be heard are the waves on the beach. The nine celebrities are totally silent. The Adventurous Mother actually has her mouth wide open. Philip sticks his neck out to take a closer look, as if he cannot quite believe what he is seeing. When the donkey and its handler reach the end of the red carpet, they stand still. The donkey flicks its tail. Rupert backs off, scuffling in the sand, getting shots of the donkey, which is looking mildly about, and the reality show participants, who are still standing, staring and saying nothing. Nobody moves.

Eventually the tanned young man breaks the silence.

"Ola! My name is Francesco. And this," indicating to his side, "this is Burra. Burra the donkey."

"That actually means 'donkey' in Spanish, I believe," whispers the Adventurous Father.

"Quite, quite," says the Adventurous Mother, nodding her head vigorously.

"Who the hell is the fucking guest, the donkey or the man?" says Philip.

"Am I going mad or is the donkey our Celebrity Guest?" says Alan, to nobody in particular.

Gemma shrugs. "It seems so. Simon," she hisses. "Is this the Guest?"

Simon turns around. "Indeed she is," he whispers. "Very famous in Spain. She was once in an Almodóvar movie."

"Burra is very well trained," continues Francesco. "She will be with us most days. I am her... handler. She will take her meals with us. She will be outdoors with us on our trips. Some of you can, if you like, ride her. She is a very friendly donkey."

"Where have you flown in from?" asks Gemma. She is still staring at Burra. She wonders why Rupert is now shooting Francesco from every single possible angle. Surely it's the donkey that is the magnet here.

"Oh, just the next bay," says Francesco, disarmingly.

"You don't sound very Spanish," says Gemma suddenly.

"I am Brazilian. But I live round the corner."

"No wonder you knew exactly when they were arriving," Alan says accusingly to Simon.

"Well, you know," says Simon.

Philip strides forward. "So this, this..." he gesticulates to Burra, momentarily speechless, "this animal... is going to share the programme with us as one of the contestants? I must say, Simon, I think you, or perhaps the television company behind this... show... has gone stark raving mad. I think that bringing a... a donkey onto the show, frankly, is a bit of a liberty. I think we all do," he says, looking around.

Simon ignores Philip. "Are you getting all this, Rupe?"

he asks. "Come on guys, its all a bit of a laugh, isn't it? This donkey is a film star, don't forget."

Rupert nods his head and carries on filming.

"I thought we were the performing animals!" says Jasper. He picks up a lemon from the Tequila table, a bottle of suntan lotion and a pair of sunglasses and starts juggling them all.

"Here!" says Francesco, motioning to him.

Jasper tosses him the suntan lotion bottle. Francesco catches it on his foot and flips with his toe it upward to his hand, where he grabs it and throws it back.

That was rather good, thinks Gemma. How on earth did he do that?

Chapter Nine
Gilda

Back in London, it is chilly. It is very cold in Philip's house, but Gilda is barefoot. She opens the double doors of her walk-in wardrobe and shivers as she steps forward to survey her summer clothes. She can't imagine being warm enough for this. Drawers full of tiny shorts, balcony bras and little strappy tops. The rails hold many skirts layered with netting, one embroidered with a strutting poodle. There are frilled silk dresses and embroidered matador jackets. Ooh, those would be wonderful in Ibiza, she thinks. Thematic. Spanish. She'll take them. She'll look the part. But what about her shoes?

She pushes past the autumn/winter array of suits, smart skirts and tailored jackets (which show just the right amount of cleavage), and reaches for a large see-through box of sandals. Just pack the whole box, thinks Gilda. Strappy heels, silvered flip-flops. Clogs. Anything summery. Maybe she should have a pedicure. She looks anxiously down at her bare feet. They look blue-veined and old. Her toenails gleam with black glitter nail varnish. Maybe. Before she goes.

She'd been unable to sleep without Philip beside her. Since he had left three days ago she had been almost in a state of mourning. Not opening the curtains until eleven, that sort of thing. She's currently wearing her brightest kimono and her most turquoise eye make-up but beneath the fantasy clothes, Gilda is worried. She knew she wouldn't hear from him but even so, the silence is deafening. She puts the box of shoes on her bed and sits down beside it.

What if Philip comes back from his stint on television and finds normal life, his home, studio, work, all of it, finds it just... unsatisfactory? What happens if he wants to go back to the Ibiza sun? She knows these worries are merely precursors to the main problem, which is as follows.

What if he looks at her, Gilda, and finds her unfit, sagged and old compared to the cast members of *Ibiza (or Bust)*?

She puts these anxieties out of her mind for a bit, but only because she is smothering them underneath new ones. Why isn't she on television? Alright, it's only daytime but these days, what with streaming and iPlayer, that doesn't really matter. She starts to sort out swimsuits. After all, she tells herself, her husband's status is only enhanced by her. She's no fool.

Gilda knows magazines love to profile Philip because of her, the glamorous wife who, it's known, has pornographic photographs of herself in the kitchen. Yes, she will arrive in Ibiza as if by chance, and prove to be the most fortuitous hit the television company has ever had. They'll thank her for it, she thinks uneasily.

She wanders down to the kitchen and looks at the pictures while drinking an instant coffee. Six black and white pictures, commissioned way back for *The Sunday Times Magazine*. I mean they aren't really rude, for God's sake. Just topless. It was after she'd had her second boob job too. God, her tits looked good. Huge and round and set off to a treat by that feather boa. That was all, though. Six pictures. Topless.

She looks at her tickets on the kitchen table. Open return to Ibiza, leaving the day after tomorrow. She couldn't get anything sooner for less than a fortune. But that's okay. Philip said he would be away for at least a week. She wonders how she can find out where the television house is, that's the main worry. She knows it is near the Old Town, but even Philip had not been told the actual address before they left, as the celebrities had to be cut off from everyone. She's not even sure about the name of the television company making the show, because otherwise she could just ring them up and they would tell her, wouldn't they? She could make up some rubbish about a family emergency and they would have to tell her. Then, she could just get a taxi from the airport and arrive, in her specially selected hot pant suit and tiara, standing at the front door, bold as brass, delighting the television crew. Give them a bit of real titillation.

But she didn't have the address, thinks Gilda. That might be a hurdle.

She had been a bit shocked to find out that Belle was going to Ibiza too. That was too much of a coincidence, frankly. She liked Belle, but she was going with that dreadful Jane, such a bloody nosy neighbour, always trying to come in and see the porno shots downstairs, and also Gilda's downstairs loo which had little sculptures of women's genitalia on the walls. Bourgeois cow. Gilda bets she bumps into her in Ibiza when she is trying to find Philip. They'd have already gone. They'd be there now.

Maybe the whole thing was a bad idea, she thinks. Maybe she should just relax and wait for Philip to come home. But no, she's bought her tickets and she's started packing. It would be a laugh. Think how surprised he'd be, she thinks happily, forcing herself to look at the positives.

She goes upstairs and starts to haul out armfuls of cotton sundresses and more hot pant suits. She'll go clubbing, isn't that what Ibiza is for? Gilda was a disco queen at heart. She readjusts the small flower crown on her head and puts a drawer load of matching underwear in the suitcase.

Chapter Ten
Jane

As Gilda is packing her balcony bras and tiny bikini pants, Jane is swirling the coffee round in her cup. She picks at her croissant. It's only nine in the morning, but the heat is already upon the day, and the air conditioning unit is whirring. She doesn't look up, but she can hear George and Belle in the pool, leaping in and out, splashing and shouting in the sunshine. They do this for hours. Everyday. She vaguely hopes George has got some suntan lotion on. And what about his hat? Belle is bound to have forgotten that. Yet she won't check. She doesn't want to go out, arrange them to her satisfaction, look on while they do things that she feels are too young for her, and then wander away again.

She could sit there reading by the side of the pool, but she feels prohibited by the presence of the younger woman, and although she had boasted, prided herself on the wraparound childcare she had organised, she has now to privately admit to herself that perhaps it was too much. She had brought Belle to take over so she and Patrick could have lie ins every morning, but the fact was that she and Patrick weren't having the sort of holiday, or were at the sort of age, to be honest, which necessitated long lie-ins. She knew they ought to have invited over some friends.

They have been on the island for three days and she is already a bit bored by it. She wonders what she ought to do today. Patrick would read by the pool, or work in his room. He didn't seem to find it awkward. Even through the splashes and shouts, he would soon drift off, an open book on his gently rising and falling paunch, his mouth wide open. She finds it easy to keep herself trim; why can't he, she thinks, with irritation.

After lunch, she supposes she might go shopping with George in the Old Town. Shopping is always a good thing to do. A hobby you can do everywhere around the world. George doesn't much care for markets, but he might be keen on getting an ice cream. She knows Belle will slope off and have a nap. I wonder if she suffers from insomnia, thinks Jane. That girl is forever yawning. Well, I suppose it's a cultural thing here. Still. I hope she remembers how much she is being paid to take a siesta, thinks Jane, overlooking the fact that Belle's arrangement does not cover the afternoons.

She wanders over to the central island in the large kitchen and picks up a large black ring binder. In it are copious lists of local restaurants, amusements and entertainments, provided by the owners of the villa. She sees she could go up Sa Talaiassa, the highest point in Ibiza, and look out at the scenery. Or she could visit to the Amante beach club on Cala Llonga for some yoga sessions. That would be quite nice, she thinks.

Then she sees an advert for Beachside Pilates run by a woman called Yasmin Bird. *We take our Pilates seriously. Seriously across the Island of Ibiza*, runs the blurb alongside pictures of Yasmin striking impressive poses on a mat. *From hillside watchtowers to gloriously deserted strands, you can have your Pilates fix in the world's most stunning places. Newcomers specially welcome. Every weekday, in a different venue across the island. Come and stretch out with the backdrop of the Med and Yasmin as your gym buddy.*

There is a close up photograph of Yasmin Bird, who has a mane of shiny long brown hair, perfectly arched eyebrows and a bright pink tracksuit. *Live the dream* says a talk bubble coming out of her mouth. From the pamphlet it seems that

Yasmin voluntarily gave up a fantastically ball-breaking career in the City of London to go and run holistic Pilates classes on Ibiza. Health, wisdom and happiness resonate out of her toned frame. Jane resolves to go to the morning session. Tomorrow. Yes. That's a plan. Then she sees that today's class starts in a nature reserve, in an hour's time. She'd better go. She'll feel glad if she does, she knows she will.

She goes back into the dark coolness of her air-conditioned bedroom. Patrick is splayed across the bed under a single sheet. He doesn't stir. Jane picks out an outfit from her new selection of gym clothes; black leggings, raspberry sports bra, purple singlet. Grey zippered jacket. No need for shoes. She slips on her flip-flops and checks the nail varnish on her feet. Can't be too careful. Jane absolutely hates people with chipped nail varnish on either fingers or toes, as if a poor manicure somehow reveals moral destitution. Her toenails are perfect; light blue. Her fingernails are perfect; peach. Never have the same colour on both extremities. She remembers reading that in a glossy magazine when she was a girl. Funny, the things that you remember. She can't remember a single thing about the Periodic Table, but advice about nail varnish? No problem.

She folds and puts the selected clothes into a mesh bag and ties her hair back. Now she has a plan for the morning and somewhere to go, the emptiness in her belly seems to have evaporated. Jane cannot bear doing nothing, and she feels that Patrick should have known that before booking this villa. He could have arranged one with a tennis club, at least, nearby. "I'm not one for sunbathing," she used to boast in the office when she too, like Yasmin Bird, worked in the City. "Lying on a towel frying? Not for me. I'm far too active," she used to say. Now what? She sighs, swings the bag onto her shoulder, walks back onto the terrace.

"Belle! George!" They have tired of the pool and are sitting on a towel playing a game of Uno.

"I'm going to a nature reserve this morning. Going to do some Pilates actually."

"Are you going to look for birds, can I come, please?" George loves bird watching and is a member of the Young Ornithologists Club.

"No darling. I am going to do some Pilates," she repeats.

"What? Plates?"

"Belle will explain. It's about stretching and stuff."

"Pilots? Sounds boring. Why don't you stay here with us, please Maman?"

"No, sweetcakes. You seem as if you are having fun with Belle. Carry on with your game. I'll be back soon. Tell Patrick I've gone to a health class. In a nature reserve."

She tosses her ponytail and flip-flops away with a spring in her step. She's off to do a spot of self-improvement.

"Bye everyone," she shouts. "Back at lunchtime."

"Bye," they manage.

Belle and George hear her put the roof down on the hire car, and after a minute, its tyres scrunch on the gravel. After a few seconds they can no longer hear the engine, although Belle can envisage it driving down the hillside road she now knows so well. Silence once more descends on the garden. The pool is totally flat and calm. Belle finds herself gazing at the nape of George's neck which after three days in the Ibiza heat, is carpeted with blonde down. She is getting very fond of her small companion. She is almost finding herself wishing that Jas might cancel the night time arrangement, just for once. She is so tired. She'd like to just play Uno all day long with George and drink milkshakes with him, and then have an early night.

"Pick up two," she says, smiling, throwing a card down with mock severity.

"Take that!" says George, trumping it with one of his own.

"Pick up four, and I change the colour to yellow."

Jane drives confidently off, humming a little song. After a few moments, she stops the car and taps the postcode of the nature

76

reserve into the sat nav. To her annoyance, Yasmin Bird's class appears to be quite a long way away.

Jane steps on the accelerator. She shouldn't really be driving in flip-flops, she knows. What the hell. There is no traffic around. It must have rained in the night, she thinks, noticing the roads are gently steaming in the morning heat. She drives past small settlements, low white buildings with rows of shops, typically a chemist and a café with tables on the pavement. An old lady is walking a dog. There is a white and blue church. She drives past a giant hypermarket, its vast empty car park like a grey beach. The lights are red and she is obliged to stop. She gazes at the car park. Columns of empty wire shopping trolleys are lined up, vacant, awaiting the day's commerce. Huge billboards above the car park signal bargains of the week. *Pizza! Nescafé!* A colossal woman holds up her child, who is holding an ice lolly and grinning. Next to her, there is a poster showing the single face of a man, tipping his hat and smiling cheekily. *Francesco Villa drinks it!* reads the slogan. She has no idea who Francesco Villa is, although he looks pretty pleased about holding up a glass of orange juice. Good looking guy, she thinks.

She checks the sat nav. The blue line continues off the screen. She still can't see her destination, but registers that there are three roundabouts coming up. The lights change. Jane presses the accelerator and barrels across the first roundabout. She comes to the second roundabout. There is another huge billboard of that grinning man with the hat and the orange juice in the middle of the mound. She looks at it, takes her eye off the road for a second, then looks back, correcting her position as she does so, but not slowing down. She changes gear and abruptly tilts the car. The flip-flops make it harder for her to use the pedals with precision. Suddenly, she can feel the one on her right foot bending underneath the brake, so she can't press it down. She stamps down. The flip-flop springs away from her foot and the car lurches.

As the car swerves, she over-corrects it, slipping on the

77

greasy road. It swings around and then suddenly, and with almighty force, the wheels lock. At once, Jane finds herself sitting behind the wheel of a madly spinning car, spiralling around the roundabout. Jane can do precisely nothing as the little car moves of its own accord right across the road, its wheels petrified into a position, skidding over the tarmac. The experience seems to go on for ever.

On and on she skids, the driving wheel rigid, immovable, as if it was paralysed. She spins right around, and then around again. At last, after what seems like an age, the car bumps up onto the central grass area where the giant billboard of the man with the orange juice stands. It comes to a halt, facing the wrong way in the middle of the roundabout and stalls. There is no traffic. It is too early. That is merciful, thinks Jane. She sits at the driving wheel, too shocked to move. After a moment, she turns the engine off properly. She picks the errant shoe out of the footwell and puts it back on again. She considers her position. She is on the top of a grassy knoll in the middle of a roundabout somewhere in Ibiza. There is no traffic. She is wearing flip-flops. She must get the car off, but not to drive home. That would be defeat. She must carry on her journey to her Pilates class.

She turns the engine on again. The sat nav flares into life, showing the screen with her destination now easily in view. She puts the car into reverse, warily backing up the knoll, turning the wheel as she goes. It is now responsive, dutiful, obedient. It doesn't seem to be damaged, thank Christ. Not the self-willed fairground ride of a few minutes ago. She drives forward, bumping awkwardly off the middle and onto the road again. A man is watching her from the other side of the road. She waves cautiously at him and drives away, slowly. She wants to go and be looked after by Yasmin Bird and the other people in the Pilates class.

After about ten minutes, she stumbles into the class, apologising for lateness as she runs towards the group of women assembled on mats reading *BE POSITIVE*. The class is being held on a rocky cliff top above the sea. A jagged island rears up out of the water behind them. It is perfectly quiet.

"Hi, hi, sorry I am late, am I too late for the Pilates class?"

A woman steps forward, tossing her hair back over her shoulders. It's Yasmin Bird in a white t-shirt and pink shorts. Brunette. Bare feet. Pink nail varnish.

"Of course not." She holds out a hand. "Yasmin Bird."

Jane grasps it urgently, pumps it up and down.

"Thank you so much. I've had a journey to get here. Had a bit of a car disaster. Almost a crash. You know, span the car round a bit, but it's okay, I'm okay, everything is okay."

"Okay!" echoes Yasmin Bird, looking at Jane quizzically. "Are you alright? Are you sure you want to do this class? Get a mat from the pile and just join in when you feel ready. Have you done Pilates before?"

Jane nods, runs over to the mats, gratefully grabs one and flips it down.

"Welcome to the Cala d'Hort nature reserve," says Yasmin Bird to the group at large. "Here we overlook the island of Es Vedrà, said by locals to be the third most magnetic place in the world. This is very important for your practise," she continues.

"What are the other two?" someone asks.

On tiptoe, stretching up, Yasmin Bird doesn't miss a beat. She tilts her head back up to the heavens. "Follow me, if you will. The North Pole and the Bermuda Triangle. Now bring your arms down, please."

After a few minutes, Jane notices a humming sound resonating in the air.

"Yasmin, what is that?" she asks.

Yasmin is lying on her back by now, her legs in the air.

"Singing bowls from a nearby mindfulness session," she says.

I am in the right place, thinks Jane. She tries to put the adventures in the car out of her mind. She stands up, stretches, puts one foot against her opposite knee and assumes a tree position. "I know this is yoga but I quite like it anyway," she says loudly to Yasmin Bird.

Yasmin shrugs and smiles. "Whatevs," she says calmly.

Jane looks out to the tiny magnetic island and then across the beach to the mindfulness area from where the singing bowls have been humming. It is then that she sees the unmistakably tall figure of Philip Burrell, standing by the mindfulness area, talking into – yes, she hasn't imagined it – a television camera. A stab of jealousy goes through her.

"Spinning the car was, firstly, like being pushed around by a giant hand. Then later when I saw that Philip Burrell, it was like having a bit of home transplanted into paradise by the same giant hand," she says later over lunch with Patrick, George and Belle. "Although the emotions I felt were more that I was still in a nightmare. I mean, Philip Burrell. He's so, well, pompous."

"What an extraordinary surprise," says Patrick to nobody in particular.

"And not a very nice bit of home either. He's such a weirdo. Do you know him, Belle?"

Belle is drinking a glass of water very quickly.

"Yes, of course I know him. My boyfriend Jas works with him," she mutters.

"Oh, sorry. Hope I haven't offended, Belle."

"No, no," mutters the girl.

"But how funny, and how actually very… odd that he is out here on Ibiza too at the same time."

"Yes," says Belle nonchalantly. She thinks about the night ahead of her, the drop from the window, the moment she sees her boyfriend, his face reflected in the neon lights of the café by their meeting spot. This is why she is here, she tries to remind herself. Forcing down more water in a bid to wake up.

Chapter Eleven
Patrick

He goes for his customary visit to the bathroom at 5.00 am, sighing slightly. One of the casualties of middle age. He's used to it by now, but he wishes he could still sleep through the whole night as he did when he was a young man. He's also thirsty. Too much wine at supper. He washes his hands then pads into the kitchen and pulls open the heavy fridge door. Juice, how lovely. The heavy sweetness fills his mouth. He stands gulping in the dark kitchen, hearing nothing but the fluid in the glass and the sweeping tick of the kitchen clock, which is decorated with a map of the island.

He pours himself two glasses. Afterwards, on a whim, his stomach drum-tight with liquid, he decides to visit his sleeping son. He used to love stealing into the nursery at their home when George was tiny. He would sit beside the cot for hours, looking at his child's perfect eyelashes curled on his rounded cheek. He'll do that here, he thinks. Patrick pads down the corridor leading to George's and Belle's rooms. He hasn't been down here before, he realises, slightly guiltily. They are outdoors all day long, aren't they? And Jane always does bedtime. Always has. He feels a bit like he is prying, and then dismisses the thought as ludicrous. After all, he is paying for the place. He allows Jane to have the illusion of being in charge, but it is he who foots the bill. He doesn't tend to remind her of this.

He pushes open the white door which he assumes leads to his son's bedroom. He has guessed correctly. The small form of George is lying beneath a white lacy bedcover. He is breathing gently. Patrick goes up to his son and looks down at him. George is fast asleep and perfectly still. He emanates a childish warmth. Patrick sits down on the bed, carefully positioning half a buttock on the very edge of the mattress so he doesn't disturb him.

It is past the very dark centre of the night. When he looks at the sky he can discern a gradual paleness in the east. It is enough for him to see George's shiny hair and his slightly rosy face. Patrick leans over him, inhaling his child's fragrance and his heat. He kisses his son's downy cheek. He dreads the time when he will feel stubble there. George's eyes are tightly shut, almost as if they are sealed. He is breathing deeply, regularly. He has had a tiring day, leaping in and out of the pool for hours on end, thinks Patrick, glad to see how relaxed the boy seems. He is filled with protective love for him.

A sudden noise outside makes him turn round, peer across the room to the window. Maybe nothing. Silence resumes. But then, suddenly, he hears it again. It is the distinct sound of the electric gate swinging open. What on earth? Patrick gets up quickly and fearfully from the bed and pads in his bare feet to the window. He sees the gate, ghostly in the dark, swaying open and a small figure running through it. Fucking hell, we are being burgled, thinks Patrick, wildly looking around the room for a suitable weapon. Christ Almighty. To his alarm, the figure swings around the terrace and comes trotting past George's window. Patrick's heart is pounding. I am going to have to fight this person to the ground. I am going to have to surprise him. Or her. He looks at the burglar more closely and sees to his astonishment that the person is indeed Belle, who by then is in the process of swinging her body up to the balcony of her room. She does it with such accuracy and speed that Patrick is in no doubt she has done it before. Blimey, he thinks, looking at her with something approaching awe. She pushes the unlocked French windows open silently and slips inside.

Patrick stands in the bedroom, scarcely believing what he has just seen. His heart thumping, he goes to George's door and peers round it to Belle's door. He sees a sliver of light flash on inside, and hears the bed creak as she gets in. The light goes off. There is silence once more.

Patrick wonders how to process what he has just witnessed. George turns over and murmurs something unintelligible. Then he scratches his head. Best go back to bed, thinks Patrick. He's worried, though, and he wishes he hadn't witnessed this. What was the girl doing out at night, getting back so late? Does she have a secret life here in Ibiza? Does she know people? Surely not. A thought grabs him by the throat. Maybe she's on drugs. Maybe she left her room from addictive compulsion, went into the Old Town to do some sort of a… a deal and is at this precise time injecting herself. Should he storm into her room, demand an explanation? He hates conflict. The very idea of apprehending Belle, who is only seventeen, in her bedroom, makes him shudder. She was too young to come with them on holiday. They could have easily done without her. Maybe she should be sent home. Then they could have their Family Time.

He decides to leave everything to the morning. Or until some unspecific time during the next day, one of those non-hours between lunch and supper. He wishes he was back in London, where everything was familiar. He walks softly back to his bedroom and climbs in beside his sleeping wife. The experience of seeing his child so soundly asleep, protected yet vulnerable, and then the whole strange behaviour of the person who is meant to be caring for him has disturbed him. He feels agitated. Why did he ever allow Jane to do this? He nestles down into the pillows and is soon asleep again.

Chapter Twelve
Belle

Belle had been obliged to tell Jas that Philip Burrell was only round the corner on his reality show.

"Philip fucking hates television," Jas kept saying with glee. "Or at least, he keeps up the appearance that he does. But I guess like most people, he's desperate to be on it."

"And he's on the show with Alan Makin, you know that financial whiz who has moved in next door."

"Unbloodybelievable," said Jas. "Let's toast them. Mojito, babes?"

She and Jas had a great night out together. Unfortunately it had only left her with three hours available for sleep. That is okay, she thought, as she arrived back at the villa at 5.15 am. Three hours before George gets up. Three is enough. Three hours is better than two. Yet when her phone sounded three hours later it was almost physically impossible for Belle to open her eyes.

Her bed is so comfortable, the morning light filtered through the curtains so soft and calming. She would so love a lie-in. She would so love to carry on sleeping. She needs to be in bed, she thinks. Lying down. Asleep. Damn those mojitos. She sits up. Her brain feels like it is cladded with insulating felt. Her mouth is chokingly dry. She forces her stinging eyes open. Something is on the bottom of her bed. Or someone. She concentrates on focusing her eyes on the shape.

It is her small charge. He is already clad in his formally tied swimming trunks and French Legionnaire hat. He is wearing the t-shirt decorated with dancing fruit. She looks at him. Couldn't he have just this once had a lie-in? Just this once? She thinks of Jas lying down on the mattress in his monastic room at the hostel. She knows he won't wake up until about midday. She thinks that after everything, including the money she will earn, he has still got the better deal. Although he's probably quite lonely during the daytime, with nobody to talk to. She at least has the engaging company of George, which she is enjoying more than she had anticipated. But just not this morning. George. Where is he again? Oh, yes. Sitting on the edge of the bed.

"Morning George," she mumbles, after an effort.

"*Bonjour* Belle," says George brightly. "Shall we have breakfast? I am very very hungry you know. Come on. Why are your eyes still closed? Open up!"

"I know. Yes, I know. Two minutes. I'll just be in the bathroom."

She somehow raises her body into a vertical position. She manages to stumble to the shared bathroom, splashes cold water on her face. She gazes at herself in the mirror. She looks terrible. She makes herself step into her swimsuit. She ties the halter neck behind her head and puts a towelling robe around her. She slips on her flip-flops and clatters back to the bedroom. She very badly wants to lie down. She knows it is out of the question, but every muscle and sinew in her body, every cell in her brain is urging her to return to bed. She defies them. Later. Just get through the morning. The sunlounger is a possibility.

"Belle, where are you?"

"Here, here. I was just brushing my teeth. Have you brushed your teeth?"

"Of course I have."

"Come on then."

As she walks into the kitchen, automatically pours George a bowl of cereal and blindly gets the plastic milk bottle from the giant fridge, she thinks, not for the first time, about why Jane and Patrick have hired her. Who hires a helper to come with them on a family holiday? The whole point of the exercise is in the name. Family holiday. Maybe their marriage needs a bit of a spark into it. A bit of a boost. They have been here for four days; it's now Wednesday. After the first evening when they all ate together, they have been out every night having supper at a different restaurant, leaving her and George to eat alone.

They then typically get back at about ten and Belle is free to climb out of the window and spend the night with Jas. Every night she has done this. Then they don't get out of bed until well after she and George have had their breakfast and are out by the pool. What are they doing in there, thinks Belle. Not having sex. She's sure about that, thanks to a giveaway comment from Jane over lunch yesterday. What was it that she called her marriage? The Gobi Desert or some such. It was embarrassing. She felt sorry for Patrick, who had just looked at his salad with a strange smile. No wonder he had snogged that nanny. She hopes Patrick will not try to snog her.

She cuts some bread and chews it absently. Was this what being married for two decades means? She could simply not imagine living in such a way.

"Belle?" says George quizzically. She looks at him blearily.

"Yep." More of a statement than an answer.

"I came into your room very early the other day."

There is a pause.

"You weren't there."

"Really?"

"Yes, really. I patted the bed."

"Oh. Oh, I remember now. I was doing a bit of beach Yoga. Yoga. On the beach. It's quite big in Ibiza, George. I forgot."

"What, in the dark?"

Oh for God's sake.

"They have floodlights."

"Can you take me with you next time?"

"No." Too quickly.

"Why not, why can't I come too? You know you are meant to be my official 'holiday friend'," says George, providing the quotation marks with his small fingers. "You ought to take me, really."

"Well, maybe," yawns Belle. She is so tired she actually feels nauseous. "I am a bit tired this morning. Let's go outside and eat this." The sunlounger. She has to get to the sunlounger.

She carries a tray of bread slices, each one buttered with the lovely white butter favoured by the Spanish, and spread with glistening maroon Morello jam.

"Would you like a glass of milk?"

Milk and jam. George could live off the combination.

She gives him his plate and cup full of UHT milk, and hastens to the sunlounger, the parasol casting a welcome shadow over her face. She stretches her legs out on the towel. The pool glitters before them. Thank God she is lying down. Just a quick kip. Thank God.

"No swimming without me, remember."

Ninety minutes later Belle wakes up from insensible sleep. To her horror, George is nowhere to be seen. The water is blue, undisturbed. The pool is empty. George has vanished.

Chapter Thirteen
George

She's asleep. Good. That was the plan. He'd noticed she was often sleepy in the mornings, but not quite so tired as this. What a stroke of luck that she went off to Beach Yoga early in the morning. George never knew yoga was so tiring. Maybe it was doing it on the beach that makes it tiring. Anyway, it's Wednesday morning and he has an appointment to keep. He had told Belle about it, hadn't he? He feels a tiny qualm of guilt, but he remembers he had talked about it to her at the airport. He'll say that in case he gets into trouble.

He slips away from the pool terrace, walking delicately behind her chair, and returns immediately to his darkened bedroom. He considers leaving his bed untidy, but that might indicate he was still back in the house. No. He wants to show he has thought about things, and that he has left. So he carefully pulls the covers back over the mattress, plumps up the pillow.

He has already left a neatly folded pile of clothes on the floor by his bed, which he knew nobody would touch. It's been there since Monday. Now it's Wednesday, his favourite day. He pulls off his dry trunks and puts them back in his drawer. He slips on his readily prepared pants, shorts and Lego Star Wars t-shirt. He looks down at his bare feet. He hadn't thought about shoes. But he needs them. Where were they? He pads out to the kitchen and almost falls over his sandals. Good. But what is that noise? He stands completely still, one sandal on, one off, listening to a sort of sawing groan. Oh. It was his father, snoring. Everyone in the villa is asleep. It's still too early. Belle is motionless out on her recliner. His father is snoring. He knows his mother will be asleep. 'Her beauty sleep' she calls it. Why is sleep beautiful, thinks George.

He swiftly does up the straps on his red sandals. He remembers to take a banana from the fruit bowl on the kitchen table. He puts it into his pocket. That's it. Now, he thinks happily, he is off to see Jack and Sam at their caravan in Camping Caller Amanter. Or whatever it's called. He's sure it will be nearby.

He walks out, past Belle on her chair. He sees her sleeping peacefully. He feels sorry that he is leaving like this. He knows she will be anxious, but there's nothing to be done about it. His mother would never sanction his meeting Jack and Sam, and Belle is a version of his mother. A version who is a lot more fun in the pool, but a version none the less. He walks confidently up to the large metal gates and presses the green domed button that he has seen his father pressing. The gates swing satisfactorily open as he had predicted. It's all gone very well, so far. Aware that he might need a bit of time to find Camping Cal Amanta, or whatever it's called, he breaks into a jog as he passes through them.

As he trots down the road, George takes time to think about why people go away on holiday but then do nothing when they get there. They simply lie down all the time. Or go shopping. At least this seems to be the case for some people. He knows that Belle has done some Beach Yoga and there was that Plates thing that his mother did the other morning, but frankly not much else. What has his father done in Ibiza? Not much, he is pretty sure. George finds he is pretty sure about most things. He doesn't find time for deliberation. Once he's made his mind up, he acts on it. His teacher said that about him in a Parents' Evening and now he finds that is how it is.

He carries on running. After a while, he gets a bit fed up with running and slows to a walk. A lorry goes past him with a rush of air which he finds a bit disconcerting. What was it that his teacher said he must always do on a road without pavements? Walk on the right or the left? If you walk on the right, which in England would be the left, you are on the right side of the road. Which is good. But then the cars come from behind you. So perhaps he had better walk on the other side of the road, but then that is the wrong side. George doesn't want an altercation with a Spanish policeman, so he sticks to the right hand side of the road, and flattens himself against the embankment when a car comes whistling past. Mercifully this doesn't happen too often. He thinks he ought to count cars and their colours. When the fifth red one comes past, he sits down on a small patch of grass by the road and eats his banana. He holds the skin and then throws it away with a regretful air. He knows it is wrong to be a litterbug but if anyone asks him about it, he'll simply explain there were no bins. He's not going to carry a banana skin around with him, that would be disgusting. Funny how a banana skin is fine when it has a banana within it, but the minute it is emptied of its contents, it becomes repulsive to hold.

He continues walking. After a while, he reaches some big official gates, and a box in which a man in a peaked cap is sitting. George waves jauntily at him, who tips his hat in acknowledgement of his greeting. George is aware he is leaving some form of compound. He walks a bit further and gets to an area where the road opens out to form a giant carriageway. There is at least a pavement. Smaller houses appear, along with a dog or two. George likes dogs, but he knows there is rabies in Spain, so he gives them a wide berth. He has no intention of picking up rabies.

He looks at the signs on the road. *Ibiza Airport* reads one. *Ibiza Town* reads another. Es Canar reads the third. He has no idea which to choose, but he doesn't think Jack and Sam would be staying near the airport, so he heads along the direction marked *Ibiza Town*. He tells himself that he is having fun. This was a good idea, he thinks stoutly. They are his friends, after all. His good friends. It's not as if he is Running Away. He's just going to see his friends, on a Wednesday. He carries on walking. It's quite hot, thinks George. He wishes he had brought some water with him. And where did his hat go?

Chapter Fourteen
Jas

Jas props himself up on his rollmat on the floor and surveys his room. It is very small, but precise. Whitewashed, wooden-floored. He thinks it is in a building that might have been some form of a seminary or school in the past. There is a single window at one end, a door at the other, a chair and a hook for his clothes. Although he hasn't unpacked.

He looks out of the window to see brilliant sunshine outside. The hostel is absolutely silent. Everyone has gone out for a morning walk; he knows they will be back soon for lunch, after a visit to the local supermarket. The walkers never eat at cafés. They always retire to the hostel, bringing bread and cheese and water that they have bought down the street.

After lunch, they take a siesta and then always go out once more to another venue on the island, possibly taking binoculars with them for a bit of bird-spotting. One of them will stay behind to cook supper, which is always vegetarian stew. After supper, they gather round, drinking water. One of them has a guitar which they all sing to. It is a good routine, thinks Jas. He admires the walkers, their properly fleshed out interests of birds and folk music, the fact they are always doing something with purpose. He even likes the idea of what they actually do, although he has yet to go on any walks with them.

He realises he is thirsty, takes a swig from his water bottle on the floor by his mat, and lies down again. He mulls over last night's news. He's not too fussed about bumping into Philip Burrell. He's on holiday, so why should Jas not be? He can't really see their paths crossing. In a nightclub. How on earth would that happen? Even so, it is a surprise. It also makes him slightly nervous, a tension which won't dissipate arising in his stomach whenever he considers the news.

Well, let's forget about that, he tells himself. Focus on the day ahead. He's getting into a bit of a routine himself with Belle. The routine is as follows: laze around all morning, get up, have a coffee, then have some bread and cheese for lunch with the nutty walkers, shower and change. Do a bit of emails, Skype a mate back home, that sort of thing. Chew a beer. Wait for Belle to arrive. She has been with him every night, loyally running down the hill in the velvety dark to meet him at some point between nine and eleven. At which point, his holiday begins.

They go out clubbing, then back for sex.

As a formula, it's pretty much perfect. Last night was amazing. They had been to Teatro Pereyra, a live music bar in the Old Town. The bands were still on stage in the early hours, playing everything from jazz to soul and Latin. Plenty of mojitos. Jas slides back into the body of his sleeping bag, remembering the night and how beautiful Belle had been, dancing and laughing alongside him. Such a shame she always has to run off back home at dawn. "I'll start to call you Cinderella," he had said to her as she hurriedly got back into her clothes in the tiny room at daybreak. "Don't forget your shoes!"

She had laughed, wiped her face with a cloth, tiptoed down the stone steps. There was no carriage waiting for her, of course. She has to run the three kilometres back to the gated community. He had leaned out of the window, waved to her as she sprinted back to her air conditioned villa and her job.

Now it was nearly midday. He has the whole day before him before he sees Belle again, holds her body, dances with her. He switches his phone on, flops back on the mattress again, listening to the cars passing by outside. If he closes the window, it's more peaceful. But boiling hot. So hot. He'd rather have air than quiet. So he has the window open. He lies on his futon, musing about the choice between heat and noise and why both are so thrilling. Suddenly, he hears a familiar voice coming up from the road outside.

"Well, I am not fucking leading a donkey. I don't care what you say, or how you put it. I don't care if you have the entire legion from the BBC here, or *Panorama*, or frankly, the *News at* cunting *Ten*. I am simply not co-operating. It's not on my contract."

Philip.

Jas leans out of the window. Down below him on the pavement he sees a film crew walking backwards in front of a group of people. One of the people is indeed Philip, wearing head to toe white linen and a Panama hat. He's never seen him looking so smart. Usually when he is working, Philip wears an old boiler suit.

Beside Philip are a collection of other adults surrounding a small brown donkey. The donkey is wearing a floral crown. Its harness is being held by someone else, whom Jas vaguely recognises. It's out of context, though. Who the hell is that alongside Philip and the other reality stars, he thinks. He squints down at the group, which has come to a halt outside the hostel door. He looks at the donkey man, harder. He knows that face, that way the man has of carrying himself, of squaring his shoulders. He knows him. Suddenly, it dawns on him.

Jas can't quite believe what he sees, but he thinks that the person holding the harness of the donkey is the famous Real Madrid and Brazil international striker Francesco Villa. He looks at him again, leaning out so far he is actually in danger of falling from the window. Impossible. But if it isn't him, it's his bloody twin, thinks Jas. After a moment or two, the group carries on walking. What are they doing, thinks Jas. They are walking along a road, practically ignoring Brazil's most celebrated and wealthy footballer. Philip is marching ahead while at the same time being hugged by a young woman dressed in a boob tube and very short shorts. The whole scene is compelling and ludicrous at the same time, and Jas finds it astonishing.

"Come on Philip, yer old sulkypuss," says the young woman. She tosses back a head of impressively tonged curls and bumps hips with him. "Let's go have a beer."

They head off up the hill, Francesco Villa pulling the donkey into an ambling trot beside the group, the television crew fussing around them. What a sight, thinks Jas. What a thing to make a television show out of. A bunch of British people on holiday with a donkey. Alright, Francesco Villa is cool but that is about it.

He turns, hears his phone buzzing. Belle. Why is she calling him so early? He wonders lazily, now looking forward to telling her about Philip Burrell.

"Hello?"

"Thank God you're there!" she sobs down the line. "I've been ringing you all morning, for God's sake."

"Sorry, sorry. I've only just switched my phone on and didn't see the missed calls. What? What's wrong?"

"He's gone! Gone!" she almost screams.

"What? Who? What is happening?"

"George, George, George has gone! It's all my fault, oh Jas, what am I going to do!"

"What? What? George? No! Oh my God Belle, are you sure?"

"Yes, I am. I am. He's gone. I fell asleep by the fucking pool, didn't I? I got back too late, too late," she wails. "Then when I woke up, I woke up and he was just… gone."

"You're sure he's not in the pool, Belle, it's a terrible thing but I have to ask you. Is he in the pool?"

"No. NO. Of course not! He's not in the pool."

"Thank God. Well, that's a start. Where are Mater and Pater?"

"Jas, cut the fucking crap. His parents are still in bed. They obviously have no idea. Oh God Jas. George has disappeared! My little boy! What shall I do?"

"We'll have to search for him. Have you looked everywhere in the villa?"

She is properly crying now.

He hears the door slam downstairs, chairs moving. The walking party is back. He grabs at an idea for her.

"Tell you what, we'll send out a search party."

"How the fuck will you do that?"

"I am living with fifteen walkers aren't I? With binoculars and everything. Come down here and we'll sort something. We'll find him. Come down now. I'll hold you and we'll sort this out together."

"Really? What, on a Wednesday morning?"

"Yes, really. What else can you do? He's not at the villa. He's not in the pool. He must be somewhere else on the island. How old is he?"

"Eight. Oh God Jas. How could I have fallen asleep?"

She'll be blaming me in a minute, thinks Jas. He tries his best to sound authoritative.

"Come on. We'll fan out across the island. We'll find him. See you in a little while, okay? Just come straight to the hostel. Now."

She hangs up.

He pulls on some shorts and a faded t-shirt, and runs down the stone flagged stairs to the kitchen where the walkers are congregated around a table, drinking tap water.

"Guys, guys. I need your help."

They gather round, earnestly listening.

"My girlfriend, you know my girlfriend? She's been up the road looking after a young boy, sort of holiday babysitting for him during the day. Well it seems the little blighter has gone for a wander. If she loses him, she'll get the sack, no question."

He looks at the group expectantly.

"I mean, the important thing is not her job, but to find the boy. He's only eight. I'm sorry, I know you have your afternoon walk, but basically the thing is, can you help me?"

The leader of the group, Vince, pats Jas on the arm.

"Of course we can."

A slight murmur runs through the party.

"We were meant to go and inspect a local church, but no question. Where did you say your girlfriend was living?"

Vince stands up, spreads his walker's map of South Ibiza on the table.

Jas immediately feels a bit better at the sight of something official. It's a positive move, he feels.

Vince gets out his propelling pencil.

"We are here," he says, defacing the map with a tiny cross. "And your girlfriend is where?"

Jas doesn't know. He realises he doesn't know. He's never been there.

"Oh, up here somewhere," he says, vaguely pointing towards a golf course. "Is there anything of danger around here?" He looks around the tanned faces.

"What do you mean?" asks Vince.

"Cliffs, dangerous rivers. Pools. Water. Vagrants. He's eight."

Someone in the party laughs. Jas immediately feels a boiling hate burn within him.

After twenty minutes, he hears the hostel doorbell ring, twice. Belle bursts into the dining room. She is wearing a white dress and trainers.

"Oh my God," she sobs. "Jas. You have to help me."

She runs across the room to him, buries her head in his chest.

"My girlfriend," says Jas to the group, by way of explanation.

"Right," says Vince. "Can you tell us where you are living, please?"

Belle turns, pores over the map, wiping her nose.

"Oh God, I don't know. No, it's here," she says finally, pointing.

"I see. So the little chap might have simply run down the hill to the town?"

"Might have. But he might have done anything."

"What does he like doing?"

"I don't know. He's eight years old. Things an eight year old would like to do. Swimming. Lego. Star Wars. Please can you help me? Can't we go out and start looking now?"

"Of course," Vince says. "I'm just covering all the bases. It's what we do in the Scouts. I lead a local Beaver Colony."

Belle feels as if she has been parachuted into a parallel universe. "Beavers? Can we just please go and find George?"

Vince stands up again. It is clear that within the last few minutes, he has assumed full Scout leader-mode. Jas finds this deeply comforting.

"Alright everyone. You, Fran and Richard, you go through the village. Check all the obvious places. Bars with a TV, football pitches, anything like that. You, Jo and Neil, you should probably go back up the road to the villa, combing all these little side roads here... and here," he says, pointing with his pencil to areas on the map. "Everyone else, follow me. We are going to the coast. Boy is called George. He is eight years old. Call me at any juncture. If you don't hear from me, we will meet back here at 1700 hours."

"You see?" Jas says proudly to Belle. "These guys are the dog's bollocks. We'll find him, no problem."

Chapter Fifteen
Jane

Jane has been lying in bed for about an hour. She knows she really ought to get up. She stares at the fan, incessantly grooming the ceiling. What's the point in a fan when the villa has air conditioning? She wonders what she ought to do today. It's a Wednesday. Maybe this could be the day to take George to the aquarium. On her own. Give Belle the morning off for once. She's always so bloody tired, that girl.

She tosses back the single sheet they have been sleeping beneath, stretches and wanders, in her long silk nightdress, out to the kitchen where she languidly pulls open the door of the giant silver fridge, feeling like a New York starlet in a film. She notices how quiet everything is. She pours some orange juice. Then she walks across to the terrace, drinking her juice, expecting to see Belle and George. The terrace is empty. The pool is silent.

She returns to the kitchen, puts the glass down and goes into the unfamiliar side of the villa, opens Belle's door. Everything in the room is messy and awry, as if it had been abandoned in a hurry. She opens George's door. Everything is neat and tidy. His bed is made, his trunks folded and on the bedspread, as if it had been left in a planned manner. Where the hell were they, then? She glances out to see the hire car still sitting in the drive.

She walks back to the kitchen, reclaims her drink. She feels a bit piqued that her employee has taken her son out without asking her, or even including her. The day seems rather empty, now. She goes back into the bedroom and sits on the edge of the bed. After a minute, she elbows her sleeping husband.

"Seems as if everyone has gone out," she says to Patrick.

Patrick slowly rolls onto his back, squinting up at her.

"Belle and George. They're not here."

"Really? That seems odd. Where could they have gone?"

"Well, darling, I don't know, of course. That's why I am saying it SEEMS as if everyone has gone out. I am ASSUMING they have gone out."

She looks at her phone. Surprised to see it is 12.15. As she looks at it, it rings. *Belle Babysitter* announces the screen.

"Oh, good. It's Belle. I expect she'll be letting us know when they're back for lunch," says Jane, letting it buzz a few times.

"Well answer it, darling!"

"Alright, alright. I don't want her to get the notion that I've been hovering over the phone waiting for her to call."

Eventually, Jane presses to answer.

"Jane!"

"Hi Belle."

"Jane, I'm afraid I have some bad, well, not too bad, but perhaps worrying news for you."

Jane shift further up the bed.

"Oh yes?"

"George isn't with me. I'm just in the process of finding him."

"Finding him? What? Is he lost?"

"Yes. No. I don't think he is actually lost, but I don't know."

"What? What are you saying, girl?"

There is a pause as the carefully constructed, mutually respectful relationship between the two women crumbles into ash.

Jane stands up.

"Belle, for God's sake," she shouts. "He is your charge. He

is under YOUR CARE. Did you see him this morning? Did you get him up?"

"Yes, of course. I got him up, gave him his breakfast, all of that was fine," says Belle, as if she is delivering a rehearsed speech, which she is. She has gone through her lines before with Jas, just to check that they don't sound too bad.

"Well, how is he…"

"I took him outside and then I turned around and he was, like… gone."

"You turned around? And then he was gone?"

"Yes," falters Belle.

"Gone. Just like that? Well, how long did it take you to turn around? Children don't just vanish into thin air! Was he ever out of your sight?"

"No," she says truthfully. I mean my eyes were shut, thinks Belle, but he was right beside me. She's not going to tell her employer that she was asleep. That must never be known.

"Well, how did he vanish?" says Jane. "My God, he could be anywhere!"

Patrick is now pacing the room. He remembers what he saw last night, how he witnessed Belle coming back into her room in the early hours. He wonders if he should tell Jane, and then thinks probably this is a bad idea. He feels anxious and uneasy.

"What has happened, what is going on?"

Jane takes the phone away from her ear.

"George is LOST," she announces dramatically.

Patrick feels as if his insides have turned to water.

"Well we must go and find him. Now."

"Belle, where are you?"

"Walking out towards the coast, with some walkers. We are all trying to find him."

"The coast? Oh my God. I am coming. Right now. We are both coming."

Having thrown some clothes on, Jane and Patrick run towards the car. She thinks about when she drove it to the Pilates class. She's not wearing flip-flops, at least, but trainers this time.

"Get in, get in," she shouts at her husband.

"Jane. Please calm down. We don't want another crash in this car. George has probably gone off to see something he is interested in."

"Like what? A new branch of the Lego Store, just opened in Ibiza Old Town? Don't be so fucking idiotic, Patrick!"

"Well, maybe he has gone to find something, or someone. George isn't the sort of child just to leave. He always has a plan. He's not just run away, has he?" Patrick feels the need to try and keep normality in the picture, although he has mounting terror within him.

"Oh my God, maybe he was abducted," says Jane, starting the car and leaping it forward as she struggles to put it in the correct gear.

"Well, how on earth could that be the case? This is a gated, locked and surveyed community. We are very safe here."

"Yeah, not safe enough to stop our only child being lost though you fool."

They are driving down the steep road to town.

After a few minutes, they pass the gates of the resort, where the security detail in his box is sitting drinking some coffee.

"Stop, stop here," says Patrick. He gets out of the car and trots over to the box. The guard opens the door languidly.

Jane sits in the car, tapping her fingers on the wheel. Fucking hell. They will have to spend the whole morning in a drama, then George will turn up, and then what will that have achieved? She's definitely going to fire Belle, no question. After the girl has found George, she is off on the next flight home. Immediately. Jane will sack her and take great pleasure in it.

Patrick climbs back in the car.

"Good news. Well, good and bad. The security guard here saw George."

"What? When?"

"At about 8.30 am."

"Bloody hell. What was he doing?"

"Jogging along quite happily, it seems. On his own. He even waved at the man. So bang goes the kidnapping theory."

"Jogging? What does that mean? Which way did he go?"

"Not sure. The man thinks he headed into the Old Town, but he didn't watch him because he thought George looked so confident he didn't need any help or overseeing."

"Yes, right," says Jane drily. "So confident that we didn't need to spend £500 and a fucking flight hiring someone to 'look after' our only child," she says, mimicking quotation marks in the air. "She is fucking dust after this."

"Belle?" He remembers how small she looked last night, in the dark. "Don't be too hard on her. She is out there going spare, looking for him right now."

"Patrick, she was HIRED to take care of him. I am absolutely going to sack her."

They are bouncing along the road to the Old Town. Suddenly, Jane spots a familiar figure walking towards her. It is Philip Burrell, surrounded by a television crew. She instantly speeds up. She does not want to engage with people having a good time when she is in the middle of a household upset. Plus, she has no make-up on. Plus, she hates Philip Burrell.

But as she nears the group, she thinks that actually, they might be able to help her. TV crews always have huge amounts of facility and money, don't they?

She screeches to a halt.

"What the hell now, Jane?" yells Patrick. "We need to go and find George. Don't bother with this lot."

"They might HELP US, you imbecile," she hisses.

She winds down the window.

"Is that Philip Burrell, my famous artistic neighbour?"

The TV crew wheels round. Rupert focuses his camera on Jane who is looking through the window at the group.

Philip, who has seen Burro the donkey be taken back to

the house while he has enjoyed a beer with It Girl Cresta, is now contentedly walking along the road, his eyes focused on her cleavage. Hearing his name, he looks up absent-mindedly from the task of surveying Cresta's surgically enhanced breasts and fantasising about playing with them.

Who the hell is this? Not that awful woman who lives across the Square from him in London? Could it possibly be a look-alike?

He adjusts his Panama hat.

"Philip, Philip, it's you! I'm so glad to have seen you."

"Oh yes, hello, hello there. Just doing a bit of, er, television work."

Despite his dislike of the woman, he is delighted to have been recognised. That would piss in that fucking Alan Makin's porridge. Pity he isn't here to witness the event.

Jane is out of the car, walking towards the group. She acknowledges Rupert and the camera with a meek smile.

"Can you please help me, I mean us?" she says to Philip. "I'm so sorry to disturb your filming but we are in need of some help. My son is missing. I wondered if you might be able to help us look for him. We only have one car and I thought you might have some manpower. I don't want to bother the police. I'm sure he's just wandered off to see something or do something. Could you help us?"

Philip Burrell looks over to Simon for guidance. Simon shrugs his shoulders. "Go for it," he mimes.

Cresta barges past him.

"Poor little blighter. We'll find him for you. How old is he?"

"Seven," says Jane. Who on earth is this tarty woman, she thinks.

"Of course we shall help you. Actually, you know what?" she turns to the rest of the group. "Why don't we get the chopper out?"

For a brief blinding moment, Philip Burrell thinks this is a reference to his splendid genitalia.

He stares at Cresta.

"The helicopter," she says slowly, as if talking to someone of limited intelligence.

"The one wot that sweet donkey you hate so much came out of. Come on Philip. Keep up."

She appeals to Simon.

"Could we use that helicopter again?"

Simon turns to Kate, his fellow producer. She nods at him.

"Might make an excellent episode as long as this lot haven't been chucked off yet," she whispers.

"Fair enough," says Simon. "We'll make sure they are still on board."

He walks over to Jane.

"Simon Courtney. I produce *Ibiza (or Bust)*," he says, cringing inside. No matter how familiar the title is, he still can't utter it without shame.

"What, so all of you are on a TV show?" says Jane innocently.

Simon nods. "Yes. Well, they are. Marvellous people. Now, as it happens, we have access to a helicopter. We could easily send it out there and have a scout around for your son. I'm so sorry. I'm sure we'll find him very soon."

Jane's phone rings again. It's Belle. She turns away from the camera, she doesn't want to be seen being angry.

"Have you found him yet?" she barks.

"No," says a small voice. "Should I call the police?"

"No," barks Jane. She wants to stay with the television people for as long as possible. "Not yet, anyway. Keep looking. Patrick and I have hired a helicopter. We'll be overhead."

Belle turns to Jas. They are walking along a cliff top with Vince and two other walkers from the group. "She doesn't do things by halves! She's only hired a fucking helicopter. George! George!" she carries on shouting hoarsely.

"Can I come with you in the helicopter?" says Jane. "I know what my son looks like, of course. You'll need me there with you."

"Right, right," says Simon decisively. "Rupert, you go with Jane and, er, Philip, you are Jane's neighbour, you'll know what the child looks like too. And Cresta, this was your idea. You go along too. Rupert, you know where the helicopter base is in town, don't you? We'll head back to the house. Patrick, we can make some calls from there."

The group starts moving away. As they go, Simon calls after them. "Rupert? Don't forget to do an establishing piece to camera with, er, the mother, will you?"

"It's Jane," calls Jane.

"Sorry, yes of course. With Jane. Nice and long."

"Right boss," calls Rupert.

Despite her anxiety about George, and irritation with Belle, whom she had paid to look after her son, Jane is silently triumphant. A piece to camera! She searches in her bag for some lipstick, and grasps it, hurrying after the other three on the way to the helicopter base.

Chapter Sixteen
George

Now he's actually in the Old Town and his plan has worked very well so far, he's not very sure about how to close it. George is not at all sure how he is going to find Camping Calle Amante. He had thought there would be signs to such a place, but there don't appear to be any even though he has walked all around the town to find one. He looks up at the clock in the middle of the market square. Eleven in the morning. George's feet are sore. He sits down on the kerb. It is hot and he is very thirsty. Camping Calle Amante. The three words have gained mystical provision. They present themselves to him, almost touchable, and then disappear. As if the place was now almost something of myth, like Atlantis. Or Camelot. It is Wednesday, he reminds himself cheerfully. He should be playing with Jack and Sam.

He looks across the market square. There, in the middle, is a large glass building marked INFORMACIÓN. Below the title is another word. INFORMATION. When he sees his own language written in such big letters, George cheers up. He gets off the hot pavement and limps over to the office, pushing open the door and breathing in the freezing air conditioned draught. There is a huge water bottle filled with clear water and slices of cucumber.

"*Hola*," says a lady in a pink and red silk scarf and matching jacket.

"Hello," says George, standing on his tiptoes to see over the counter.

"I am looking for Calle Camping Amante. No, Camping Cala Amente. I think…"

His voice trails off. Tears fill his eyes. It is Wednesday and he did so want to get there, but everything has been thwarted and he doesn't know what to do. He knows he will be in big trouble the minute he gets home. Maybe he should go home now.

"Okay, no problem," says the lady.

"You have heard of it?" George says, incredulous.

"Of course," she replies.

He smiles. Hope embraces him. The place emerges with bricks and tiles out of the mists of myth, it becomes real. He feels he is there already.

"I am trying to find it. Can you show me how to get there, please? I am playing with some friends there. I have a playdate."

"Playdate?"

"Er, well, you have a date to go and play. It's a special day."

The lady brings out a large map and spreads it before George.

"You are… 'ere," she says, brandishing a large black pen and marking the spot with a cross.

"Your friends are… 'ere," she continues, marking a circle quite a long way away from the cross. George looks at it doubtfully.

"Camping Cala Amante. Is lovely place, but about fifteen kilometres out of town. Too far for you to walk, I think. Does your mama know you are going there?"

George nods vaguely. "Yes," he lies.

"How are you travelling?"

George looks hopefully up at her. What would his mother say? What would she do?

"Could you organise me a taxi?"

Fifteen minutes later, after he has had plenty of water from the large bottle with the cucumber slices, and been shown to the staff lavatory which he discovers is hidden behind a small door, George is ensconced in the back of an Ibiza Town Taxi, emblazoned with: *We Take U There*.

The lady gave the driver a piece of paper with the name of the campsite. George assured her that yes, his friends could pay for the taxi, and asks if the taxi driver might stay until he has found their caravan. He wants to hold onto the confidence, the surge of hope he has got from the lady and her links. He thanks her very politely. The taxi driver, who is married to the lady from Information, winks at his wife and makes sure that George is strapped into the back seat. Then the car drives off out of the Old Town.

George looks idly out of the window. He is on his way. He looks up at the cloudless sky and notices that there is a helicopter circling the city. Within minutes, the car has left the city perimeter. He is on his way to Camping Calle Amante, after all.

Within the helicopter, there is a slight state of urgency. Jane is in the front, face pressed against the window. "What are we looking for?" she says over the intercom attached to her headphones. "We're never going to see a small boy wandering around."

Philip leans forward from the back seat.

"We are looking for places he might go to. A circus? The beach, although that's a bit dangerous, scrap that. Let's not think about him falling into the sea, shall we? What does he like doing?"

"Lego," says Jane. "And football." She looks directly into the camera. "I must find my son," she says dramatically.

Cresta wriggles forward. "Does he have any school friends here? People he might have gone to visit?"

Jane looks at her, irritated. Why has this awful person tagged onto her drama?

"No. This is a Family Holiday. We are here quite, quite alone. Well, apart from a girl who is helping me with… things. We are meant to be having a Family Getaway."

Rupert, who is also in the back seat, waves the camera at Philip.

"Wanna say anything, Phil?"

Philip draws breath and gives a statement in deep tones appropriate for the situation,

"We are flying above Ibiza Old Town looking for someone who is related to a good friend of mine. I think that's about all I am licensed to say at the moment."

Back on land, the taxi is nearing its destination.

"Ave you reely told your mama that you are going to see your friends?" says the taxi driver, in a more pressing fashion than that of his wife.

"Yes. Well, no, actually. I just went out of the house to see them."

A leathery hand appears in front of George, holding a large Nokia phone. The car continues to move.

"Why don't you phone 'er? She might be worried about you. I know Mamas. Do you know 'er number?"

Silly man, thinks George. He has known his parents' numbers for years. There is absolutely no way he is going to call his mother, however. His father was a much softer touch.

"I might call my father."

"You need to put in the country code. I think this is 0044." The hand waves the phone again.

Reluctantly, George takes it.

It rings for a long time in the *Ibiza (or Bust)* house.

"Hi, Father," he says, formally, when Patrick answers.

"George! Oh my God! My God! George! Everyone! It's George!"

George hears a vague commotion going on around his father.

"George! Where the hell are you! We have been so worried! Where are you?"

"Going to see my friends Jack and Sam. In a campsite."

Patrick sits down with emotion. He finds he is close to tears. He thinks it is important not to berate the child. He remembers now that George had seen these two friends on arrival at Ibiza Airport. Why had anyone not thought of that? Why had they, or he, not remembered what things George holds dear, and catered for them? Why had Jane just set him up with a nanny? He feels choked with guilt, relief and love for the boy.

"Do you know where the campsite is?"

"Yes. I'm in a taxi going there."

Well, at least the boy has initiative, thinks Patrick. He finds he is grinning down the phone to his son.

"Right. Whose phone are you on?"

"The driver's."

"You must call me when you arrive at, where is it?"

"Where is what?"

"The name of the campsite, George."

"Camping Calle Amante."

"And you must give me the name of your friends' mother."

"Michelle, er, Michelle Wright."

"And George?"

"Father?"

"Don't ever do this again. We have had the whole town out looking for you. Your mother is in a helicopter as we speak, do you understand? We have been so worried."

"Wow," says George and hangs up the phone.

"God," says Patrick, turning to Gemma, Alan Makin and Jasper The Wizard, who have all been standing around him, transfixed. "He's turned up, as they say, safe and well. Thank God. Thank God."

Everyone cheers wildly.

"Seems as if he went off on his own to find some friends. I mean, friends he already has from London. Who are on holiday here. Why we didn't think about that, I just don't know. Now, if you will excuse me, I have take a moment to call my wife." Patrick makes a cartoon grimace and steps into the hall.

"Follow him," says Simon to Alex, the second cameraman.

Simon winks at Kate. What a great episode for Programme Three. He can see the billings on the now: *Reality Show Finds Child*. Alright, it wasn't actually his programme which found the child, but that is a detail. He had sent a bloody chopper up, hadn't he?

"I knew he would be alright," confides Jasper to Gemma.

"Oh really? And how did you know?" says Gemma. She has just about had enough of this character and his tricks.

"I turned over a few cards this morning. You know, Tarot. They showed me all would be well."

Gemma walks off. She can't even be bothered to be polite any more. She quite likes the unusual feeling of liberation that rudeness brings her.

Patrick comes back into the room, followed by Alex who kneels down before Patrick and points the camera at him.

"Whoo. Well. Just spoke to the Führer."

"Cut!" says Simon. "Sorry, can you just go from the top without the Hitler reference?"

"What?" says Patrick, confused.

"Sorry, sorry, we want to hear how your wife has reacted but you can't call her the Führer on daytime television."

"Oh, right. Sorry. Household terminology. Well, she's emotional. Very."

"Cut!" says Simon again. "Sorry, can you just go out and come in and start all over again from 'Just spoke to Sue, or Catherine', or whatever your wife is called. Sorry, Jane."

Patrick takes a deep breath, leaves the room and comes back in again.

"Well, I've just spoken to Jane, that is to say, my wife, and she was emotional. And I think she's flying straight to the Campsite. Anyway, all's well that end's well, eh? Is that alright?"

Simon gives him a thumbs-up, turns away and calls Rupert who is still in mid-air.

"Did you get Mum's response? How is everything?"

"Perfect," says Rupert. "Fucking top hole. Mum finds out,

cries. It Girl cries too, takes the chance to snog ArtyPants (his description of Philip Burrell). He snogs her back. Everyone is very happy. We're just about to land at the Campsite for the big reunion."

"This is GREAT," says Simon to Kate. "I was beginning to panic about the narrative arc, and there we are. A lost child! And celebrities snogging on the helicopter! Couldn't be better. Hope he looks sweet."

"What?" says Kate.

"You know, the child. Looking sweet. By which I mean no braces. Or fat. It would be grim if he was fat. I think this might be a *Radio Times* cover, you know. Mind you, his parents aren't so… bit too posh for the audience, anyway, now, I think we all probably need to go to the campsite. Well, not all of us. Let's take Dad, of course, and let's take Jasper and…" Simon pauses for inspiration, then waves a hand aloft and bends his head down to whisper to Kate. "Oh fucking hell, let's take the Brazilian! Yes! Of course! Fucking genius! How old is this boy and his friends? They are bound to know who he is. Bound to. At last we will have someone on this bloody show who will recognise him. But Kate?"

She is already running off to the office to call Francesco's PA.

"What?" she says, turning round.

"Leave the donkey behind."

Chapter Seventeen
George

George gets out of the taxi. He holds a piece of paper bearing the number of the mobile home.

When his friends open the door, they all seem very pleased to see him.

"Hi," said Jack calmly. As if he had really been expected. George was very relieved that Michelle didn't mind at all paying the driver from We Take U There. He'd been a bit worried about that, but had assured Michelle that of course his mother would pay her back. He'd seen adults doing that sort of thing all the time.

He had also been glad that the Reception at Camping Calle Amante knew where the right mobile home was, and very glad when he knocked on the door to see the familiar face of Jack looking at him through the glass.

Michelle did seem a bit surprised to see him, it's true, but after a welcome lunch consisting of Marmite sandwiches, washed down with a glass of Coke and some Haribos, neither of which he was ordinarily allowed, it was as if it had all been arranged.

After lunch, they had all settled down for some Lego. Jack and Sam had brought a set for the Lego Star Wars model of the Millennium Falcon, which George had coveted for some time and which apparently they had acquired from Ebay. He knew that his father would be on his way, and he knew there would be a commotion and a huge fuss when he got there. He wanted to get as much building time in as possible before that happened.

"Strange that your mother put you in a taxi to come here," says Michelle, looking fondly at him. "Don't you have a hire car?"

"Oh, I don't know why she did that," murmurs George. He thought wildly for a minute about the options that might have been available to Jane, which forestalled her dropping him off.

"I think she had a cocktail party to go to. Or a Plates thing on the beach."

Michelle doesn't say anything and carries on washing up the lunch plates.

"She does know you are here, right?"

"Of course," says George. "I've just spoken to my father."

"Oh, have you? That's good to know. After this, shall we go to the Activity Centre? You'll like it George, there's a huge waterslide."

"It's awesome," says Jack.

"Did you bring your swimmers?" asks Sam.

"No," says George, regretfully.

"That's alright," says Michelle. "We've got spares."

George looks around the modest mobile home and wishes that he was on holiday here, with an Activity Centre and waterslides. He likes playing with Belle, but this seems better. Belle. He'd forgotten about her, in all the drama of the morning. He hoped she would be alright. He settles down next to the brothers and searches for a special roof tile.

His quest is halted all too soon by a great commotion outside and a ceremonial knock on the door. He knows this is his father. Or, worse, his mother. He sighs, puts down the brick he is holding and waits to see what is going to happen. He knows it will be big.

Michelle, who is not expecting anyone, puts down the tea towel and opens the door, only to be confronted by a group of people including Rupert wielding a camera, and Simon wielding a Release Form.

"What is going on? Who are you?" says Michelle.

"Michelle Wright? I am Simon Courtney and I am here from TooTuneTV, we are making *Ibiza (or Bust)* for Channel M Daytime, but which will probably be screened sometime by a BBC outlet, would you mind just signing this?"

"What?" says Michelle. "I'm not signing anything. Who are you?"

Patrick jumps up and down, waving urgently from behind a large crowd of people.

"Michelle! It's George's dad here. Bit hard to explain just now, but we are wrapped up with a television reality programme, better just to sign, I'll fill you in later."

Michelle gives Simon a hard look, and signs on the dotted line.

"Wonderful, thank you. Can we possibly come into your mobile home? Would you mind?"

Michelle stands aside, opening the door wide.

Simon leaps into the mobile home and indicates furiously that Rupert ought to follow him, which he does.

"Here, here he is."

Rupert points the camera at the three astonished small boys holding bits of Lego.

"Which one?" he hisses to Simon.

"Er, I don't know. Which one of you is George?"

"I am," says George, standing formally to attention. It was as he had feared, only worse. Much worse. This was terrible. Why was his father surrounded by a television crew?

"Right. Pop back down again, that's it, carry on playing with your Lego with your mates, that's a good kid. Now, Rupert, let's go."

After a brief moment in which the boys self-consciously continue playing with the Millennium Falcon, Patrick is readied.

"And... Action!" says Simon.

Patrick bursts into the mobile home. George is already on his feet.

"George! We've been so worried!"

He enfolds George in his arms. George stands stock still, hands by his side. He has never been so utterly embarrassed. Not only his father, but a whole load of other adults, none of whom he knows, have invaded his friends' home. With a television camera. He glances at Jack and Sam who are sitting silently on the carpet, surrounded by the Millennium Falcon.

"Okay, Dad."

"And here," says Patrick with panache, "is your mother!"

Jane, who has had time since the helicopter landed to apply a full face of make-up, courtesy of Cresta, rushes over, arms wide. George's heart fell. He knew he would be in deep trouble, now.

"George! My darling child. Never do this again."

She holds him, a tight ball of guilt and confusion choking her. She buries her face in his motionless neck. She can't speak. She knows she has failed him. She knows she can't help it.

"Can someone explain to me what the hell is going on?" says Michelle acidly.

"Oh, Michelle, how lovely to see you," manages Jane as she releases her son. "We were so worried about George, we didn't know he was out here. I mean, visiting you. Of course, we knew he wanted to come and see, er, your sons, is it Jack and… Sam? But we just didn't quite have a date in mind. Yet."

"You have to give Michelle twenty Euros for the taxi," says George sitting back down on the floor.

"What? Oh of course, of course," says Jane.

"Told you he would go straight off and find his mates," whispers Cresta to Philip.

"Silly cow wouldn't have it."

"George told me you knew he was here. I don't get it. Who are all these people?" says Michelle, gesturing to Philip Burrell, Cresta the It Girl, Jasper The Wizard and the crew from *Ibiza (or Bust)* who are currently standing within her mobile home.

"Oh, we are doing a bit of television work while we are here. Sort of reality show stuff," says Jane, who has fast overcome her guilt and tears and is now trying to combine pride alongside a fear that she would be found out for not knowing where her son had been all morning.

"Really."

"Yes, really! It's quite fun!" says Jane. She considers that Michelle has had enough attention for now. She turns to her son.

"Guess what, George, I even went up in a helicopter today! Darling. We were so worried about you."

"This is going on for too long. It's probably time to bring in our special guest," mutters Simon to Kate.

"Go for it," she says.

"Rupert, make sure you get this. Patrick, remember your lines?"

"Er, yes," says Patrick anxiously. He had no idea that reality television was so scripted.

"Boys, boys. Listen up. We thought we would bring a bit of a surprise in, to make up for bursting in on you," announces Simon loudly.

"And me too!" interjects Michelle.

"Yes, of course, Michelle, and you too, well to make up for bursting in on you ALL, we thought we would bring in someone who is on the show with us. Now boys, this... is Francesco!" Patrick grandly waves his arms.

The big moment is partially dented by comments from the *Ibiza (or Bust)* contestants.

"So bloody what," mutters Philip.

"Why is he here without his donkey?" says Jasper loudly. "I thought he went nowhere without his donkey."

Francesco Villa walks nonchalantly into the mobile home. He has lost his demeanour of anonymity and is now shouldering a friendly, but public manner.

He clearly indicates that he expects to be adored.

To his calm satisfaction, his arrival has an electric effect on the three young boys, who are still young enough to accept that a multi-millionaire Brazilian superstar who plays football for Real Madrid might indeed just wander into a mobile home, indeed their mobile home, on a campsite in Ibiza and want to meet them.

"Wow! Sick! It's Francesco, Francesco Villa!" They crowd around him.

"Why aren't you in your Number Seven shirt?"

"Can I see your shoes?"

"Can you do some keepie-uppies for us, now?"

"Can you do Around the World? I've seen your YouTube channel."

"Francesco, can I have a selfie with you, can we go and play football? We've got a Real Madrid ball here just for you! Awesome!"

They drag him towards the door. Francesco shrugs happily at the camera and hops down outside.

"*Obrigado*, boys," he says.

Back in the mobile home, there is a stunned silence.

"What just happened there?" says Jasper The Wizard. "I didn't see this coming in my Tarot cards."

"Your fucking cards didn't alert you to the fact that Francesco seems to be rather well known?" asks Philip, acidly.

"I think he might be a striker for Real Madrid," says Patrick timidly. "At least that's what he says," he mutters, jerking his thumb at Simon.

Simon is bent double in the tiny kitchen, weeping with laughter.

"Oh, très *amusant*," hisses Philip. "Get a whole load of OLDIES together, see how OUT OF TOUCH we all are, how HIGH AND MIGHTY we all are, and then get a bunch of kids to show us up. What a great plan. Because the 'donkey handler' happens to be a fucking world famous footballer. Well, I for one was never taken in by all that donkey stuff. I knew there was something in it. But how very clever, what a huge amount of planning it must have taken. You know, the lost child and all that. Ha bloody ha."

He turns on Jane. "And you, my lovely neighbour, are one hell of an actress." He pulls his microphone off his lapel.

"To hell with this," he says, storming out of the mobile home.

Jane gasps, although not without a sneaking pleasure that her acting skills seem to have been praised. "What? What have I done now?"

"Pretending to lose your son!" shouts Philip from outside.

"I certainly did not pretend," says Jane. "We had no idea where he was, really."

"No, no, she didn't, I can attest for her complete surprise and shock," murmurs Patrick.

Michelle surveys them all, hands on her hips.

"So George didn't tell you where he was off to? Well full marks to him for getting here under his own steam."

"Oh, yes, here's the money for the taxi," says Jane, holding out the note with the awkwardness over money common to the English middle classes.

"Thanks." There is a silence as Michelle shakes her head, and then comments. "Francesco Villa. Even I know he's the striker for Real Madrid. You mean he's been hanging out with you on this show and you had no idea?"

"I thought he was rather too well dressed," says Cresta, who can see the funny side.

"What a laugh. I don't know anything about football, and I don't care if I look like a muppet, because if you don't know, you don't know," snorts Michelle. "But the boys are made up, that's for sure. You're not going to see them for the rest of the day!"

There is a silence while everyone considers the phenomenon of a professional footballer pretending to be a donkey handler and fooling British celebrities.

Philip saunters back into the house on the pretence he has lost his sunglasses.

"What happens now?" asks Jane.

"Er, nothing really," admits Simon briskly. "I've decommissioned the chopper. We'll be going back to the house in a while. I'll leave Francesco here for a bit, his position on the show is over really, now he's been unmasked. We only had access to him for three days, in truth, so it's no bad thing this has happened. We'll go and do a PTC with him in a minute saying goodbye. But Jane, I'm very very pleased that we found George for you. Reunited him. All safe and well. Marvellous."

"What's a PTC?"

"Piece to camera. He'll probably drop in on us at a later date but that's him out of the programme. He was only ever booked for three days. We couldn't afford any more."

"I bet he's not on our pay scale, that's for sure," mutters Philip.

"So what happens to the rest of you?" asks Jane, pointing at Cresta, Philip and Jasper.

"Oh, we go back to the house. Until we get chucked off," says Cresta nonchalantly.

"Which is when?"

"I think one of us leaves tomorrow," says Philip, who knows perfectly well this is the case. "Thank God. I hope it's me."

"Do you really?"

"YES," says Philip with feeling.

"It's not going to be," murmurs Simon to Rupert. "I'll make sure of that."

"I'd love to come up and see you in the house," says Jane brightly.

"Jane, darling," interjects Patrick. He can see his wife's longing to be on television, and he is determined to quash it.

"We have to get back to our house. To our holiday. Think about George. An hour ago we thought we had lost him! Belle is probably still out searching for him."

"Oh, God, I forgot to call Belle," says Jane.

"Goodbye, everyone," says Patrick hurriedly. "Let us know when the show airs. Thank you, Michelle. Very much.

Do I owe you anything else for the taxi? No? Are you sure? Alright, we'll be back to collect George... when? Tea time? Then you must come over to ours. As they say."

They step out of the mobile home and walk together to the camping site reception, where there is a direct line to We Take U There taxis.

"Do you mind waiting ten minutes?" says the receptionist.

"You have got to call Belle," says Patrick. "It's only fair. Poor girl."

Jane snorts. "I have no idea where she is."

Belle and Jas are walking some way behind Vince, who is scanning the red cliff landscape outside Ibiza Town.

Belle is distraught, sniffing and occasionally sobbing.

"He's just such a sweet little thing. Loves jumping in the pool. Honestly he would do it all day if I let him."

She remembers the feel of his slippery thin body in the swimming pool. His laugh.

"Jas, if something has happened to him..."

For the fortieth time that day, Jas consoles her.

"Look, shall we call the police? I think we should, you know. I really do. Maybe we should call Jane? She might have found him, you know."

"Yes, perhaps. But wouldn't she have called me?"

"Call her. Vince, mate?" Jas yells towards Vince. "Just stop a while. We're calling George's mum."

Belle turns away, taps in the number of her employer.

"Jane? It's Belle. Have, have you any news?"

There is a pause. Then Belle screams.

"You FOUND HIM? You actually found him? He's OKAY?"

She sits down on the grass, crying.

"No, no, that's fine. I'm fine. Yes, of course I'm still out looking for him, but no, don't worry about not calling me. Where was he? With friends? Really? His friends? The ones we saw at the airport, oh yes."

She is silent.

"I remember now."

"What, what?" Jas is hopping up and down, waving to the other walkers.

"He's been found!" he yells to them.

"Where the hell was he?" he asks Belle.

"With two friends. I never thought… But now I remember him saying something about Wednesday. What day is it today? He went off to play with them. In a campsite. Jane?" she says, turning back to the phone. "Shall I come back to the villa now?"

She puts the mobile in her bag and lies on her back, looking at the sky.

"I want to go home. Proper home. Not back to the villa. Let's go back to London. I'm probably going to be fired anyway. Almost definitely."

Jas squats down beside her.

"Come on babes. All's well that ends well."

Chapter Eighteen
Gemma

Gemma is in her bedroom. It is very quiet. Simon and some of the others have gone out for a 'morning walk', and seem to be taking a very long time about it. She had opted to stay in, but perhaps that was a mistake, she now thinks. Maybe they are doing something important, something which will help keep her on the show.

She feels rather lonely. The lines have been drawn up and as far as she can see, it's her and Alan the financial adviser, against everyone else.

It's like being back at school.

She feels particularly vengeful towards Nigel, the Adventurous Parent. Since he was so openly insulting to her at dinner the night before, he has been practically stalking her around the place, coming out from corridors and beckoning her into empty rooms. She fears he has the worse intentions. Does he really think she would like to kneel before him and – as the papers might put it – 'pleasure' him? Does he really think that? Creep. Why doesn't he just go and make some more babies with his hideous wife Jocelyn? The woman with the perfect pelvic floor. Ugh. Some people really enjoy shoving their candour down your throat, thinks Gemma. As if we are all interested, which we are not.

Well, probably some people are, she reasons, and she's sure the television show will unveil a certain audience who might like to know about it, but she doesn't. She doesn't want to know any more about people who lead such lives. She had no idea they existed, and she is rather sad now that they do, and also sad that she knows they do.

She's nearly worn all her outfits already, and some of them need a dry clean. Her hair is beginning to look ratty. Her nails need manicuring. Up against Cresta, whose entire body is a groomed, tattooed glory of chemical and surgical perfection, she feels ugly, and old. She wants to go home. But she also feels a strange power beginning to wax within her, what with all that nonsense about the Beach Olympics, and nearly drowning, and being hailed as a feminist.

She doesn't want to be chucked off the show first, that would be an utter humiliation.

There is a knock at the door.

It's Cresta's other half, the idiotic 'celebrity farmer' known as Moo. Moo is closely followed by Alex, the second cameraman.

"Wanna go for a swim?" says Moo.

"What is happening today, do you know?" says Gemma. There is no way she is going in that weed-infested pool with this man. "What are... people doing?"

"I don't know. I don't know where Cresta and the others are," says Moo in his strange, whiny voice. "No idea. They went out for an early coffee with Simon and Rupert and it's now almost lunchtime. Fish is meditating and I think Alan is... I have no idea where Alan is actually."

She stares at him.

"Skinny dip?"

She slams the door in his face.

She lies down on the bed. She'd better start being nicer to people, she knows. Otherwise she actually will get chucked off the show. The way the programme is arranged is that after the first week, everyone votes for everyone else. That's what will happen tomorrow.

The person with the least votes gets has the early exit.

125

And then the next, and then the next. Brutal. Who could bear being the first to go, knowing that they were the least popular? However, sucking up to everyone would just look pathetic, particularly as it will be aired on television. Gemma, not for the first time, thinks of the money. It wasn't even that much, when you considered it. Four thousand pounds. Why did it seem to matter so much at the outset?

There is a second knock on the door. Oh, God.

She opens it. To her horror, it's Nigel. Her nemesis. And of course Alex with his camera.

"What?"

"Hey sunshine," says Nigel. "I've just had a call from Simon. He's on his way back with the others. Seems as if they got caught up in rescuing a child or something. A big drama anyway. Well, I wondered, before they come back, would you like to come and play boules with Jocelyn and me outside by the pool?"

Gemma looks at him without speaking.

"We have our own special way of doing it."

"I bet you do," says Gemma politely.

She slams the door again.

She can hear Nigel laughing in the corridor. God, she hates him.

"Sweetie if you want my vote you're going to have to calm down a bit. Calm down and smell the coffee. We're all human beings on this planet together."

"Fuck off," says Gemma. She had no idea she could be this rude.

"Why don't you go and stroke the donkey?"

"Why don't you go away?"

"Touching an animal is meant to be very calming if you are stressed out," he says, through the wooden door.

"I guess I can be a bit of an animal you know, Gems."

"Don't call me Gems. With regard to your invitation I refer you to my previous statement."

He has no shame, thinks Gemma. This is all going to be

on television, doesn't he care? Or at least, if he doesn't care about himself, he should care about his eight bloody children, and how they are going to feel when they are teased about it at school. Or perhaps they don't HAVE a television, and of course, she now recalls, they don't go to bloody school, do they, because naturally they are all homeschooled. So he can say what he likes, because he and his family and his awful Free Love wife have just opted out of the modern world and live in some sort of weird bubble. Great. She feels like crying out of frustration and disappointment that this whole television experience is proving to be so unbearable. She had such high hopes of it.

She wonders if Nigel and Alex are still out in the corridor.

She opens the door slightly. To her joy, the corridor is empty. She tiptoes across to Alan's room, and taps gently on the door.

"Who is it?"

"It's me, Gemma," she says.

"Come in," says Alan. What a relief, she thinks. Someone normal to talk to. She'd go mad without Alan's calm ordinariness, his essential Alan-ness. He is the most normal celebrity she has ever met.

She walks in, finds him sitting on the bed in front of his computer.

"Alan! You CAN'T do that! This is meant to be an internet-free zone!"

He folds the computer away hastily. "I know, I know. Just had to catch up with some stuff."

He puts it underneath the duvet.

"I didn't even know there was Wi-Fi here."

"There isn't. I'm on 4G."

Gemma looks at him anxiously.

"I hate this experience so much I actually want to be the first to leave. But also, I don't. Do you think I will be the first to be chucked out?"

Alan smiles at her. "For the last time, no you won't. Things will improve. You're just having a bit of a dip. You're one of the stars of the programme."

"Am I really?"

"Sure! You're about the only person here who truly speaks their mind, although everyone is pretending to."

"Well who will then?"

Alan leans back easily on his elbows. "Get chucked out? I think it will be Philip. Or maybe Jocelyn."

"I hope to God it's Nigel. That would be the answer to my prayers. Don't know how you can be so sure. Would you mind if it was you?"

"No. Well, maybe a tiny bit, but that's just ego. But I'm not going to get chucked off."

"How can you be so sure? It's about people voting, isn't it?"

Alan shrugs, and smiles. "I just know I won't. I'm too useful in the mix. And so, my dear celebrity estate agent, are you. I don't think it's about voting at all. I think it's about the production team choosing. Now. Isn't it time for lunch?"

There is a clatter of feet along the corridor. She hears Francesco talking, and wonders if this is the moment that Burro is to pay a visit to the bedrooms.

Then she hears the unmistakable tones of Philip Burrell.

"Yes, well, all's well that end's well I say, as I have said several times already on this quite extraordinary morning. Footballers and all."

Alan looks at Gemma.

"You don't think it's about voting? I'm just too naïve for this world. I'll just go and put some make-up on," says Gemma. "See you in the dining room."

She leaves his room and quickly flits into hers. On the floor she sees a letter which has clearly been pushed under her door. It has her name on the envelope. Picking it up and opening it she gasps.

Chapter Nineteen
Jane

Jane faces Belle in the kitchen. "What more is there to say, Belle? You were charged to care for George. You were employed to care for George, and you were to be paid to do so, and you failed. Not just in a little way. In a big way. He vanished. He could have been in danger. He could have been killed."

"I turned my back for a second and he simply slipped away. He'd planned the whole thing. He even had his clothes laid out. He murmured something to me about it in the airport, but I forgot about that in the panic of the moment."

She is sunburned and weary. She delivers the lines she and Jas have rehearsed all afternoon.

"When I realised he had gone I immediately went looking for him. Right away. I was scared. Look, I'll go home if you want. I think I want to go home anyway. Don't worry about paying me for the work I've already done. Please let me go home. I'm really sorry."

Belle looks dully at her employer, expecting to be told to go and pack.

However, now she is actually faced with the resignation of her only resource for child care, Jane isn't sure that she wants to trigger it.

What with the joy of George being found, and banishment of her guilt at the excitement of the television crew, and the

129

fact of actually being on television, and the possibility of being on television again, all the talk of sacking Belle now, somehow, seems to wither slightly in the afternoon light.

Because if she gets rid of Belle, which is the obvious course of action for her as an employer, who will look after George? All the time? She will have to.

She runs through the options in her mind as she pours herself a glass of water.

"Want some?"

"Yes, thanks Jane. Jane, please believe me. I am so sorry."

Here Belle departs from the script.

"I have loved looking after George." She sips the iced water. Her eyes fill with tears. "I love him."

She took the job because it signified a free holiday for her and Jas, and would give her money to fund a ticket for The Reading Festival but the real discovery for her this week in Ibiza has been the joy in getting to know this odd little only child, this boy with his formal ways, daily habits and small pleasures.

She was horrified when she lost him. Now he's been found, she wants to cherish him. Even though she would still like to leave this nasty, over-luxurious villa.

Jane doesn't want Belle to love George. She simply wants her to look after him. Loving wasn't part of the deal. Jane loves George and thinks that is enough for the child. But still. Of course, Patrick could always be drafted in to look after him but then what about the babysitting they had anticipated? Plus, if Belle goes home early then she, Jane, would probably have to pay for a fresh ticket back to London for her. It all suddenly seemed too unnecessary.

Jane also knows she has asked too many hours of Belle. She really ought to have been there as George made his great escape. If she, Jane, sends her home, then there will be absolutely nothing to stop her badmouthing her, and explaining to everyone, all their neighbours on the Square, how very irresponsible she, Jane, had been. And how lazy she and Patrick had been in the mornings… On a family holiday no less. And also how nasty she had been in sacking her. She might even take it to the papers. Particularly as the episode looks likely to air on something like BBC1, Jane thinks hopefully. Belle's parents would never speak to her again. No, she needs to keep Belle close to her.

"I'm glad you love George," she lies. "He is a very lovable child. I think he loves you too. The other important thing is, Belle," she says, playing the mother card, "that I don't want George to feel he has done something very wrong, and that you are being punished on his behalf. He is after all, only seven."

"He's eight, actually," murmurs Belle.

"Yes, of course. Eight. Of course. Well, I think as things stand and now that everything has ended well, I think I would like you to stay, Belle. Of course if you insist on going home, there is little I can do about it, you are free to go and buy a ticket if you want…" pausing to let that particular point drill home, "but I think you should stay. Let's draw a veil over this," she says, using a favoured phrase belonging to her mother.

To Jane's horror, Belle breaks down completely, and hugs her frantically.

"Thank you, Jane. I'm so sorry. I'll never take my eyes off him again. Thankyouthankyouthankyou."

They hear a merry hoot from outside. Patrick comes driving into the compound, with George in the back of the car. The boy can hardly get the door open quickly enough.

He rushes over to Belle and Jane.

"Francesco Villa was sick! We saw Francesco Villa, he came to Jack and Sam's caravan. He signed my shirt, look, look!"

Jane steps back kindly to let Belle have her moment.

"Fantastic," says Belle. "He really came round to the mobile home? Francesco Villa. Well, that's television for you. Oh George. It is so good to see you. Please don't disappear like that in the future. I have been looking for you all over the island."

"Belle, I am so sorry. I went, well it was because it was a

Wednesday and that is my favourite day and I really really wanted to see Jack and Sam. But everything's fine now, and we saw Francesco Villa, you know he plays for Real Madrid and Brazil of course, so it was in fact quite a good thing that I went to see them, wasn't it?"

She can't speak. She buries her face into her hands.

"Just don't do it again," she says, muffled.

"Were you worried, Belle? Were you really?" He smiles, looks into her wet eyes. "Don't cry. I was fine. I was just doing the Millennium Falcon with Jack and Sam. I knew they had a set and I really wanted to help them. Do you know it has over 4,000 pieces, and is really meant to be for people aged over 16? And they got it from Ebay. Can we have a look on Ebay to see if there's another one, so we don't have to wait until I can get it for Christmas?"

"How did you get to see Jack and Sam in the end? Sounds like it was miles away."

"I took a taxi," he says proudly.

"His mother's son," says Patrick, laughing.

"And your mother was up in a helicopter. Goodness George, you do know how to cause a commotion. But let's only do that once."

George is happy, but he hasn't forgotten about that anxious moment eating the banana on the side of the road, or the bad moment with the lady in Information, when he felt lost and worried. He nods his head.

"Of course."

"Shall we all have supper by the pool?" says Jane briskly. "Darling, can you fire up the barbeque?" She turns and hugs her son.

"Never do that again, never."

George stands stock still, letting the waves of emotion and guilt lap around him. After a while, he thinks, everyone will calm down and let him explain about Francesco Villa and how he has a selfie with him.

Later that evening, Patrick watches his wife kissing George

on the sunlounger. Thank Christ the boy has been found. Poor little mite, walking all the way into town, although it has to be said he is rather jaunty despite the mileage. And getting a taxi, that showed initiative. But still, Patrick considers he probably needs to be a bit more on George's wavelength now he is growing up. They do. He and Jane. What did she want? He looks at her, with her bright lipstick, laughing as if nothing had happened. She was jolly pleased to have found herself at the midst of a TV show, he knows. But why was it so important to be immortalised this way?

He glances at Belle, sitting beside the pool. What on earth was the girl up to? This morning has been a revelation across the board, considers Patrick. He needs to speak to her.

He turns the barbeque down to a low heat. "Belle, come here a sec," he says. That chicken will take a few minutes.

They walk inside the kitchen, leaving Jane hovering over George outside. Belle looks at him, worried. He takes in her red eyes and nose.

"I'm as delighted as you are. And I was as worried as you were. More. I know it wasn't your fault, and you behaved very well in the circumstances," he says. He is anxious to have everything on a fair footing. "However, Belle, I think there are mitigating circumstances here."

She looks at him, uncertain. "Mitigating?"

"Causal links."

"Causal?"

"Yep. You see, Belle, I saw you arriving back into the house in the early hours this morning. I saw you climb in the window. I saw you."

She flushes, looks down at her feet.

"Does Jane know?" she says, huskily.

"No. Where were you, Belle?"

"I was with Jas. My boyfriend."

For some reason, this reassures Patrick, who had been wildly imagining Belle to be at the centre of a drugs hub ran by Spanish narcotics barons.

"Oh, is that all? Jas? The boy from around the corner in London?"

"We went, er, clubbing. I came back and then... I fell asleep out on the lounger. I am so sorry Patrick. It won't happen again. Jas helped me search for George. Please believe me. Please don't tell Jane."

"No, I won't. You can't go out again with him like that, though."

"No. I know. I've already told him that."

"Go out with him for supper earlier, but be back by eleven. We'll say no more about it."

It would give him a chance for Family Time with Jane and his son. It was what he had wanted anyway, in this holiday. Let the girl go and do her own thing. He'd have this over her if she slips up again.

He saunters back out into the blinding sunshine, and begins to put the cooked chicken bits around the plates sitting on the table he has already set up beside the barbeque.

Chapter Twenty
Gemma

When Gemma sees what is on the card, the shock is such that she has to sit down on the bed.

She turns the card over.

There is a short inscription on the back.

Thinking of you?

Gemma turns the card back over again and stares at the photograph. Then she puts it back into the envelope. Suddenly, she is overcome by nausea. She rushes into her bathroom and vomits into the toilet.

She spends a long time in the bathroom, washing her face. Then she comes back into the bedroom and stands before her wardrobe. She takes off her jaunty, striped playsuit and pulls out a long plain blue top and trousers.

She doesn't care to seem summery or fun. Not now.

There is a low knock on the door.

She opens it. Alan. Thank goodness. Her only true friend in the house.

"It's lunch. Everyone's back from the trip and Simon wants us all gathered on the terrace."

She looks at him silently.

"What's wrong?"

Gemma draws back dramatically. "Come in. Close the door. Have a look at this."

She hands him the envelope. He pulls the card out.

"My God. My God," says Alan quietly. "This is unspeakable."

He looks at Gemma. Her face is full of red and white blotches, and tears are in her eyes.

"Let me give you a hug. Is this from whom I think it is from?"

"Can you doubt it? I've just been sick. It is disgusting, and depraved."

"I'm not surprised. We have to show it to Simon. Get the so and so off the show."

Despite herself, she laughs.

"Nobody else would say 'the so and so', Alan! You are funny."

"Well, I could say Total Arse, or worse. But I opted not to," replies Alan, with a wry smile.

"Come on. Put this in your pocket. We don't want it going astray. It's too inflammatory."

She slips her shoes on and tidies her hair.

On the terrace, Philip Burrell, despite his earlier outrage at the situation, is holding court in front of the other contestants, Simon and Rupert.

"… and so there we were, all hovering anxiously outside this rather SMALL caravan."

"Mobile home, actually babes," interjects Cresta, who has developed a rather close camaraderie with Philip after the helicopter ride.

"Yes, well, said mobile home, and said child is within. Parents outside with us. A full emotional moment awaits. We get in, and what do you know but they are playing Lego! What a brilliant encapsulation of the classic British holiday!"

"Er, isn't Lego Danish?" says Moo.

Philip chooses to ignore this interjection and continues.

"Parents rush in, find the child, hugs, tears, all that. Very stirring. But what the three little boys really love is what happens next. And that comes from our wonderful donkey guardian. The delightful Francesco. Who has been hiding

136

around the corner, and turns up to reveal to the world that he is really a FAMOUS FOOTBALLER. Of course, we all knew he wasn't a fucking herdsman all along, well I almost certainly knew. It always seemed far too unlikely."

"Yeah, he was far too good-looking frankly," says Cresta.

"What?" says Gemma. "I don't understand."

"Well, the kids go wild about him and everything is suddenly a triumph."

"Simon, I have to talk to you," says Gemma into his ear.

Irritated, he turns away from the action, which is going very well.

"What, what is it?"

"Could you come over here?" She checks that nobody is watching her. Apart from Alan, who smiles encouragingly and gives her a small wave.

"I have just had this put under my door."

She gives him the envelope.

"Jeepers!" he says, jumping away as if he has just been bitten. "What the hell? When did you get this? Just now? Who is it from? Whose…?"

Gemma closes her eyes. "I can only surmise 'it' belongs to Nigel."

"Blimey," says Simon, examining the photograph closer. "Are you sure?"

Gemma snatches the card back. "Of course I'm not SURE, you twit. You can't tell, can you! I mean, it's just an ORGAN. But frankly this is harassment and it's not funny. And it has to stop."

Alan, who has heard all of this, walks over to Simon.

"I am going to front him up about this, if you don't."

In a different world, Simon would like to have had a different career, but this is not a different world. This is the world he has chosen, and he is a television producer. He can't resist. This is gold dust, he tells himself. Gold Dust. It would make a brilliant episode for Programme Six. After the kid moment, and Francesco Villa, to come back to the house and find sexual harassment and, well, what one could only describe as a Pornographic Moment going on, and now something equating a duel between the two men, it is frankly unmissable. Isn't it? Only how was he going to get away with showing that card on Daytime Television? Maybe, he thinks quickly, going through the options, maybe he wouldn't be obliged to show it at all. Maybe that is more powerful. Maybe this event is strong enough to push this show onto PEAK TIME. Simon feels butterflies in his stomach at the very thought of it. Producing a show on Peak.

Although what would Ofcom say? What were the guidelines about nudity? He'd have to go online at the first opportunity, although he thinks this sort of thing would be out of bounds at any time of day on a terrestrial channel.

Simon had actually planned that the ineffectual and frankly dull Fish would be the first to go, tomorrow night, but now he feels duty bound to kick Nigel off the show. Jocelyn will have to go with him, which would be a shame. She and he were simply the most outrageous people on the programme, what with their loose ways and her pelvic floor and everything. And now this.

Damn.

"Are you sure it's Nigel?" he says again to Gemma.

"Simon, please. It's hardly from Jasper the bloody Wizard, is it? Or Francesco the donkey handler who we now find out is a famous footballer? This man, Nigel, has been hounding me ever since that awful dinner. And now it's reached Peak…"

"Penis?" says Alan, snorting.

"Alan!"

"Sorry, sorry. I know it's not funny. Look, you know I don't approve of his harassment of you. I think it's disgusting and in very bad taste. I've offered to front him up about it. Which I will. After lunch. Out there by the pool."

"Alright, you do that," says Simon. "We'll film it. I'll sack him from the show afterwards. In private of course. But to have you publicly accusing him – although please no mention of penises, this is Daytime Television, remember, and that word can only really be said after the watershed – yes, a public accusation by one of the contestants, sorry, guests on the show, will give me a good dramatic rationale and explanation to the viewers as to why he has suddenly left. I think people would be sad to see him leave but," seeing Gemma's increasingly exasperated face, "of course with such an action, there is no option for him but to go. And his wife. Pity. No, I mean, it's a pity they are behaving like this. Strange people."

"Well, you invited them on," says Gemma. "Where the hell did you find them in the first place?"

"We advertised," admits Simon.

Chapter Twenty-One
Simon

Everyone sits down to a very late lunch. The table is set with treats from the local market: Sobrassada sausage, Bellota ham, Mahón cheese from Menorca and tall, dusky green bottles of olive oil.

"I suppose now we all know Francesco is a global star and not a donkey hand, that Burro's been dismissed from the show already?" asks Jocelyn loudly, as she reaches for a Mahón cheese crisp biscuit decorated with ham, mint and slices of peach.

"Er, yes," admits Simon out of shot. "Sadly, yes. The donkey has gone, everyone. Of course you realise that her main purpose was as a prop for, er, the Brazilian. Francesco Villa. Who is, if anyone didn't catch that, a very famous footballer. In the end we decided not to go with the Bedroom Visits," he continues. "Seems as if the *Radio Times* changed their mind about the shoot, which is a pity."

"I will have to say goodbye to her," says Jocelyn firmly. "Is she still in her stable?"

"Gone already, I'm afraid," says Simon bluntly.

"No!"

"Yes."

"You are heartless, you know that!"

He shrugs. "It's a television show. Don't forget it."

"Probably already on its way to the canning factory to be made into dog food," says Philip loudly.

"How could you!" hisses Jocelyn.

"Well, I always knew that was a hopeless idea, if you don't mind me saying so," says Philip, with satisfaction. "Bedroom Visits! I ask you." He takes some bread and dunks it aggressively in a saucer of oil.

"There was no way that donkey was coming into my inner sanctum. With or without an apparently World Famous Footballer."

Simon gazes at him with hatred. Maybe they ought to have told Gilda where the house was when she called for the umpteenth time. That would have cramped Philip's style somewhat. That would have ruined it for him, the lecherous old man. Well, he might do. In time. Right now he just wants to put him down.

"Francesco, who is very nice as well as famous in real life, Philip, is going to pop by later and say Ciao. Or whatever Goodbye is in Spanish. Or Brazilian. He speaks about five languages, actually. Anyway, if you want to say bye to him, be around the pool," he says, raising his voice so everyone hears.

"He popped by briefly earlier to pack some things and his people have already collected his stuff, but he'll be back in person later. We are having a little drinks thing for him. At teatime. All welcome."

A moment that has cost the production company a small fortune, he feels like adding.

Dealing with Villa, who was a real celebrity, and who had naturally therefore had an agent and 'people' with him, including a team from Make-up and Hair, had been painful for Simon. Coping with Villa was a totally different thing compared to coping with this mob, people who were not famous although the programme pretended they were. People such as Philip. Simon looked at him. His celebrity status was about as firm as the scales on a butterfly wing. Or Moo, the 'celebrity farmer' who nobody had heard of. Or Cresta, the It Girl.

No, dealing with the likes of Francesco Villa was an enterprise requiring very different skills.

Villa's fame inhabited a world Simon realised he heartily disliked, because it was a world in which he had no power. In the world of minor fame, he was in charge. He could dictate what happened. In Villa's world, he couldn't. The talent dictated what the production did. Villa's agent demanded not only money, and a lot of it, but also an impossible schedule. The Brazilian was only to be called at certain times, he was only obliged to be on television for a set amount of minutes, he would only wear certain brands of denim and he could only eat certain foods. He had to have special mineral water provided for him in a separate bottle. Donkey handler, indeed. Frankly, the donkey was the easiest part of it (and something that Simon could see that Villa himself rather enjoyed). They had even had to buy a brand new helicopter.

Although, Simon has to acknowledge that after only a week in the *Ibiza (or Bust)* house the others – mere asteroids compared to the planetary fame of Villa – have changed. They actually believe they are famous. They no longer flinch, or laugh, when he calls them 'Celebrities'. They like having an official Celebrity Bus. They have started to demand accoutrements in their rooms such as hairdryers and ironing boards. They walk around with their heads held high. It is as if a Famous Persona, dormant all along within each, has awoken and hatched out in all its terrible glory. Apart from Gemma, Simon thinks.

She's the only person on the show who still seems normal, shy and undemanding. Still, that will change. This is the fourth series of *Ibiza (or Bust)* that Simon has produced. He is long used to how it changes people. Contestants forget they are being filmed. They also forget they are nobodies. This can make them unreasonable. The whole format is actually quite dangerous, thinks Simon. It plays with people's minds. Replaces reality with fantasy. 'Reality' is actually not what it is at all. It is made-up, all of it. The illusion lasts until the punters get kicked off. It's a foul concoction. And he is part of it. Well, it's a Faustian pact that pays his mortgage.

He sighs, and drinks some sangria.

What was it that he had to do now with them, his puppets? Oh, of course. That bloody postcard. That's the next thing to sort out. He's very cross. Nigel will have to go, of course, but what a quandary it puts him in. Nigel and Jocelyn are so good, so outrageous, so willing to say anything to anyone, that he is loathed to see the back of them. Maybe there is a way around it. He looks down the table. Maybe the card isn't from Nigel after all, he thinks hopefully. And if it isn't, then he won't have to go. Who the hell is it from, however, and how the hell is he going to find out? He can hardly have an identity parade.

He looks at Gemma, who is chatting to Alan. She's sweet, but so dull. Could she have planted the card in order to get rid of Nigel? She hates him, no question. Simon rejects this option. It is simply too outrageous to imagine the vanilla Gemma doing such a thing.

He would have to have it out with Nigel and then if it transpires that it is him, Simon and his team will be obliged to rig the voting. He had been hoping to rig it so that Fish, the boring yoga-obsessed chanter had been the first for the high jump. He had high hopes from Fish, but he simply hadn't delivered. Oh well. He can be the next one to go. Or maybe they can get rid of two at once. Three, counting Jocelyn. But that won't work with the programme schedule.

He sighs and stands up.

Rupert, always alert for a sign from his boss, jumps up too, but Simon motions him to keep on shooting at the table. Philip is explaining why the Turner Prize is a waste of time. The footage of Philip himself won't be used but it might provide a few good shots of people listening, or yawning. Simon is going to enjoy editing anything which might help to bring Philip Burrell down. He is going to make him look like the total twit he really is. Simon is looking forward to it. He wonders what Philip's wife is like. Probably a fucking saint.

He walks quietly round the table and taps Nigel on the shoulder.

"Have you finished, Nigel? Sorry to bother you but can I just have a quiet word?"

Gemma notices Nigel leave the table. She nudges Alan.

"Here goes."

Alan winks. "Keep talking. Don't react. At all."

Simon rounds the corner with Nigel, who is grinning inanely. He is wearing a white linen safari suit. He looks like someone on the 1970s TV show *Daktari*. Was it possible that he could have sent such an outrageous card to Gemma? Highly, thinks Simon.

"How can I help, Sire?" says Nigel, bowing ridiculously, and yet again Simon quails at the notion of kicking such a watchable goon off his programme.

"Well, Nigel, it seems as if, er, Gemma has received some very upsetting material tonight. And she thinks it comes from you."

"Material? What do you mean, material?" He looks genuinely surprised.

"A postcard. With a pornographic image on it." Simon feels as if he is talking like his father might. "Posted under her bedroom door. Any idea?"

Nigel stares at Simon.

"How hilarious! A porn shot and she thinks I'm the model. Well, I'm very flattered, but I'm afraid you've got the wrong idea. Is this… Is this because I have made a few risqué remarks to Gemma over the dining table? Invited her to play boules with me and Jocelyn? Now she is trying to frame me with a slur about sending her porn! And doesn't have the guts to do it directly! How very pathetic," he says, his lips whitening. "Tell you what, Simon, have you seen this picture?" He draws Simon closer to him by his lapels. Simon can smell the sangria on his breath.

"Calm down, please. Yes of course I have, Nigel. It is of a male… organ. She thinks it is… yours."

There is a pause while Nigel looks glassily back.

"Nigel?"

"Well, tell me this. Is there a piercing anywhere in sight, hey?"

Simon has to think about this. She had flashed it at him, so to speak, and then put it back in the envelope. He can't actually remember seeing anything on the card, more than a lot of… flesh. He's pretty sure there was no piercing around.

"Er, I don't think so."

Nigel smiles at him. "Well, mate, I have to assure you then it's not mine. Unless it's a very tight close-up. No siree! I am the proud possessor of a wholly pierced penis and scrotum. Innocent as charged. Ha ha!"

He pushes Simon away, laughing helplessly and, Simon thinks, nastily. Thank God Rupert isn't recording any of this.

Nigel puts his hands up. "Not guilty. I did it myself too. Not the picture. The piercings. While watching a very long and dull documentary series on TV. Did a couple, thought well, it's not too bad. Might as well do thirty. Can I go back to the table, sir?"

Simon smiles at him. Pierced scrotum. This man is a find, and no mistake. Well, at least he won't have to chuck him off the programme. He sighs. He'll have to speak with Gemma and calm her down.

He walks back to the table and catches Gemma's eye. He shakes his head and shrugs his shoulders. "Nope," he mouths.

She frowns.

"A song, a song!" Moo is shouting at Cresta. "Go on baby. Give it to me one more time!"

"Alright." Cresta stands up rather unsteadily.

"Keep it clean, Cresta!" shouts Jocelyn. "Actually, don't!"

Rupert stands up and focuses the camera as Cresta, standing on a chair, in a pair of microscopic hot pants, starts to sing Beyonce's 'Single Ladies'.

"But of course, she's not!" yells Moo rather unnecessarily as she begins.

"Don't be so sure," rejoins Philip, who hasn't forgotten the snog in the helicopter. He looks approvingly at Cresta's conical breasts, which are almost immovable on her chest. God, they are big, thinks Philip. He mentally takes off her tiny top and revels in the notion of seeing her in a lacy bra.

Simon finds himself looking at the groins of the men on the show, wondering whose genitals are pierced and whose are not. This isn't a real job, he thinks.

As Cresta continues to warble and wobble on the chair, Alan gets up from the table and walks behind Nigel. He taps him on the shoulder.

"What now?" says Nigel, irritably.

"Come out here, sunshine."

"My, I am popular this lunchtime. What is it?"

Alan is leading Nigel to the terrace. Alex trots behind them.

"I've seen it."

"What?" says Nigel. "What the hell are you talking about?"

"The card."

"Oh yes, the pornographic card that I am supposed to have sent in order to terrify and harass the comely maiden Gemma. I've heard all about this card. Bor-ing. Next?"

Alan suddenly grabs Nigel's linen jacket by the collar and pulls Nigel close.

"Look, you weirdo. Leave her alone, alright?"

"No you look here, you stuffed shirt. I may have been a bit cheeky to Gemma but that is categorically not my style. It's not even my dick, or whatever the image is. Not guilty. I've said as much to Mr Producer, who has already hauled me over the coals for this, alright?"

Alan is vaguely aware of Gemma looking at him over the terrace and frantically waving to him. He tightens his grip.

"You think I'm going to believe that?!"

"Yeah, have you seen the amount of piercings I have on my balls? Have you any idea? I tell you, it's not my card and it's not my cock."

Alan leaps back from Nigel. "Piercings? God, you just don't care do you?"

146

Jocelyn wanders up. "Hello boys," she says. "Are we talking about piercings, because if we are, I have a lot of expertise in that department, frankly."

"Not you too," says Alan, despairingly. "Whoever encouraged you both onto this show ought to be had up in front of Ofcom for…" he pauses slightly, "detrimental effects on broadcasting."

He walks stiffly back to the dining table, leaving Jocelyn and Nigel cackling into each other's necks.

"Keep your wig on," shouts Nigel, winking at Alex who has recorded the entire encounter.

Chapter Twenty-Two
Jane

George and Belle are out on the terrace in the morning sun, playing Uno. It seems like weeks ago since they last played, but as Jane reminds herself, it's only been two days. So much has happened since then. What was she doing when she last saw them doing this? She remembers. Of course. The Pilates class. Maybe she could go back. Get on with what she was progressing. Life, for Jane, is a series of advancements.

She walks over and kneels down on the towel beside them.

"George? Are you alright this morning? After everything?"

George looks at her calmly.

"Of course I am, Mother. Are you?"

She ruffles his hair. It's complicated, thinks Jane. She loves her son. But she doesn't want to devote her life to him. She doesn't want to sit on a terrace in Ibiza and play Uno with him. She wants to do things for her, and love George in the abstract.

"Never better. Just as long as there are no sudden expeditions which you haven't told a grown-up about."

"Yes, Mother," George says wearily. "*Bien sûr.*"

"Belle, everything okay?"

"Yes, fine," says Belle. She had explained to Jas that she absolutely could not abandon her bed that night and go dancing. Hence she had gone to bed at a normal time, woken George up as normal in the morning, and they had had their customary banana milkshake in the kitchen followed by bread and jam. Everything screamed holiday normality. This was how it was meant to be. It was good. She had to admit, it was a relief not to cope with the day under a cloud of exhaustion, deception and the shade of a hangover. Jas had understood but she missed him.

"Pick up four, Belle," says George, putting down a card carefully.

"How could you do this to me?" she says to him in mock anguish.

He smiles at her, rounding soft apples in his cheeks.

Belle smiles back at him, and then glances at Jane, still hovering over them. She wonders if she ought to invite Jane to play Uno. She probably doesn't know the rules, thinks Belle. World's easiest card game, but Jane wouldn't know it. After all that has happened you would have thought she might have made a bit of an effort. Never mind, thinks Belle. The treat of playing with George had been hers.

Jane looks around. She has no idea what this card game is all about. Everything looks calm, she reasons to herself. Normal. She might as well go to Pilates. After all, what is the point of paying for childcare if you aren't going to use it?

"Well, I think if you are happy with everything, then I am going to go to Pilates."

She thinks about the advertising strapline. *Come and stretch out with the backdrop of the Med and Yasmin as your gym buddy.*

"No problem," says Belle. She puts a card down. "Miss a go," she says nicely to George.

"Oh no," says George in sing-song. "Miss a go too."

He giggles, slapping down the same action card.

Belle remembers what they had planned to do. "We thought we might go to the market today, Jane. Is that okay? Patrick said he'd organise a taxi for us."

"Well, I think that's fine, Belle. Would you like to go to the market, George?"

"Maybe."

"No running off now."

"Very funny."

Jane pads back into the bedroom, picks out the freshly laundered clothes. Same as last time. Black leggings, raspberry sports bra, purple singlet. Grey zippered jacket. She's not going to drive in flip-flops though. Special mesh Nike shoes will do it. She ties her hair up and collects her sunglasses.

"Bye then," she calls to George. "No sudden trips out of the house, remember."

"Non Maman," calls George, wearily.

She drives back along the same route towards the Nature Reserve. Takes the three roundabouts very gingerly this time. She passes the same smiling man holding up a glass of orange juice on the posters. She glances a bit more acutely at his face. He looks rather familiar. She goes round the roundabout again to be sure and manages to read the name beside the product the man is promoting. *Francesco Villa drinks it!* Of course. No wonder. The same bloody footballer. The same one that turned up on the shoot. She ought to have been a bit nicer to him, paid him a bit more attention. She might have got to know him. She makes a mental note to bring George down and show him the poster.

When she arrives at the class, she hurries over to the small group that is assembling on the cliff top again. Yasmin Bird is looking just as fresh and elegant.

"Morning Jane," she says, tossing back her hair.

"Oh, good morning Yasmin," says Jane, flattered that she has remembered her name.

"That's a great outfit," says Yasmin. "I noticed how nice it was last time."

"Oh, just an old thing," says Jane, delighted. "But I think the colours work quite well here."

"Perfectly."

The sun is making the sea glitter into a million separate diamond shapes. It casts long shadows on the magnetic island of Es Vedrà.

"Move to your mats. Let us start our practice with a few leg stretches," instructs Yasmin. "Bend your right knee, deepening the crease at the hip socket, as you would in knee folds, until your thigh is upright and your shin is parallel to the floor. Don't let this move take your right hip off the mat. Keep your tailbone anchored to the floor at this point."

I must have missed this bit last time, thinks Jane, as she assumes the position.

"Take your right knee across your body toward the floor on the other side. Allow it to lead your hips into a gentle back stretch," continues Yasmin. "Jane, as you turn, don't take your whole upper body with you. Try to leave the right shoulder behind and send your gaze past your right hand."

She watches Yasmin carefully and tries to imitate exactly what she is doing. Yasmin tosses her hair back again and looks at Jane over her shoulder, smiling. Then she stands up and comes over to Jane.

"You have to have your shoulder like… so." She says to Jane, getting very close. Jane can smell a delicious lavender fragrance from her hair.

"Like this?" says Jane, smiling.

"No, like this," says Yasmin, gently moving Jane's arm. As she does so, her hand brushes Jane's breast.

Jane looks quickly at Yasmin, but she has moved away and resumed her position at the front of the class. Was that on purpose? "Experiment with the stretch that is right for you. Don't forget to breathe," she says. This always makes Jane snigger. How could you forget to breathe, she thinks.

"Let us all now stand," intones Yasmin. "Keeping your spine fully erect, go into your demi plie, bending the knees without allowing your heels to lift off the ground. Not easy for any ladies who spend their lives in high heels, I know. That used to be me!"

She shakes her hair, as if ten years of London irritation has been erased by life on a higher plane involving yoga mats and kale smoothies. "Work your abs in and up and keep your chest lifted. Knees open over the toes, not wider or narrower. Breathe and exhale. Remember to keep your gaze straight forward. Look at the island. Feel the magnetism. Now let us go onto the floor position, everyone," she says.

Jane lies down on her mat, looking up at the endless blue above her. She points her toes and flexes her feet as Yasmin orders. Suddenly, the face of the teacher is above her again.

"Can I just move your leg to the right place, Jane?" asks Yasmin.

Jane simply nods silently.

Yasmin takes her leg and moves it. Again, it could have been nothing, Jane tells herself. But Yasmin allows her hand to slide along Jane's belly.

Is she making a pass at me, Jane thinks wildly. God, I hope she is. Maybe she is just making it up, what with all the excitement and fuss of the last few days, maybe my brain is going a bit crazy. And Yasmin is so beautiful and young, she is much younger than me, why on earth would she be doing this to me? Can't she see I've got a wedding ring on, she thinks, and then dismisses the thought immediately for being ridiculous.

"Let us stretch uuuup," says Yasmin, reminding everyone once again how important it is in their practise to breathe.

The class gets to its feet.

After a few more stretches in various positions, Yasmin seems to be drawing the class to a close.

"And relax," says Yasmin. "Well done." She leads the applause, customary after Pilates classes across the world. The soft clapping dies out, the women bend over in their leotards and leggings and roll up their mats.

Yasmin comes over to Jane.

"Well done."

"Oh, thanks."

"Are you having a good holiday here? Is Ibiza being kind to you?"

"Yes, of course. Well, I had a bit of a drama yesterday."

"Oh?"

"My son got lost… we had to find him… I mean, me and my husband."

She felt annoyed with herself admitting she had a husband. Yasmin nodded seriously. Jane looked at her closely, hoping for a flicker of dismay. There was none. If she was disappointed to find out Jane was heterosexual, Yasmin seemed to be taking it on the chin.

"Oh how terrible. I assume you found him? Was he okay? How awful."

"Oh yes, he was fine. Just fine. I felt a bit foolish, to be honest. He had gone to play with some friends and forgotten to tell us. In the end we collected him with the help of a TV reality show which is being filmed out here, did you know that?"

To her amazement, Yasmin nods.

"Yes, I'm filming with them the day after tomorrow, actually. I'm thrilled."

"What, the *Ibiza (or Bust)* crew?"

"The very same."

"What a coincidence. Well, Yasmin, I know half the people they are using. I mean, they are my neighbours. I know them!"

She wants to be seen as part of the group, someone in the charmed circle.

"Great," says Yasmin. "But your son, that is a relief."

"Yes, yes of course," says Jane hurriedly, remembering her priorities. She looks at Yasmin and smiles. To her great joy, Yasmin doesn't seem in a hurry to stop the conversation.

"If you want to come along while we are filming, we are at a new venue. I could do with some other people in the class who know more or less what they are doing. And the fact you know them is even better. Means you won't go silly over meeting famous people."

"Oh, they aren't very famous," says Jane hurriedly. That bloody Philip Burrell. And Alan Makin! They aren't famous at all, she wants to say.

"Do you want to have a look at the map and come and find us?" continues Yasmin. "Sorry to pick you up on a few of your stretches. You're so good at this, you know."

Jane nods "Thanks, well, I do a lot of Pilates at home in London."

"I can tell," says Yasmin seriously.

Can she really tell if Jane has an aptitude for Pilates? She rather guiltily recalls she hasn't actually attended a class for over a year, but maybe once you know the moves, your muscles just do it.

"Thanks, Yasmin. I really enjoy it."

"I enjoy having you in the class," says Yasmin, brightly.

What on earth does that mean, thinks Jane. Does she say this to everyone? She hardly knows me.

"Water?" says Yasmin, getting out a frosted plastic bottle from her cooler.

She hands it to Jane, who opens it clumsily, spilling the water over her top.

"Bad luck," says Yasmin, brushing away the beads of water that have fallen over Jane's breast. Her fingers glide over Jane's nipple. Jane wonders if she's dreaming. No, this is reality. The woman is making a pass at her.

"Shall we go and have a coffee?" says Yasmin Bird.

Chapter Twenty-Three
Gilda

While Philip Burrell is delighting himself by looking at Cresta's luscious cleavage, and fondly imagining burying his head there, his wife is seven miles away, nervously pushing her trolley through Ibiza airport. The trolley is piled high with cases; two big ones for her clothes and shoes, and a small round one for her jewellery, hairdryer and make-up.

Gilda is wearing a long zebra striped coat, Ray Ban sunglasses, knee length suede boots and a black crêpe de Chine jumpsuit. Her hair is swept back from her face in a simple black band. She is promoting the look of international jetsetter. Just in case she is spotted.

She moves slowly through Arrivals, not really wanting to arrive, because arriving means she will have to make a decision. She hopes she might not need to make one. She hopes she will see someone she knows, or has a link with. Anything. Someone with a sign saying TooTuneTV. Well, it's a possibility. There might be someone else coming to join the programme, like her. She looks hopefully down the line of the drivers, tired looking Filipino men carrying name boards. There is nothing recognisable.

She swallows and carries on pushing her trolley. Where should she go to find Philip and the television programme? Where is this special house where they are all secreted? She has no idea where to start looking.

TooTuneTV. That is the name of the company. Simon Courtney. That is the name of the producer. She hangs onto these points.

She hails a taxi, allows the driver to put all her stuff in the back, and gets in.

"Where to?"

"The centre of town please. Actually, no. The Hilton." She'd need somewhere to put her stuff.

"That is in the centre of town. Gran Hotel Montesol? Is that the one you want?"

She shrugs. "Yes, that's fine."

They drive along the motorway for a while, but arrive too soon at the destination. When she is moving, Gilda feels fine. It's when she stops that she starts feeling nervous about what she is doing out here, in the heat, looking for her husband on a secretive reality TV show.

The hotel is yellow and white and elegant. She walks in and asks for a small room with a nice view. A porter takes her baggage and puts it onto a trolley with a huge shiny arch above it, for hanging coats. The hotel is recognisably expensive and international. It calms her down a bit. Thank goodness Philip is a successful artist, she thinks. She's got her Mastercard. She's got a £20,000 credit limit. She could stay here for a month if necessary.

When she gets to her room she is comforted by seeing the expected accoutrements: the Nespresso machine, the vast television, a shoe shining order form. A white laundry bag. One giant bed. Flowers. Fruit. There is a nice view over the harbour. She thanks the porter and tips him and sits down on the bed.

At least she has the number of TooTuneTV back in London, maybe that would be the best thing to do.

After a while, she rings the number.

"Hello, TooTune?"

"Hello, good morning. My name is Gilda Burrell. I am married to Philip Burrell. Well, I am in Ibiza and I was hoping

156

that I might go and visit my husband Philip who is taking part on your programme, you know, the programme where everyone is in a house together?"

"We have lots of programmes here. Sorry, who are you?"

"Gilda Burrell," says Gilda faintly. "My husband, Philip Burrell, is on your show, the show which is in Ibiza at the moment. A daytime show. Ibiza Getaway I think it is called."

"Do you mean *Ibiza (or Bust)*?" says the receptionist.

"Yes, I think so. I might do."

"Sorry, Mrs Burrell, I have to let you know that there is no communication between our contestants and the outside world. Unless this is an emergency. Is this an emergency?"

Gilda adjusts her black hair band, which she thought would be a nice touch in case of any paparazzi in the airport. She's been fobbed off with this excuse before.

"No, no it's not. I just wanted to pop by."

"Well I am afraid that is against the contractual arrangement for the contestants on the show, which I am surprised have not been explained to you, and I am not allowed to connect you with the production."

"Can I at least have the address? I am his wife."

"Sorry," says the receptionist. "Data protection. I'm not allowed."

"Could you give me the number of the producer, then. Mr Simon Courtney?"

"No, that's not allowed. Sorry."

Gilda swallows hard. She looks at the boats in the harbour outside. She has to get in touch with Philip. She wants to be part of whatever he is doing.

"Alright. Well, could you please, please contact Simon Courtney and tell him that Philip's wife is in town?"

"Of course."

"I am his wife."

"I understand that."

She puts the phone down. A few minutes later she realises

157

she never gave the receptionist her number. She calls back but the number rings out and is answered by a machine. She records her number on the machine. Maybe someone will ring her back this afternoon.

She looks dully at the television, on which some adverts for local attractions are flashing up mutely.

Thursday market reads one. *The famous old market, centre of town, every Thursday.*

She thinks she will go and wander around.

She goes downstairs to reception and asks where the market is. The smiling receptionist opens up a thin paper map in front of Gilda and circles the market. Then she circles the hotel and indicates the relationship of one to the other. She does this while the map is upside down and with such speed that Gilda assumes it is something she performs twenty times a day.

"Ten minutes," smiles the receptionist.

Gilda walks out of the hotel and allows the outside heat to wash over her. She looks at the map. Ten minutes.

About fifteen minutes later she arrives at the market. It is full of women carrying baskets, men chopping giant pieces of fish on large plastic boards, toys hanging from the ceiling and seemingly endless arrays of brown cured ham still on the bone, featuring the shiny trotters of the pig who originally bore them.

Gilda walks down the aisles and stops by a tower of batteries because she hears an English voice. She thinks she knows it. The voice starts up again. It is the voice of a child, over the other side of the food display.

"Oh, Belle look, there is another pig's foot here, in a funny holding thing, and its actual leg, yuk, can we buy it, can we?"

She retraces her steps around the aisle and sees Belle holding George by the hand. He is looking, entranced, at one of the many giant porcine limbs which like all the others, is clamped into a metal and wood device hanging above them.

"Of course we can't. But it looks good, doesn't it?"

"Belle!"

Belle turns round, surprised to see Gilda helplessly smiling at her.

"Oh, Gilda," she manages to say, masking a gasp, "hello. How are you?"

"Belle, I've just arrived, about two hours ago. How funny to bump into you. And so soon! I'm staying at the Hilton by the harbour."

"How lovely. We're just here for the morning actually. Patrick, er, George's father, he ran us down in a taxi. This is George."

"Hello," says George.

"Oh yes. I think I know you from the Square, George."

"Gilda, I'm so sorry, but we were just about to…"

Gilda holds up a hand.

"Belle, I know you are busy, but I do need your help. Do you have any idea where I might find Philip and the TV programme? It would help me so much if you did." She laughs lightly. "I rang the production company and can you believe it, they said they weren't allowed to tell me. Something about data protection. Honestly! Unless in case of emergency, which of course I should have said I was experiencing. Might you know? Have you seen him on the island at all?"

Belle shakes her head vigorously. There is no way she wants to get close to Philip and the television team, even if it is to help out Gilda, who looks anxious and slightly flustered.

"I'm sorry, Gilda."

"But I've seen them all!" squeaks George. "The television company? Yes, I've seen them all."

Belle looks crossly down at George.

"No you haven't," she says.

"Oh yes I have," responds George.

"What? Did you see Philip?" says Gilda.

"Er, I think so. Do you mean that old man from back home, the artist?"

"That is my husband," says Gilda. "Philip Burrell. Have you seen him?"

"Oh YES," says George. "Yes I have. He turned up in the mobile home, that is Jack and Sam's holiday home, oh yes, actually, with a very sexy lady!"

Gilda stands very still.

"I don't think he means quite that," says Belle hurriedly. "I remember now. I haven't seen Philip, as I said, because I wasn't there that day. But I think George bumped into Philip and the rest of the television team when he was out, visiting his friends. Jack and Sam. In a mobile home."

"Yes, they all arrived, with Francesco Villa, you know, the Brazilian footballer."

Gilda shuts her eyes, bombarded with extraneous information. This is too much. There is only one thing she needs to know about.

"And the sexy lady?"

"Yeah. She was in shorts! And she had been on a helicopter with that artist. Your husband."

"Shut up, George," says Belle quickly.

Gilda takes a deep breath. She's not going to mind about the fact that Belle said she didn't know where they were, when she clearly had known about their presence all along during this conversation.

"Well, could you possibly find out where they are now?"

Belle shakes her head. "Sorry, Gilda, but I have no way of doing so. I really would help you if I could, but I don't think I can."

"Mother might know," George interjects. "I bet she knows where they are. I'm sure she wants to go on the show."

"George, please," says Belle, fervently wishing George would just stop talking. "Can we just discuss this, I mean can I just talk to Gilda about this on my own? Please go and have a look at the piggy's feet. Go on. Now." She turns back to the older woman.

"Gilda, I am so sorry but I am almost convinced that Jane

has no idea where the house is either. Regardless of what George thinks."

Gilda smiles weakly at Belle. Her lipstick is feathering the lines around her mouth. Her brightness has drooped. Belle feels sorry for her. She might try and find out for her, silly old thing. Maybe in a week or so. Gilda's got lots of money, reasons Belle. She can afford a couple of days longer staying at the Hilton.

"I might be able to find out for you, but not straight away."

Gilda looks up hopefully. "Oh, thank you so much. You are a darling. You have my mobile number don't you Belle, dear? Please can you try to find out from Jane where, where the house might be? Can you?"

Meanwhile, at the house, Simon's phone bleeps with an incoming email.

"Simon, Belinda on reception. The wife of one of your contestants has turned up. In Ibiza. Do you want more details? It's not an emergency. She just wants to say hello. I think. Someone called Gilda Burrell."

Simon is so shocked he has to read the email two or three times.

He beckons Kate over.

"Kate, Kate, what the hell! You know Philip Burrell's dotty old wife?"

"Vaguely, why?"

"She's only fucking turned up on the island. She's here! Wants to pop over and say hello to Philip."

"Well, she can't. It's going to be bad enough writing that Jane woman into the show, with her child, the kidnapped George. We can't handle anyone else just turning up."

"I know, but it's difficult. Do we tell him?"

Kate looks across the terrace to the pool where Cresta is sitting on Philip's knee and feeding him a bunch of grapes, to the amusement of Jasper.

"Are you mad? No."

"Okay. If you say so."

"No. Apart from anything else it will stop... this sort of thing going on. We've never actually had one of the contestants hit on another so openly in four seasons of the whole damn franchise, have we Simon? Can you think of the ratings if Philip really goes for it with Cresta?"

"I know. I feel a bit bad though, she wasn't a bad old thing when we met briefly during the research period."

"Too bad. Email reception back and say no dice."

Simon, feeling like a snake, sends an email.

"If she rings back, tell her that under no circumstances can we divulge the position or location of the house, at least not while the show is being recorded. Tell her to hang around on the island if she can. We can reunite them at the end of show party. Thanks, Simon."

He turns back to Kate and shrugs.

"She's not our problem. At the moment. If she turns up, she will be."

Chapter Twenty-Four
Gemma

That afternoon, there is complete commotion on the terrace of the house. Rupert and Alex are everywhere. Young men carry trays bearing wine glasses and canapés. They thread their way through the contestants who are standing in a line beside the organic pond. Fairy lights dangle from the bougainvillea; a local guitarist has set up in one corner and is playing gently. Everyone has dressed up.

"Well, true to form. She hasn't disappointed," says Philip to Jasper, pointing at Cresta as she arrives on the terrace. Cresta is wearing a gown consisting of two long pieces of material, one covering the front of her body, one the rear. They are attached by a tiny piece of transparent mesh on either side. It is clear she's not wearing any underwear at all. Her hair has been curled and cascades down her back in hoops, as if she is a fairy tale princess. She is in very high heels.

"You could say that," observes Jasper, who has donned his cloak and is looking extremely hot in it. Both men look at her body as if surveying something they are about to buy.

Philip Burrell is back in the white linen suit, which has been laundered and pressed since its experience in the pond.

Gemma looks at the men looking at Cresta, and sees the way in which Philip's eyes rake her body. She rather wishes she had a new piece of clothing to wear. She looks down at her dress. It is made from lilac silk, cut on the bias like a sheer slip, trimmed with brown lace. It was always one of her stalwarts, a designer frock bought two years ago that at the time cost her a fortune. Now she worries that it's rather old fashioned and also that it is not fitting properly. Has she put on weight since she arrived? She feels aghast about the prospect that she may have done, and pulls in her stomach, tidying up her hair with a freshly manicured hand, remembering to smile and throw her head back, laughing, whenever one of the cameraman walks past. Have they only been here for a week? The pressure of not only being cut off from her home and all social media, but also potentially having every single gesture, comment and action recorded by a television camera, is becoming unbearable.

Simon said everyone would forget about the cameras very quickly. It hasn't happened for her. What if everything she says ends up on screen? What if nothing she says ends up on screen? Both options are horrendous.

She turns quickly around. Alan Makin is behind her.

"You look nice," says Alan. "Charming dress."

"Oh, do I? Thanks. I feel a bit underdressed, to be honest. Look at Cresta."

"Don't be silly. She's just doing it for effect. You look great. At least you're not wearing a bloody cloak like Harry Potter over there. How're you feeling?"

"Sick."

"Come on. You're not going to leave this show before I do. Any more porn posted under your door?"

She laughs. "I don't know what to think about that, now. Apparently it wasn't Nigel at all."

There is a huge fuss at one end of the pool. Alex and Rupert switch on the lights on the top of their cameras and walk backwards. Someone has arrived on the terrace. It's Francesco Villa. There's a huge transformation. Gone are the ripped shorts, the casual t-shirt, the smiling 'Ola' of the friendly donkey handler from a local village. Francesco is in full football star mode. His body is wrapped in a perfectly cut navy suit, an immaculate white shirt open sufficiently to reveal just a trace of smooth chest. His hair is shiny and gelled.

"Hello guys," he says, smiling briefly, with no trace of accent bar a gentle sense of Mid Atlantic. "It's good to see you all now that I'm here as myself."

"He could hardly speak English before," murmurs Jocelyn. "He's a very good actor."

"So, everyone," says Simon loudly. "Francesco has very kindly agreed to come and say goodbye to you. Now is the time to have a chat with him, don't ask him anything about donkeys of course because he doesn't know much about them!"

Francesco rolls his eyes comically. Everyone laughs.

"That lovely donkey. Dear little Burro. What a cutie."

"Dog food," mutters Philip.

"He's going to be with us just for a bit, then after more food and sangria, Francesco will leave us, we'll be doing the voting and then, sorry folks but we will have the first expulsion from the show. Has everyone packed?"

"This is the worst bit," murmurs Gemma to Alan. "Just awful."

The contestants have all had to put their fully packed cases in the hall. This is a requirement of the rules of the show so that when the first person is kicked off, they can leave straight away, case in hand. No goodbyes, no embraces, no farewells to the bedroom or one last dip in the organic pond. It's straight off in a taxi.

"Brutal," agrees Alan. "That's showbiz for you."

Jasper is doing one of his tricks at one end of the pond. He is swooping his cloak around and flashing a deck of cards. "Where is your three of diamonds?" Gemma can hear him saying to Cresta.

"Oh gawd, Jasps, I dunno," shouts Cresta, looking down at her hand where she was sure she had been holding the named card a second ago. She looks up at Jasper. He is holding the card in his mouth.

She screams with pleasure. "Aw, Jasps. You're so bloody clever you know that!"

Jasper bows low and swoops the cloak around for effect.

Gemma rolls her eyes and turns around. Alan is nowhere to be seen. Probably gone off in search of a drink. She is aware of someone else behind her and turns round. To her astonishment, it's Villa.

"Good evening. How are you enjoying the show?" he asks.

"Oh, thanks, well, it's okay," she says cautiously. "I loved you with the donkey."

"Thanks. I'm sorry to leave this show you know. Very sorry. I was only booked to appear with you for a few days, but even so. You're a nice group."

"Are we? I mean, oh, thanks," says Gemma. Now that donkey husbandry has been dropped as a potential conversational topic, she really has nothing to say to this sporting hero.

"Look, good luck with the season ahead. I'm sure you'll do... really well."

The Brazilian inclines his head courteously. "That's my hope. But thank you. Come over to Madrid and see a game sometime."

"Oh, well, yes, that would be lovely," says Gemma with surprise. She has never sat through an entire football match. "Thank you." She remembers she cannot actually recall which team Francesco plays for, and is suddenly gripped by anxiety that this famous man will ask her something about it.

"What did you like best about being on the show?" she says, inanely.

"Oh, meeting all of you, for sure," says Francesco. "Say, Gemma, tell me this."

"What?"

He leans closer. She can smell his aftershave and toothpaste.

"Did you like the little card I dropped into your room?" he whispers, sniggering.

"What?"

He laughs, claps her on the back and turns around to find Simon hovering behind him.

"Francesco, sorry to bother, but the boys are ready to film your exit, if you are ready?"

"Sure, sure." He leans over and kisses Gemma on the mouth.

"*Ciao*."

She has not been able to even draw breath.

"Alright everyone it really is *ciao*. Now you see me as I really am. And you know, good luck. Good luck to the eventual winner. You are all fantastic!" says Francesco loudly. He waves his left arm and points a single finger to the sky, his favoured post-scoring gesture.

Gemma is standing still, her mouth open.

She watches the back of the beautifully cut suit leaving the terrace, watches as the cameramen dance backwards, shooting the footballer's every move, gesture, comment. He gets into his Ferrari and accelerates loudly out of the compound.

Rupert and Alex walk back into the pool area. Everything seems a little bit flat. Then Simon claps his hands, which has the effect of turning up the fairy lights around the terrace and kicking off some darkly throbbing music around the pond. The guitarist takes this as a cue to shuffle off.

"Alright folks," he says. "Now that Francesco has gone, back to business. A few more drinks, if you wish. Then you will each be taken separately into the living room to cast your votes. This is the last time you'll all be together!"

Gemma pokes Alan.

"You'll never guess what just happened. The card. You know that bloody card."

"Yes, what?"

"I found out who sent it."

"Go on."

"Apparently, and you probably aren't going to believe this, but it was from him! The Brazil player, or Real Madrid, or whatever! Francesco Villa!"

"What the hell?" says Alan.

She nods at him, incredulous.

"He just came sauntering up to me, leant over and after a few comments about, oh, I don't know, the football season, about which I know precisely nothing, he asked if I liked the little card he'd dropped in my room. I was gobsmacked."

She pauses for effect, looks at Alan, laughs out loud.

"Can you believe it?"

Alan looks at her.

"Alan! Can you believe it?"

"Yes. Yes I can actually. It's all part of being famous," he replies.

"What? What do you mean? I mean, you are famous, aren't you? Well, as a famous person, do you go around posting cards of your genitals to women, Alan?" She laughs, in spite of herself.

"No, obviously not," says Alan, pleased that she has acknowledged his status. "Because I am used to my fame. And my fame, if you will, is miniscule compared to his. A non-event. Someone like Villa," indicating the recent presence of the superstar footballer with a dismissive jerk of the thumb, "who probably came from some hovel somewhere in Rio, and who now has everything he has ever wanted, simply likes to behave like a rogue. I once did a show about the finances of footballers, and you wouldn't believe what their lives are like. They have so much money and so much power... they can do pretty much what they want. And they see women as..."

"Conquests?" says Gemma, rather wishing that she had known all this earlier on the show. For a brief moment she lets her imagination run. She envisages Francesco Villa conquering her. That devastating smile, that body. Imagine. She thinks about him dipping his head to kiss her neck, sees lines of paparazzi snapping them on the red carpet at public events, what an amazing trajectory that would have been for her. A fairy story. From an estate agent who had turned up on TV a couple of times, to... a footballer's wife. She'd certainly get to know about the offside rule. Disappointment wrenches her stomach.

That is madness, she thinks. Hadn't he done something utterly disgusting to her, disgusting and disrespectful?

"Yes, conquests. He was playing with you."

Gemma thinks about the card. What if she were to, by happenstance, leak the story to the papers? What a story that would be.

"Of course, there's no proof," says Alan, as if he was reading her thoughts.

"And you wouldn't be believed, and you would be *persona non grata* with the show. So if I were you, I would simply tuck the experience away as a life memory."

"Ugh, no thanks," says Gemma, remembering her earlier revulsion. "I'd rather just forget it. Weird, though."

"I wouldn't tell Simon."

"Yes, but what about Nigel?" She looks over at the Adventurous Parents, who are standing by the pond, wine glasses in hands, not saying anything much. She feels a bit sorry for Nigel, now. She even hopes he won't get chucked off the show. At least, not first.

"He'll live," says Alan. "Unfortunately."

"Right, everybody," says Simon loudly. "You know the score. I'll be calling you one by one to come into the lounge where we will take your vote. An hour later, you will all be assembled by the front door, at which point one of you will leave the show, by taxi, with Rupert, so he can record your thoughts. Do you understand? We'll start with Alan."

The contestants of *Ibiza (or Bust)* stand silently around the organic pond in their finery, anxiety written across their faces. They don't look famous now. They look like the nonentities they have always been, thinks Simon. Each is desperate to stay on the programme. Jasper has gone quite pale.

"I read my cards this morning," he whispers to Philip. "You and me should be fine."

"Oh, do give it a break," says Philip. "I don't fucking care, but if you are asking me, the first off the show is going to be that Class A bore Alan Makin. Who has been drooling over Gemma since he turned up. He should be kicked off for sexual harassment."

"Oh," says Jasper. "I hadn't noticed."

"Yeah, that's because you're too busy doing tricks with tiny metal hoops," mutters Philip, stalking off to find another glass of wine.

Jasper sighs. He is particularly anxious to stay on the programme. Before leaving the UK his agent had called him with two pieces of bad news. Firstly, the agent told him he was retiring and clearing his books. So he would have to find someone else to represent him. The Magic Circle might help with that, but things had changed so much there. It was all about television people like Dynamo, not old school men like Jasper. Secondly, Jasper's annual booking for the Brighton Winter Season on the Palace Pier had been cancelled. It hadn't sold well last year, and he knew it was touch and go for this year, but still. But this show might do wonders for him.

He was putting all his hopes on *Ibiza (or Bust)* rescuing his profile and helping him towards another booking. Plus, if you stayed on the show for another week, your fee went up. He could do with the money, to be honest. Very much so. He was behind with his rent and he wanted to take his wife away somewhere nice. And there were no so many other things he had to find the finances for; he had learned during this week, for example, that all other celebrities paid people to send out witty and charming messages on social media. Who knew about that? But how to find such a person, and how much should they be paid? Jasper was learning quite a lot about climbing the immense mountain of celebrity during this week, and it frightened him. He licks the sweat off his top lip, and adjusts his cloak.

Chapter Twenty-Five
Alan

Alan walks into the lounge, where Rupert is hovering behind his camera, perched on a tripod. There is a single chair in front of the camera.

"Shall I sit down?" says Alan to Rupert.

"Of course, yes. Simon will be here just… oh, here he is!" says Rupert as Simon and Kate both walk into the lounge and slide shut the doors.

Kate pulls a filmy curtain across the glass, just in case, she says.

"In case I suddenly burst into tears, or something?" says Alan jokingly.

He is surprised to discover he's actually quite nervous.

"We always do it like this," says Kate.

"Alright Alan, you know the score," says Simon.

"You have to give us the names of five people whom you would like to be kicked off the programme, in order of preference. Each name will get a score as to their position on your list, so the first person, the person you want booted off first, will get five, the next person four and so on. We ask everyone the same thing. Then we add every score up. The person with the most points leaves the show tonight."

Alan takes a deep breath.

"Can we name the same person twice?"

Simon laughs. "Funny how that question always comes up.

Sorry, no. So, who would you like to leave the *Ibiza (or Bust)* house? Speak directly into camera, if you can."

Alan takes a deep breath. He thinks about the group that has been here for a week. Only a week, he thinks. Yet they have all grown attached to one another, like tendrils from a fast-growing plant. Despite his frustrations with some of them, he considers that at the moment of dismantlement he doesn't want to change anything. Still, this is a show. This isn't life. It is entertainment, although God knows who would want to watch it, he thinks.

"Do you think this show is really going to work?" he says, suddenly to Simon.

"Alan. Give us the names of the people you want to leave the house."

"Philip Burrell."

Simon looks surprised.

"Really, Alan? Why?"

"Because he's a cunt."

"Cut. Rupert, can you switch off the camera, please."

Simon leans forward.

"Alan. Please. Come on. We'll have to start again."

"But he is. He's been one since he arrived on the show. Utter knobhead, prancing around in that white suit as if he was Tom Wolfe or something. Thinks he's above everyone. Not knowing about football or popular culture, and yet desperate to have his own culture admired and adored and talked about. Plus, he's sexist. Furthermore, he's clearly so desperate to get his cock into Cresta."

"Alan, can we continue? With no bad language?"

"I suppose so," says Alan moodily.

"Okay Rupert, turn over. Now, Alan Makin, who would you like to leave the *Ibiza (or Bust)* household? You can name five people in descending order, but let's start with the holiday companion you would like to see packing his or her bag most of all."

It's so negative, thinks Simon. This programme is all

about enmity, and fracturing relationships, and falling out with one another. That's the only point of it. Bringing up differences between people, heightening argument and dislike. That's what the producers back in his Manchester office see as a success. He talks to them on Skype every night. "Who fell out with whom?" is always their first question. He sighs. He wishes, again, that he was working on *Panorama*.

"Right, Alan, come on."

"I think Philip Burrell should leave," responds Alan sullenly. "Because he's such a great artist, I think his time is wasted here. He ought to get back to the Square and carry on making his golf courses. Do you know, we are neighbours?"

"No, I didn't," lies Simon. "Back to the list."

"Can I vote myself off?"

"No."

"Alright, then I would advocate Gemma next."

"Gemma? Really? Why?"

"Because she is hating this whole experience and I think you should see that, and release her from the programme."

Outside, Gemma sits on the terrace in the heat, and waits for Alan to come out. Someone is playing the guitar again. Gemma watches Cresta in her semi-clothed state dancing underneath the fairy lights, arms above her head, swaying on her heels. Moo walks around her slowly clapping his hands. The whole image is of some mad Spanish flamenco.

Nigel progresses past the bullrushes and ferns by the organic pond and wanders unsteadily up to her.

"Tell you what," says Nigel.

"What?" says Gemma. She sips her sangria and looks at him from over the rim of the glass.

"Well," says Nigel.

"Well what?" replies Gemma, exasperated with this twit.

"I know you thought I sent you something outrageous, some naughty postcard, but it wasn't me, really."

"I know. I know that now."

"Good." He looks at her blearily. "Do you want to leave this show?"

"No. Well, I'm not really enjoying it very much, but it would be such a blow to be voted off first. So I suppose the answer to you has to be no."

"Tell you what, Gemma." He leans forward. "I was thinking of voting you off, and so is Jocelyn. Because we were so fed up with what you thought I had done. It threatened our position, you see."

"Really?" She hadn't thought Nigel capable of such a calculating move. "But that's horrible. Horrible. Getting rid of me like that."

He laughs at her. "I know. And with two of us voting against you, you probably would end up leaving."

"Well, thanks a bunch. Is that all you came over to say to me?"

"No. Stand up, Gemma," says Nigel. She obeys him.

"There's one thing you can do for me which will make me stop voting you off the show. Do you know what that is?"

Gemma thinks she probably does, but shakes her head.

"No, no I don't know. Must you tell me? I'm not sure I want to know."

"Come under the terrace, here, just come away from everyone."

They walk into the shadows.

"Now Gemma, you know I think you are gorgeous."

Oh, God. She can't believe this is going to happen. She knows that it will happen.

"If you and I go into your room, I slip my trousers down and, you, and you give me a, you know, lovely and quick blow job, then I promise that both Jocelyn and I will leave you off our voting slips. What do you think about that?"

She rears back, looking at him, disgusted. Then she pours her glass of sangria over his head, turns away and walks off.

Nigel stands laughing, shaking the drops of maroon liquid from his head, wiping them out of his eyes.

"I guess that's a no, then!" he shouts. "So long, Missy!"

Gemma, shaking slightly, walks back past Cresta and Moo and crosses the terrace. She needs something to do with herself and is relieved when she spots Philip standing by the pond looking out over the bullrushes.

"Hi Philip," she says.

"Ah. Gemma. The fragrant soul of the programme. I think we all will keep you here, without question."

She has to acknowledge to herself that this experience is bringing her up against some complete nutters.

Chapter Twenty-Six
Jane

Jane follows Yasmin for the promised coffee. She had never been to bed with a woman before. Fantasised about it, of course, but never done it, even at university, which is when everyone was meant to be experimenting with bisexuality. Well, thinks Jane, calming her nerves, I'll just try and do what I would like done to me by a man. But the act of touching a woman, rather than the unyielding frame of a man? She shivers. Sex is important for Jane. It is so important that it has been allowed to threaten her marriage. But she can't help herself. Time to indulge in sexual experimentation which, Jane is sure, is about to happen. She feels almost sweaty with excitement.

"Shall we have a drink?" says Yasmin, leading Jane into the clubhouse by the sanctuary. What? We're going to do it here? That's daring, thinks Jane, following Yasmin's lead. In a public place? Well, I suppose we could use the toilets. It wouldn't be the first time for Jane.

"Coffee or water? I prefer iced water at this time of day," continues Yasmin breezily.

"I think by the time the hours are in double figures it's over for caffeine, but you might feel differently."

Jane is longing for a strong coffee but feels that Yasmin might take a bit of a dim view of this.

"Oh, iced water is fine."

"Water is just so good for you," says Yasmin.

Maybe there was a coded message going on here. Was Yasmin going to pour water over her and lick it off? Was water a sign of some sort of rebirthing into the lesbian world?

She looks at Yasmin's long tanned fingers. Was she imagining it? No, the woman had practically stroked her stomach and then honed onto her breast. That was an erotic sign. She had given her a sign. Maybe that wedding ring on her finger was because she is married to a woman somewhere on the island, maybe back in Britain. She thinks about Yasmin Bird peeling off her sports bra.

"Ice in your water?"

"Oh, sorry, yes, that's great. Thank you."

She sips it slowly.

At least she's had that Brazilian, before she left, thinks Jane. Although was waxing accepted on the lesbian scene? She felt confident that most men were up for being faced with a Brazilian. Her lover Jay always said they were a delicious part of oral sex, and Patrick, back in the past when Patrick would go down on her regularly, well, he never complained.

Jane knew it wasn't regarded as a wholly feminist gesture, and so women might not be so up for it. And what about Yasmin herself? Was Jane going to encounter a waxed pudenda? Well, she had seen lesbian porn. Everyone looked totally hairless there, but then they do in porn anyway, so perhaps that was no guide. And perhaps the lesbian porn was actually not lesbian porn at all, but porn made for heterosexual men who... what happens if Yasmin has a piercing? She suddenly becomes aware that Yasmin is talking to her urgently about something.

"Sorry?"

"Oh Jane, forgive me, I was just saying that I am really quite nervous about having the television team over tomorrow, and the fact that you know them all makes me feel much, much better."

Yasmin Bird, nervous? Jane can't see her being anxious

about anything. Let alone people like Alan Makin and that awful Philip Burrell.

"Oh, you do not want to be nervous of that lot. They are pussies."

She looks at Yasmin closely to see if she reacts to the word. To her irritation, Yasmin continues drinking her iced water, looking into the far distance somewhere above Jane's shoulder and musing about mats and how many she is expecting will come tomorrow.

"It's happening on the beach. Demands of the TV company. Of course I'm really hoping it will do wonders for trade."

Jane slowly starts to wonder that she may have been mistaken, if she has got everything completely wrong. Maybe Yasmin wasn't making a pass at her after all. She actually starts listening to what the woman is talking about, waves of embarrassment passing over her. How had she let her imagination to race away? Even thinking about waxing and how she would get her tongue around a labial piercing. For God's sake, thinks Jane. Right now, Yasmin probably has a huge, muscle-bound boyfriend preparing smashed avocado on sourdough toast for a late brunch together.

"And so I am just going to do a bit of Yoga, you know, some Downward Dogs and key stretches and then a spot of my normal Pilates lesson. Because it's all only for show, and to have a chance of flashing up my Twitter handle," Yasmin continues.

She smiles brightly at Jane. Jane looks at her angrily, furious that Yasmin Bird is in fact not about to lead her into the toilets, roll down her pants and put her tongue gently between her legs. She is even more furious about the fact that she, Jane, was fantasising about such things. Is she a sex obsessive? She thinks she might be.

"Are you sure these people are really the business?" says Yasmin.

"What?" says Jane. "What people?"

"The television crew. And the famous people themselves. I mean, they aren't going to just mess me around are they? I'm not good at dealing with famous people."

"Yasmin, they are fine. You'll be ideal. I mean, they are not even proper celebrities. They are people hoping to be celebrities, after being on television. Now, I have to fly. What time tomorrow?"

"No problem. Here. On the beach. Starts at 8 am. Looking forward to it, Jane. Thanks."

Yasmin leans forward to embrace Jane. She smells the lavender fragrance, feels Yasmin's hair brush against her bare shoulder. Yasmin puts her hands squarely around Jane's collarbone and draws her face in towards her, kissing her pertly but definitely on the mouth.

"You're a star. Thanks for making me feel relaxed about everything. I'm so pleased you are going to be there, supporting me. See you tomorrow."

"See you," mutters Jane.

She walks back towards her car, shaking her head. What were the boundaries these days? She suddenly feels very old. Everything has changed and she feels adrift. She knows younger women were forever hopping into bed with men but also women, she reads about it online. But a women of her age? She hadn't had that sort of chance, didn't do that sort of thing. What happens if I hit my fifties, say, I mean, real middle age, without having had a sexual encounter with another woman? It's a life experience, Jane thinks. It is one she feels she needs to have, and she doesn't really care how she gets it.

Chapter Twenty-Seven
Gemma

The voting is complete. Everyone assembles at the front of the house. Moths dance around the spotlights from the television cameras. Everyone has drunk too much sangria. Gemma finds her hands are actually sweating, clutching her fully packed suitcase.

Simon and Kate have summoned them into the living room and they have all condemned one of their kind to exile. How can everyone smile and chat to each other, when they have each been a betrayer to at least one person, thinks Gemma. What happens if it is her? She knows the drill. A taxi will roll up, and the taxi driver will come out holding a card on which a name is written. What if it's her name? How will she cope? She knows she would have to speak to a camera in the taxi, but she's sure she will be crying with the humiliation of it all. She takes deep breaths.

She knows it's all fleeting. This will be something she will look back on in time. She knows this is not part of her life, and never will be. But there has been something about the intensity of the week, about living with this group of adults, which makes her want to cling on. It will be something she will never do again. She feels choked about the thought of the community being split up. She knows it is the demands of the television company, and the show, but it makes her feel tearful.

Simon steps in front of the group.

"Now, celebrities. You know tonight is the first night for departures. Only, things are going to be a bit different this evening, for the first time on the show."

"A stay of execution!" calls Philip Burrell.

"Yeah, I feel as if we are all on the way to the guillotine," says Nigel loudly.

"The tumbrils, the tumbrils," yells Jocelyn. "I shall take the role of Marie Antoinette, whose hair went completely grey on her way to the Place de la Revolution in the cart."

"It is a far, far better thing…" starts Nigel.

"Could you two please kindly shut up?" says Philip. He feels like punching Nigel. "I can't hear what Simon is saying," he comments loudly.

"So the thing is," continues Simon, "that for the first and the only time on this show, we are actually going to say goodbye to TWO of you this evening. Sorry. Schedules, all that. Anyway, there's safety in numbers."

Gemma feels as if a great chasm has opened up beneath her feet, and there is nothing holding her back from diving down it. Two people! So her chances of being thrown out have just doubled! She's definitely going to be chucked off, she knows it. And if she stays, with two less of them, well the dynamics would change entirely.

A pair of headlights arrive at the bottom of the drive. The taxi! This is the moment. Gemma feels as if her entrails have turned to ice. Everyone stands very still, holding their luggage. A large seven-seater rolls up to the front of the house. Gemma looks back at the house, the house where so much emotion and angst has been spent during the last week. Was this the last she would ever see of it? Was this the last she would see of her fellow celebrities? Silly word, but she feels they are a discrete group. And that word is no better or worse than any other, is it?

The driver gets out. It's Robin, the thin, harried looking man who had collected them from the airport.

"Good evening everyone," says Robin.

The group looks at him with hostility. Everyone is preparing for the worst. Nobody wants to leave. Surprisingly, they all hold hands.

"Everyone hates everyone else, don't they?" mutters Kate to Simon. "But look at them all. Suddenly, they are in unison."

He smiles wryly. "Always happens. Always gets very emotional. Why do we make this stuff? They can't stand one another."

Robin coughs. Rupert and Alex crouch down. One is focused on Robin, one on the group.

"So I have two names tonight," says Robin.

Without any more warning, he suddenly brings out a giant placard he has been concealing behind his back. It reads:

1. FISH

2. MOO

The group sways. Fish shrugs his shoulders, drops the hands of Gemma and Alan and lightly steps away from the group. He is barefoot and has no luggage with him.

"Where's your stuff?" whispers Gemma, feeling a little bit sorry for him.

"I burnt it all in a cleansing ceremony on the beach at dawn this morning," says Fish cheerily. "I knew I was going to be leaving tonight."

He reaches the car, turns to everyone and gives a high salute.

"Goodbye. Good luck. Good riddance."

The group watches him, open mouthed. Fish disappears into the darkness of the taxi.

"We'll have to cut that last comment," mutters Simon to himself.

Rupert, camera on his shoulder, leaps in behind the evicted Fish. Gemma sees the interior of the taxi suddenly bathed in light as Rupert turns his spotlight onto Fish and starts shooting his reaction. It seems as if Fish is not about to give any other reaction as he is sitting on the floor of the taxi in a lotus position, eyes closed.

Meanwhile, back on the terrace, reactions to the second eviction are not going well. Cresta is draped around Moo, crying loudly.

"No, no! Moo! Babes! Off the show! What arse could have done this to you my darling? How did this happen? Don't leave me! Simon, Simon, we are a couple, what is going on?"

Simon, who can't say anything, merely shrugs. He's very pleased with how the evictions are going. He hadn't had to doctor the votes too much this year. He was disappointed with the underperforming Fish, and although Moo was fun, he could do with a bit of illicit sexual behaviour or something scandalous on the show, and on that score he wants to see more of Cresta snogging Philip. That was always going to be hard with her husband lurking on the sidelines. It would give the show a welcome mid-series boost, and he knows the tabloids will love it.

There always had to be a sacrifice.

Moo, unaware of Simon's moral struggle, manages eventually to disentangle himself from her clinging arms. He looks surprisingly unfussed.

"Look, love, don't worry. It's only a game. I know, I know. I'm fine. I need to get back to the farm anyway. You stay on, babe. Don't worry about me."

"But we are a pair, how could we be separated?" she wails.

Moo picks up a large rucksack and follows Fish into the taxi.

"Goodbye everyone," he shouts over his shoulder. "Great knowing you. Look after my bird. Hey, Fish, get up off the floor, mate."

Fish reluctantly sits on a seat. Moo sits down beside him. They both wave to the remaining candidates. The taxi spins off in the gravel outside the house and disappears into the darkness.

"Don't worry about that, she'll be looked after," shouts Jocelyn to the receding taillights. "Eh, Philip?" she continues, nudging Philip's gangly frame.

"I don't know what you are talking about," says Philip loftily.

"Oh yes you do," says Jocelyn. "Don't he, Cresta? Are you alright, love? Tissue?"

Cresta giggles, pushes back her hair behind her ears and wipes her eyes.

"Course I'm alright. I was one of the people what voted him off, the silly bugger. More sangria, anyone?"

Chapter Twenty-Eight
Cresta

Everyone goes back to their rooms, pulling their luggage behind them. Gemma gets inside her room, closes the door and starts hanging up her clothes. She feels a mixture of relief and disappointment. But mostly relief. She wonders what Moo and Fish are saying to each other in the cab. She feels sorry for them. Off the show, away from the magical circle held fast by the people still in the house. What a bunch of oddballs they really are.

There is a knock at the door.

"Come in," she calls merrily.

"Gemma, it's me," says Alan, wandering in.

"Oh, hi. Well, that was a damp squib in the end."

"I know. Entirely predictable, although I suddenly caught myself wanting to get into that cab with that bloody loony Fish."

"Really?"

"'Fraid so."

"Actually, so did I. For a minute. But then, back there, when we were all lining up outside, I didn't. I was terrified it would be my name on the board. I'm really glad to be back here with everyone. It seems like home. It's weird, because it's not, but it seems like it. Almost more real than my own home."

There is a pause. Alan smiles at her.

"This hasn't been what you thought it would be, has it?"

"It's been strange. Intense. I think I'll, you know, I'll find it hard to be myself when I get home. I think I'll keep on looking around and wondering where you all are. I do hope we'll keep in touch. Don't forget. You said you would sort out my finances when we all get home. I still have no idea what bonds are."

Alan laughs. "You're not alone."

"Team winners, survivors, whatever, there are drinks on the terrace," Simon calls down the corridor.

"Shall we?" says Alan, chivalrously opening the door.

Gemma drops the rest of her clothes on the bed and hurries out of the room. The corridor, once so strange to her, is now as familiar as her own house. It is her own house. Alex walks beside her, shooting her. Being observed all the time is not strange, but part of it. Her undocumented life back in London seems rather hazy and undefined in contrast.

Outside, Nigel and Jocelyn are lolling around beside the organic pond with Jasper. Jasper has cheered up immeasurably. He is back in his cloak and performing his favourite trick, Entourage, on Jocelyn.

This involves losing all the Queens and then finding them again.

"Where are Cresta and Philip?" asks Gemma, as Jasper slaps down each card.

"Where is the Queen of Hearts?" says Jasper sunnily.

"Who knows," says Jocelyn, momentarily looking away from the pile. "I can probably hazard a guess, however."

"Joce, I need your focus," murmurs Jasper.

"Sorry, sorry," she says. "I'm with you. All the way."

Gemma makes a face at Alan. "Sorry I asked."

Meanwhile, Cresta hadn't even bothered to pack her bag, because she knew she wasn't going to leave. She had been holding a completely empty case. She considers this show is going pretty well, all considered, and is fully intending to win it. Not just because of the popularity that will come in its wake, but because of the £20,000 prize money, which she and Moo need. In order to win, Cresta knows she must be indispensable. Outrageous but not disgraceful. It's a precise target.

She and Moo had done their best as a pair but in the end, she had to be on her own.

"I've gotta cause a scandal, babes, and I can't do that with you lurking in corridors. So it's back to the farm for you while I work my wonders on that old arty chap." They had both voted for him to leave, Moo pleading the health and safety of his cows to Simon.

Now she is free to get on with her plan. She takes off her gown and pulls on an entirely different outfit, checking her make-up in the mirror as she does it. This will be the moment when command of social media and online gossip will be hers. She smiles at her reflection and hums gently. She puts her hair up in a bandana. Her feet are bare. She hopes Jocelyn has understood the plan. Timing is all. She quietly opens the French windows at the back of her room.

Five minutes later, Cresta is climbing around the window ledges on the ground floor to arrive, cat burglar style, outside the glass doors leading into Philip's room. She watches him wandering around like a phantom, unpacking, repositioning his toiletries. Then she taps softly on the window.

Philip leaps back as if he has been stung.

"What? Yes? Who the hell's that?"

He marches up to the glass and peers through it. It is very bright in his room, so he can hardly see outside. Slowly his eyes adjust and he sees the unmistakable frame of Cresta. She is wearing bright pink hot pants and a matching boob tube. Her hair is swept off her head and held by a pink bandana. She is barefoot.

She taps again on the window.

"Well, come in," says Philip testily, pulling back the door. "Why the hell are you coming in through the window?"

"Didn't want the cameras to see me. Or that cow Jocelyn for that matter. You know what she's like, how she hates me. Oh Philip," she sniffs. "Can we turn the lights down a bit. I've got such a headache. I need comforting after all that. Can I come in? Thank you," she says, not waiting for an answer.

"Really? You didn't look too sad about your husband departing, my dear."

"Oh I was gutted. Be here without Moo?"

"I thought you said you voted him off?"

"I was forced to. He wanted to go, didn't he? He had to get back to the farm. Things are bad between us." She sniffs again. "He was desperate to leave. Don't you want to comfort me? But Philip," undoing the bandana from her head and shaking out her hair, "I think I have some bad news for you."

"What?"

"I think you might be the next to be evicted."

"What? How do you know?"

"I just know," says Cresta, fumbling behind her for the bed and lying down on it.

"Bloody dark in here, innit."

"You asked for the lights to be turned down," says Philip, exasperated.

"Well, could we just keep the lights off but perhaps open the door a tiny crack, so we can get some light from the corridor?"

"If you say so," he says irritably, opening the door, peering down the corridor. He can hear everyone out by the terrace. The corridor is empty. He turns back to the project in hand. He is flattered by the arrival of this young woman into his bedroom. He prides himself on his sexual allure and what he considers his undimmed erotic charge. Let other men go to seed when they hit sixty. Not Philip Burrell. Now, it seems as if he is going to have no choice in the matter of

188

whether to seduce Cresta the It Girl or not. Plus, if what she says is true, and he is going to be kicked out, he might never have another chance like this. He might as well give the girl a treat.

He turns round, sees her lying on the bed in front of him.

"Now, I could help you here Phil. I could put my vote towards keeping you on."

"I thought you would vote for me anyway, my dear."

"Well I might not, you know. Certainly not if you aren't going to comfort me this evening. Will you just give me a hug? I'm so lonely and sad. I just need to be held."

He stands above her. Was this sexual blackmail? He runs through the options of going to bed with Cresta.

1. They have sex and nobody finds out, which is the best option, but quite unlikely.

2. They do it and Alex bursts in with his camera, which is pretty disastrous yet probably untransmittable, being daytime television and all. Plus, he can hear Alex chatting over by the pond. Why would he suddenly venture down here? He's pretty sure he's safe.

3. He slings her out of the room right away. He thinks of his wife Gilda at home waiting for him. He should really sit this silly woman bolt upright and command her to leave. Well, that's not going to happen, is it? He can already feel his cock moving in his trousers. Why shouldn't he have a bit of pleasure in this show? He remembers kissing Cresta on the helicopter ride, remembers touching her body and how exciting it felt. It was all good, thought Philip.

Cresta writhes encouragingly on the embroidered rustic Ibizan counterpane, her hair fanning behind her like a mermaid. In an almost Pavlovian response to the sight of a woman on a bed before him, Philip undoes his belt and drops his trousers. He is very keen to take Cresta's clothes off as soon as possible. He is unaware of the door sliding open slightly.

"Come on then, Daddy," she says, opening her eyes very

wide as behind Philip's back, through the open door, she sees the wholly satisfying sight of Nigel and Jocelyn. Alex, his camera peering past them, brings up the rear.

Oh Cresta, you clever thing. This could not be better. She flutters her fingers, decorated with three inch long false nails, in acknowledgement to the assembled company.

As Philip reaches out and dips his head down towards her fully clothed body she puts her arm around him and whispers.

"Whoops."

Philip whips round, sees the fully open door and charges to close it, forgetting that his trousers are by now around his ankles.

"Get out, get out!" he yells, stumbling at Nigel and Jocelyn, the Adventurous Parents and Alex. "What the fuck is going on? Get out of my room, you dreadful lot. I was just unpacking and... helping Cresta with something." He wrestles his trousers up his body.

"Oh for Jesus' sake."

Alex, Jocelyn and Nigel scurry back down the corridor. Cresta, sitting upright on the bed, gives her tinkling laugh.

"What the hell was all that about?"

"Don't worry about it baby," she says. It was perfect. Good old Jocelyn. Philip still had had his pants on, so no nudity. But a lot of suggestive behaviour. The tabloids would go mental over it. She might end up with a spin off series. No question about her staying on the show, not once Simon hears about this. She yawns. She might as well have a good night of it now.

"Well, now we are on the bed, why don't we finish it off eh, babes?" she says.

"What? With that lot hanging around outside? Are you mad?"

"They'll have gone off now you've slammed the door. They got what they wanted. It'll be alright. Just you see."

Unfortunately, Philip has been thoroughly alarmed by the turn of events. He wants nothing greater than to be alone.

"Cresta, my dear, you are very beautiful but I must insist on your leaving my room." He holds the door open. "Door, or window. The choice of exit is yours, but exit it must be."

"Alright, keep your wig on. Toodle-oo," says Cresta, sashaying out of the door and down the corridor.

Chapter Twenty-Nine
Jasper

In the morning light, Philip considers his position. He could deny everything. He could admit everything. But admitting being seduced by the It Girl, and then being found out so outrageously was embarrassing. He had been framed, he realised. By someone who was almost a teenager, too. And someone with no social standing at all. Probably best to brazen it out and just pretend nothing happened. Gilda must never find out. He thinks about Gilda with fond nostalgia. He wishes he was back at home, in his studio, with his art and his routine. Rather than here, in a place where reality moves and changes shape with alarming rapidity and frequency.

He knows the cameramen, Rupert and Alex, would be waiting in the corridor. Particularly after last night. Especially after last night. He suspected someone had even camped out there. He sighs. This programme was proving more challenging than he had ever thought it would.

The trouble is that he keeps on forgetting it is going to be transmitted. Tempting though it was to relax into the moment, and do something momentarily entertaining, such as go to bed with Cresta, he now envisages it repeating on him like some sort of dreadful piece of food, only months later, on daytime television. In front of Gilda. In front of his dealer. In front of the world.

Last night he had given into temptation. But it was

unexpected. How was he to know that Cresta would come onto him like a whirlwind, arriving at his window with that outfit on? Yes, they had had that kiss in the helicopter, but honestly. The silly bitch. It was probably quite a blessing, to be honest, that he and she had been interrupted. He was pretty confident that without the interruption, they would have gone all the way. Of course they would.

He puts on his robe and peers out of the corridor, closing the door quietly behind him.

"Hi Philip," says Alex, bearing his camera.

Oh God.

"Hi."

"Off for a swim?"

"Yes, I think I am."

He stalks off, head held high, in the direction of the organic pond.

As he walks down the corridor, he senses he can hear giggling. He ignores it. These idiots. At least he hasn't been evicted. Not that he ever really thought he would be, but one never knew.

On the terrace, Jasper is doing a few card tricks to the Adventurous Parents, Nigel and Jocelyn.

"Ah, good morning, survivor."

For a brief moment, Philip thinks this is a veiled comment from Jasper to his evening frolics but he doesn't think Jasper is actually capable of saying something knowing like that, so he assumes it must be a reference to the evictions.

"I know. Good to stay alive."

"Wasn't it!" gushes Jocelyn. "I never actually thought any of us four," she says, proudly indicating the group, "would go for the fall, but when Simon said there were two people to be chucked out I did get a bit nervous. Didn't you?"

"No," says Philip. "I never get nervous."

"You might do when your wife watches the show," snorts Nigel. "That is if they keep that moment in."

"I don't know what you are talking about," says Philip.

"From last night," presses Nigel.

Jocelyn simply smiles and looks at Jasper.

"Silly old fool," she mutters. "Where is the Queen of Hearts now, then?"

"Well, talk of the devil," says Nigel.

"Morning babes!"

Philip turns around, dreading what vision he will see. Cresta is clad for the morning in a leopard skin bikini, accessorised with gladiator sandals. A long golden chain is wrapped across her tattooed torso and up past her torpedo-shaped breasts. Her hair is pulled away from her face and has been wrapped into a cone. She looks like someone from a sword and sandals epic film.

"Hello, naughty," she says, coming up and slapping Philip vigorously on the bottom.

"Get off me," hisses Philip. Why did he ever come on this show?

"Whoo-oo," Cresta giggles. "Don't pretend you don't like it! You certainly did last night!"

"And… cut!" says Simon, who has tiptoed up behind Cresta with Rupert in tow.

"Fantastic," he whispers to Rupert. "Fucking brilliant. Get his grimace. He doesn't know where to look. Right, everyone," he continues, beaming. "We are going to do Beach Yoga today. With an additional extra which should sort the sheep from the goats."

"I thought the sorting had already been done last night," says Nigel.

"We're onto the next challenge. Where is Gemma and, er, where is Alan?"

"Probably in the same room," sniggers Nigel.

"Oh my, were you all at it last night?" says Jocelyn. "I thought we were the only ones to be…"

"Yes, Jocelyn, we all KNOW about your amazing sexual appetite. Can you please spare us the details at least until after lunch today," says Philip grandly.

194

Jocelyn walks up to him. "I really don't think you are in any position to be high and mighty with me, dirty old man. You should have seen yourself last night. On your hands and knees behind Cresta, panting like a lapdog about to get a biscuit. It was actually pathetic."

"Social media and the papers are just going to love this series," says Simon ecstatically to Rupert. "We'll probably all get a fucking bonus."

He sees Gemma and Alan standing by the breakfast buffet chatting and stands up. "Could the rest of you all get breakfast?"

Two hours later the celebrities are all aboard the bus and on their way to the beach, where they are to meet Yasmin Bird for a spot of Beach Yoga. Philip is doing his best to hold his head high and laugh along with everyone else.

"What is the other surprise?" says Gemma to Simon.

"It's a good one. Everyone, listen up," announces Simon. "The last challenge as you remember was focused on Water. Well, today we are going onto the next element, Fire. We've got a spot of fire walking ahead of us. On a fire bed. Over hot coals."

"Whaaaat?" screeches Cresta.

"Yes, Cresta. And if you don't do it properly, you'll be going over broken glass. That's an additional extra. After that, you can relax with some yoga from the very lovely Yasmin, who's been doing Yoga and Pilates on Ibiza for years and is something of an institution."

There is a silence around the group. Eventually Gemma pipes up.

"What, so after Water and Fire, we will have to go through the next round and meet something do to with... Earth?" she says, cautiously.

"That's the notion. Do you like it?"

"Well, it depends what Earth consists of. Frankly I'm not happy about being buried alive, but I'm hope even *Ibiza (or Bust)* wouldn't be so stupid," she mutters. "Although I'm not sure."

When they arrive at the venue, the celebrities bundle off the bus, preceded by the cameras. They huddle together anxiously like a flock of birds.

"I've done this before at a Spiritual Festival," says Jocelyn. "Piece of cake. You simply have to look up and keep moving. Don't stop. And obviously don't wear socks."

"A thousand degrees Fahrenheit," says Jasper The Wizard.

"What is?"

"The heat of the coals, my dear. It's fine. I've come across this act quite a few times at... you know, magic conventions."

"Magic conventions?"

"Yes, where we in the Magic Circle get together and swap notes."

"I thought you weren't allowed to let on about your secrets," says Cresta.

"Well, that's a secret," says Jasper, slightly flustered.

"Oughtn't we go and find out where the bed of coals is?"

"Come this way," calls Simon.

They all walk hesitantly across the beach to a low bed scooped out of the sand, in which there is a long line of glowing coals. Gemma feels sweat starting to run down her back.

"This is a nightmare," she whispers to Alan. "I'm so frightened. I can feel the heat from the coals from here. What happens if I burn my feet really badly? What if I trip and fall onto the bed of coals?"

He grabs her arm. "You'll be fine. This is all for television. Nobody is going to get hurt."

"Yes, but we've heard that before, haven't we. What about that bloody awful swim from the pontoon?"

She stares into his face. "You and I nearly drowned. Remember? There was no facility for health and safety at all. There isn't one here. Can't we just say we are allergic or something and skip to the Beach Yoga?"

"No, Gemma. We are paid to be here and we have to

196

perform. That's our role. That's the deal. Remember? You'll be fine. We'll all be fine."

Afterwards, she can't quite remember how she did it. She simply recalls standing in front of the pit, heat, steam and smoke rising in front of her, and looking steadily ahead at Rupert, who was some way off on the sand at the other side of the pit.

"Go, Gemma!" someone shouted "And keep walking!"

At that, she forced herself to lift up one foot and step onto the hot bed of coals, which was strangely soft and pliant. A hiss came off the sole of her foot. Then she repeated the action. Twelve times. She counted. Alex ran alongside her on the sand, filming her face, her feet, her entire demeanour.

"Keep walking, Gemma," shouts Alan.

"Mind over matter," she repeats to herself, steadily continuing to pad swiftly across the bed, counting her steps. She thinks she is going to be sick. Are her feet actually cooking beneath her? She keeps going. Only a dozen steps, but the whole monstrous experience seemed to take about an hour. Was this entertainment? She reaches the end of the bed and stumbles up into the sand, grabs Alan.

"Thank God. Thank God we only have to do that once." There is a bucket of cold water. She immediately stands in it and turns to see who is doing the walk next.

It's Jasper. He undoes his cloak and bravely strides onto the pit. Immediately, he brings up the sole of his foot, lets out a shrill scream. He starts walking very quickly. In no time, Jasper is running towards her on the bed of coals, his face contorted red, hands waving hopelessly, sweat pouring off his forehead.

"Stop him, stop him," shouts Gemma. "He's running, something's wrong! Get him off the bed, now!"

"I'm burning, I'm burning," screams the magician. "I'm burning!"

He launches himself, crying and weeping, and falls onto the sand.

Simon rushes up.

"Jasper, are you alright? Stand in this bucket of water, that's it, stand here. We were assured that everything would be fine, this is a company who does this all the time at raves down the road. Are you alright? Jasper, let me see your feet. Kate, call the medical team over."

"Funny that the fucking magician is the only one to get burned," Philip says acidly, looking on.

"How can you be so cruel?" says Gemma. "It was horrendous."

"Some people can just do it, I suppose," muses Alan. "And others can't."

Jasper is hunched up over the bucket, sobbing. A First Aider is getting large volumes of bandage out of his case.

"And cut," says Simon crossly to Rupert. "We won't be able to show that bit of course. Thank fuck he was the last one to go. What happened?"

Rupert shrugs his shoulders. "Nobody really understands the phenomenon. Apparently ninety-nine per cent of people can do this, but occasionally it does go wrong. Well, according to Wikipedia, anyway."

"What a plethora of background information we are supported with on this show. Wikipedia, for God's sake," splutters Simon. "Well, the First Aider is here," he says, glancing over at the assistant who is bandaging Jasper's raw feet, "and we need to continue with the programme. Have you got the steaks?" Simon turns to Gemma. "It seems that Jasper has come a bit of a cropper, but we need to carry on. Now, I want you to do something for me. Are you any good at cooking?"

"Are you asking me to do this because I'm female?"

"Of course not. Now, can you do this for me? Take this frying pan, put it on the coals and simply fry up these steaks. It's just to show that the coals really are hot."

Gemma points at the shivering Jasper, whose feet are now completely bound in white bandages.

"I don't think anyone doubts you, Simon."

Nevertheless, she fries the steaks, their fragrant smell wafting across the beach. Nobody does the broken glass exercise, out of respect to Jasper, who is eventually encouraged to sit down on a beach chair and drink a milkshake. Hunched and miserable, he sips it slowly through a pink straw.

"What next, I wonder," says Alan calmly to Gemma.

"What, before we all get buried alive? Or have to eat dunghills or something?"

"No, what next today? Aren't we doing Downward Dogs?"

"Ah yes. And here is the ever present Simon to guide us."

Everyone walks over the beach to find Yasmin surrounded by five or six attendants and seven empty mats. One of the attendants is Jane, who waves enthusiastically as they approach.

"Hi everyone! Remember me? You know, George's mum! Hi to my neighbours, Philip! Hi Alan! It's me!" she shouts.

"Oh for fuck's sake," mutters Simon. "Not her. What is her name again?"

"Jane," says Rupert.

"Jane!" calls Simon. "Can we tone it down a bit? Viewers will have no idea who you are and what's going on. You are just background here, I'm afraid."

"Oh, sorry," says Jane, aghast. She runs up to him, tossing her hair, smiling. She is wearing a lot of make-up.

"Aren't I going to be in the show from the bit, you know, with my son George, and you lot finding him, and all that?"

"Maybe. Maybe not. Thing is, Jane, you never know what's going to end up on the cutting room floor," says Simon grandly. "Sorry, but this bit is for our seven Celebs. We need you in the background here. Can't have you yelling like this. Now, can we go for the entry and arrival shots again, everyone? Back to positions by the fire pit. Jasper, can you walk?"

Jasper nods nobly, and hobbles back over to the pit.

Jane stands, aghast, watching everyone return to their original places. She turns away.

199

"Sorry, sorry," she says to Yasmin, humbly. She wishes she had stayed at home. She had built this whole morning up to be something. Now it was turning out to be nothing. She wishes she was back beside the pool. She'd even go as far as play Uno with Belle and George.

"No matter," says Yasmin, tossing her perfect plait over a bronzed shoulder.

How could I have thought she was gay, thinks Jane for the twentieth time.

Everyone sits down on a mat.

"Good morning," announces Yasmin. "Now, for your practise today you must assume the position of Downward Dog."

"Blimey," mutters Philip, who is positioned directly behind Cresta's shapely bottom.

The night after the fire pit filming, the second eviction is almost a formality. It has been decided that Jasper, who has suffered second-degree burns to his feet, must go home at the first possible occasion. The seven contestants have a quiet dinner. There is no voting. They gather outside the house with their cases as before, but the cases are empty and when the taxi driver turns up with the note bearing Jasper's name, it is not so much a nasty surprise as a wholly welcome event.

"Jasper, you are on your way home," says Philip grandly, as if he was a Victorian father in the colonies waving off a child aboard a steam ship.

Jocelyn rolls her eyes.

"Please come and see me at Blackpool next year," says Jasper as he embraces each of them. He is clad in his magician's cloak, but has to wear slippers because his feet are still so sore. Gemma finds herself crying when she kisses him goodbye.

"I wasn't sure of him at first but I soon realised he was harmless," she says later to Alan. "With his lemon tricks and his little card surprises. I had him pegged as a potential winner!"

"This whole week has been one hell of a learning process," says Alan.

"Poor Jasper," says Gemma, too weary to expand the conversation. "I just hope he gets a lot of work out of the exposure."

Chapter Thirty
Jane

Belle opens her eyes and looks up at the whirring fan. She goes through the programme of the day. Jack and Sam are coming over for a playdate. She knows Jane is out. With something that involves that television crew. At seven in the morning. Funny how she seems to only now be enjoying the holiday. When there's a camera involved. Anyway, Belle thinks, absence of her boss means she can relax. Maybe after Jane gets back she can get the address of the house and send it to silly old Gilda.

She would have to keep an eye on the boys, of course, but she won't have to entertain George. The day stretches out ahead of her. There is always Patrick. She is becoming rather fond of him. He had been very kind to her on that awful day, particularly as he had known the whole truth of the incident. Things had been much better since then. She and Jas had spent the early part of the evening together most nights. She didn't mind missing out on the clubbing scene. She'd had enough of it anyway and she was running out of money.

Patrick had said it was good, her being away. "Giving us some Family Time." he had said. He was a gentle presence in the household, ineffectual beside the brutal force of his wife, seemingly happy to go off with his iPad. Spread betting and playing the market online in his bedroom was his idea of a good holiday. It certainly wasn't Belle's.

Three hours later, Belle is on her sunlounger by the pool.

She can hear the boys playing with George's Lego Nexo Knights in his room. She turns a page of her holiday book, continues to read until distracted by a noise outside the compound. With a spin of gravel and a rather jolting halt, the hire car arrives back at the villa. Far too early, thinks Belle. Why is she back? Belle puts down her book. Bang goes her relaxing day. She can see from the way Jane stomps up to the house that she is in a mood.

Throughout the fifteen minute drive from the beach, Jane has been castigating herself. Firstly, for the whole business of thinking that Yasmin was gay and had made a pass at her. That still hurt. Secondly, for believing she, Jane, was a key player, almost a celebrity to be valued by the television crew. The whole business had been an utter humiliation. Being told to shut up by that producer, Simon. In front of all the yoga class. To whom she had boasted, earlier, about her connections. It had been mortifying.

She had enabled them to shoot the whole George-in-the-mobile-home escapade, hadn't she? As she parks the car back at the villa, an idea comes to her. She might as well find Simon. Complain. And deny him access to the footage of George. As a minor, his presence on the show was her responsibility. Wasn't it? Hold the whole programme to ransom. Then they would let her on it. Furthermore, if she goes to the 'Celebrity' house itself, she might be on the show again.

She walks past Belle and gives her a cursory wave. Look at that. Reading when she is supposed to be working.

Jane can't be bothered to tell her off or make a pointed comment. She just won't employ her again as a babysitter when they are back in London. That'll teach her to read books on holiday.

She passes into her bedroom and checks her face in the mirror. It had just been so embarrassing. To be told off. To be told to shut up. To be told not to wave at Philip and Alan, both of whom were, after all, her neighbours. What an arse. She is filled with rage and anxiety. She leaves the bedroom and slams the door, remembering her ebullient mood earlier that morning, with the chance of being on television ahead of her. She had looked forward to it so much she had even gone into the old town the day before and had her hair done specially, plus a mani/pedi.

She longed to be on that reality show. And not just as an extra. Well she would show them. She was going to be on it, come what may. Let that Simon regret the moment he had told her to shut up. She wasn't going to take it lightly. She knows she holds one key card, which gives her power. Access to the footage of her son. She would withhold it, wouldn't she? Until they gave her a special place. Maybe a starring role. She was a star, Jane thought. She just hadn't been discovered, yet. But there was a place for the mature woman, wasn't there? You didn't have to be under 20 in order to be discovered, did you? Look at that Martha Kearney on BBC Radio, nobody had heard of her until she was about 40. And then what about Theresa May? Tootling along in the Home Office until bang! Prime Minister. Who saw that coming? And she has A LOT more going for her than Theresa bloody May.

"Hi Jane!" calls Belle. Stupid girl.

"Hello Belle. Where are the boys?"

"In George's room, playing Lego. They wanted to be out of the sun."

"Oh. Well, I suppose that's okay."

"How was the shoot? You're back early! Did your new hairdo go down well?"

"Oh, it was fine," says Jane airily. "Yes, it was okay. But much shorter than we had told it would be. Someone got their feet burned on a fire walk. Rather badly. Where's Patrick?"

"I think he's having forty winks," says Belle. "Or he's online. Feet burned? How dreadful."

"Yes. Very bad. Well, why don't you do some of George's laundry?"

"Done it."

"Very good," said Jane, meaning the precise opposite. "I'm just going to have a swim." It will ruin her hair, but she's in such a temper she actively wants it to be ruined.

Belle takes the hint and walks off to her room, texting.

Hey babe. How's the walking scene today?

After Jane does her 20 lengths, she feels a bit better. They will have an early lunch by the pool, she thinks. Jane was intending a family lunch around the big table, but Belle makes sure that George has a little table to himself, to share with Jack and Sam. This is just what George wants. They spend the entire meal talking excitedly about tablets and what they would have if only they were allowed to have their own. Jack, as the older, already has a mobile phone which George covets dearly.

"When can I have a phone, Mother?" asks George, calling over as the meal begins.

"When you are at Big School, George," says Jane.

"But Maman," whispers George. "That's not until Year 9. Until I'm fourteen."

"Why do you go to secondary so late, George?" says Jack.

"Because he is at Prep School, Jack," says Jane, loudly. "It's a different system."

Jack and Sam, who had only ever thought that there was Primary, and then Secondary, unless you went to Hogwarts, are silent about this new information, and look at George for some form of explanation. He shrugs.

"Let's talk some more about tablets," he says to them.

Jane looks at Patrick and Belle. She has recovered her poise.

"Well, I got on quite well today."

"Did you sweetie?" says Patrick. "You were back earlier than I thought."

"Well, they only did their filming in the morning today with Yasmin and the class. I'm actually going to go back up to the house. Tomorrow morning." This was an invention. Now

205

she would have to go. Find out the address and just show up. She doesn't know how she will do it, but do it she will. A simple thing like an address is a minor hurdle.

"Are you? What about our plan to go to the market in the old town?" says Patrick anxiously.

"Oh, can't we do that on another day?"

"It's only open mid-week. But never mind. You go off to the TV house. Do you remember I explained to you where it was?"

Of course, Patrick has already been there, thinks Jane. She is flooded with joy. Oh, you beauty. Of course. She turns a dazzling smile onto her husband.

"I'm not that sure I do. That whole day was so fraught. Do you remember?"

"Of course I do. I'll draw you a map if you like. Now, Belle, why don't you come with us to the market? From what you said, it looks rather exciting. I'd quite like to see how they chop up those giant pieces of swordfish, that sort of thing, with little cafés selling shots of tequila while you wait."

"Yes, let's go. Sounds cool."

Belle remembers meeting Gilda at the market, and her rather pathetic plea to her. Well, if Patrick tells Jane then he might as well tell her where the house is. She feels rather sympathetic towards Gilda, now that she herself has had a brush with potential disaster, and avoided it.

After lunch the boys go back to playing Lego. Jane paces around her room. Now she has announced it in front of Belle and Patrick, and now that finding the address has proved a piece of cake, the thought of going up there has become a reality, something which is going to have to be executed. But how? She couldn't just turn up, could she? She would have to have a reason. She has no idea what the filming schedule is for the celebrities for the rest of the week. No idea if they are going to be in the house or out at another excursion like this morning. She doesn't know how TV shows are made. All she knows is that she wants to be on one. She wants to be on this one. She simply cannot bear the thought of knowing it is being shot, up the hill, with her bloody neighbours. They're going to have fame thrust upon them, while she, Jane, is relegated to the role of an extra. But her role was more important than that. The mother of the lost child! This could be her breakthrough moment. The more she thinks about it, the more it makes sense to her. Other people have chance breakthroughs. They only have one per life, however. And the thing is that when your chance comes, you have to identify that it is the one chance and you have to grab it and go for it. That is the tricky thing about chances. They have to be correctly identified. Jane feels that this is her one chance.

Simon and the rest of *Ibiza (or Bust)* have no idea that Jane is heading in their direction. On the terrace by the organic pond the next morning, the plans for the next Chuck Out Challenge are going very well.

"So, we have said goodbye to Jasper," announces Simon. "I've heard from him since he arrived home and he's going to be fine. He's been to the GP and everything is fine. Really. Absolutely fine."

"That's lucky," mutters Gemma to Alan. "Bet he's relieved Jasper's not going to press for damages to his feet."

"Now that we have done Water, and Fire, and a bit of Air in the helicopter sequence, today we are going to achieve the Earth Element in the challenge."

"Yeah, well as two of the above have been life threatening, let's hope nobody dies this time," whispers Alan.

"This," says Simon, "is going to involve a bit of cycling. Quad bikes, in fact."

Nigel and Jocelyn look at each other anxiously.

Philip sniggers and whispers to Cresta while taking the chance to look down her cleavage. "That's them screwed. Do you know they don't know how to drive? Anything. What a terrible shame."

As the bus containing the celebrities pulls out of the drive, headed for a mountainous and earthy bike trail, Jane is getting into her car. She is, she thinks, perfectly dressed for the occasion: white dress, yellow bandeau, yellow espadrilles. Ray-Bans. Pink nails, hands and feet (not the same tone of course). She is clasping a legal letter, which she has printed out this morning. She puts the letter, addressed to *Simon Courtney, Producer, Ibiza (or Bust)*, carefully in her bag and tosses her blown-dry hair. She hopes she will be filmed today.

"Are you off to the house, Jane?" calls Belle casually as she makes up a picnic for the day in the market.

"Yeah, yes, I am."

"Has Patrick told you where it is on the island then?"

"That's my little secret," shouts Jane.

Damn, thinks Belle. Well, I'll just get it off your husband.

Chapter Thirty-One
Jane

It is nearly midday, and quiet in the house. Outside, the water in the organic pond looks coolly inviting, despite its green tinge, but Jane is grateful for the fans whirring in the lounge and happy to sit indoors away from the sunshine. She has started to find the constant blue skies and sunny weather tedious.

Kate, the assistant producer, shows her to a sofa and offers her a glass of water. As usual, the table at the back of the lounge is set with enough food for about twelve people; heaps of bread, bunches of grapes, biscuits, a platter overflowing with golden mandarins, dark green olive oil in saucers.

"Would you like anything to eat? Some fruit perhaps?" offers Kate.

"No, thanks. I'll wait here for Simon."

"He might be a long time, you know. They are out filming all day on a bike trail."

"I'm happy to wait," says Jane.

Kate stands and looks at her.

"I mean, a really long time. We're not expecting them back until tea time."

Jane feels she cannot leave until she has achieved her mission. Anyway, Patrick, George and Belle are out at the market. She can stay and relax, can't she? Perhaps one of the cameramen might be around. She might get asked to do some filming. Wasn't this how people were discovered? It might happen to her. Odder things have occurred to people, haven't they?

Two hours later, Jane and Kate are outdoors, having a late sandwich lunch on a small table set by the organic pond. Kate has to admit she is quite glad for the company. Logging rushes all day in a tiny dark office is one of the downsides of this job and she welcomes the distraction.

"So, how long are you in Ibiza?" says Kate, chewing at her sandwich.

"Oh, just a few more days. You?"

"Only two. Today's the last challenge. Two more people will get chucked off the show tonight. Then there's just the final, here in the house. It's time. We are all bushed."

"Really?"

"Yes. Filming looks easy but it's hard work."

"Oh, yes."

"I can't disclose what the final challenge will be, of course."

"Of course."

There is a silence.

"Who do you think is going to win the show?"

"I can't say. All depends on the voting, really."

"Oh, yes. Yes, of course," says Jane, as if she understands.

"Who do you hope will win?"

Kate laughs. "I couldn't possibly tell you, even if I knew. They are all wonderful contestants and I would be very happy if any of them won. It's going to be quite a close call."

This is untrue on a number of counts. Kate and Simon have both decided that they are going to threaten to resign if Philip Burrell wins the show, such is their contempt towards the artist.

"I refuse to let that prat walk away with the glory," was Simon's succinct manner of putting it.

Following a conversation with the executive team back in London, everyone has decided that it will be Cresta who wins

210

this edition of *Ibiza (or Bust)*. The *Radio Times* special edition cover is underway with a picture of Cresta in a low cut dress, draped in a Spanish flag, waving a Union Jack. A series of these pictures were taken with all the contestants before they left the UK.

Rigging the voting process requires tact, but it's not impossible, as long as you can manage to stop the rest of the celebrities talking about how they voted, which is quite easy, provided that you provide distractions. Everyone hates each other by this stage in the show anyway. Apart from Gemma and Alan, that's been unusual, thinks Kate.

She looks at Jane and wonders why this anxious looking woman has broken off her family holiday to come to what is essentially a glorified TV set.

"This is obviously a lovely spot for a family holiday. We were very happy to see you reunited with your son, Jane. Makes a lovely moment in episode three."

This is just what Jane wants to hear.

"Oh, really? I'm delighted." What Jane really wants to know is whether she looks good, and how much footage has been dedicated to her in the helicopter, but she knows that's not the way to get what she wants, which is more time on camera, more time on the show. She smiles at Kate. She correctly identifies Kate as the gatekeeper.

"Of course, we weren't really all that worried about George. I mean, he had a playdate already arranged, which had slipped my mind, you know how it is. Senior moment," says Jane, laughing loudly, waiting for Kate to correct her.

"Yes of course, of course," says Kate. "I know how you feel. I'll be there one day."

"Well, I'm not THAT old," says Jane.

"Oh, I know, I know."

There is a pause.

"But in any case," Kate continues, "the whole occasion, the helicopter ride and the little tiny bit of anxiety, you know how a show needs a slice of jeopardy, it is all very nice. Brings a bit of worry to the viewers. You know, where is the child, is he going to be in danger? That sort of thing. We've devoted quite a large chunk of the episode to the drama."

"I hope you won't make too much of it. I don't think George was actually in danger for a second, you know," says Jane coldly.

"No, no," says Kate, hurriedly. She fervently hopes that Jane won't ask to see the footage. As far as she can remember, there is a lot of crying in it. Very unattractive crying. From Jane.

"Can I see the footage?"

"Impossible, I'm afraid. Company policy."

"I see. But I am his parent."

"Sorry." She looks at Jane.

"I think I will need to see the footage, you know."

What a bore. She's bound to insist on cuts, thinks Kate. She's bound to insist on losing that brilliant shot where she is weeping and huge amount of snot is running out of her nose. Damn.

"I'll have to check with Simon first, you understand. He's in charge of everything and that includes the footage. Now, if you don't mind…" Kate gets up. "Rushes! You know how it is."

"Yes, of course," says Jane, who has no idea to what Kate is referring.

In the end, Jane waits so long for Simon that she eventually falls asleep.

Simon opens the door of the house to see her, mouth open, slumped in a deckchair in the sun.

"Hello? Are you alright? Who let you in?"

"What, uh… oh, sorry, sorry, yes," says Jane, leaping out of her chair. Her mouth tastes foul. Her hair is a mess.

"Um, Kate, your assistant, Kate let me in."

"Assistant producer, but yes, alright. Can I help you? We have all just got back from a day shooting."

Simon is very tired. How can he ask this woman to politely

go away? It has not been a good day. When they had all arrived on the dirt track, Nigel and Jocelyn proved themselves utterly unable to master the quad bikes and refused after a few, rather alarming, moments, to ride them any further. So called Adventurous Parents. Simon had been obliged to read them the paragraphs from their contract which insisted that they were obliged to take part in everything that the programme saw fit to request them to do, at which point the pair had downed tools completely.

"Left the fucking show!" he said to Philip Burrell on the way home.

"Well, they're still on the coach, you know," pointed out Philip, gesticulating to the renegade pair at the back of the bus.

"Yes. But going home tonight. Apparently."

Indeed, once the bus arrived at the villa, both Nigel and Jocelyn perform pieces to camera outside the front door, explaining how the aims of the show ran counter to their own belief in a world free of petrol engines, and that they were thus forced to resign from *Ibiza (or Bust)*.

"It's been amazing," gushes Jocelyn. "Just amazing. But like all good things, sadly this one has to come to an end. And we have our children to think about, at home. So Nigel and I will wish you all goodbye from the bottom of our hearts. And from my bottom of course, ha ha!"

"Yep, that pretty much sums it up," says Nigel, waving at the camera. "Bye, folks!"

"I'm amazed they are just, well... leaving," whispers Alan to Gemma. "Do you think it's anything else? I mean, they're just abandoning all hope of a cash prize."

"I don't think they ever intended to stay on to the end. Jocelyn told me she hadn't even unpacked again after the last eviction. And they've outstayed their outrageousness."

It was true. The pair had been reduced to rerunning old shockers, such as the state of Jocelyn's pelvic floor, every night after dinner for a few days now. They had privately decided to leave, but in the most public way possible. Doing it as part of the Earth Challenge meant they would have to be included right until the final show.

"I'll get Robin to run you out to the airport. We've changed your tickets," says Simon. He has no idea how he is going to weave this late personnel change into the programme, but he'll work it out. One year one of the contestants had been bitten by a spider and left the show midway. Actually, now Simon comes to remember it, he recalls that the unfortunate contestant, who was a celebrity tabloid newspaper editor, had actually died of the bite at the Hospital of Tropical Medicine in London, a few weeks later, but by then the show had come and gone. So no harm was done, at least in terms of ratings.

In the early days, contestants were desperate to stay on. Now that the schedules were groaning with reality shows it was becoming clear that people were quite happy to walk away from reality television once the original sign-up fee had gone through their account (which it had, with Nigel and Jocelyn. He'd checked). People were bored of it, tired of it. Ratings were not good. He wondered how many more series of *Ibiza (or Bust)* and its myriad versions the public would stand.

"Two down. Four to go," says Philip, pushing open the large wooden door to the villa and walking straight into the figure of Jane who is standing next to Simon.

"Oh, hello, you!" says Jane, grinning widely.

"Jane, what a complete pleasure," says Philip grandly. He was going to win this show. He knows it, now that those two twats were off the scene. He could resume his early dominance over affairs. He is very pleased about this. Now here was his neighbour, for some strange fucking reason, but who cares, come to see his ascendance.

"Welcome to our house… again. Are you staying for dinner?"

"Oh, that would be lovely, thanks," says Jane loudly.

"Is that okay with you Simon? Philip is my neighbour after all."

"Well, no, it's not actually alright, Jane," says Simon wearily.

Jane. That's her name, thinks Simon.

"The house is the province of the Celebrities in the show. It's their house. It's their show. You have been great but you are an outsider. Sorry."

That did it. The use of the word 'outsider'. A civilian. A mortal! How dare he! Jane opens her bag and rustles in it for her official bit of paper.

"Simon, can I have a word?"

"What? Now?"

"Yes, now." She takes him by the elbow and steers him into a corner full of Iberian jugs.

"I'm afraid that we have to go through a few, er, procedures before I can release the footage of George for your show," she whispers to him. "And his friends Jack and Sam. Sorry, but that's the way it is. I've taken advice from counsel. Sorry, love." She hands him the envelope.

Simon sighs. He can see that Jane is determined to be on the show, come what may. And he has just lost two contestants. Oh for God's sake. He will just have to invent the rationale behind her arrival in the edit suite. God give him strength and a producer's job on *Dispatches*. He scans through Jane's legal letter. As he feared, she has demanded control over the elements of the programme concerning her child. And his friends.

"Give me the release form. I'll sign it. Stay for supper. You're welcome."

She had no idea he would give in so remarkably quickly. Must have been the use of the word 'counsel'. That's typical of media folk, thinks Jane. They put up a huge barrier, but when you confront them with a bit of legal smoke and mirrors, they cave in. She kisses him warmly on both cheeks.

"You are a darling. What a treat. Thanks. I'll be very well behaved."

Jane is sitting next to Philip and Cresta at dinner. Opposite her are Alan and Gemma, who eat their food more or less silently. As always, Alex and Rupert move around the table, quietly recording. Jane is the only person who notices them. Every time the cameras focus on her she tosses her hair back and smiles into the face of anyone who is willing to tolerate it. Gemma is exhausted after the quad bike experience. Alan eats his food, transfixed at watching Jane get slowly but surely inebriated.

Everyone is drinking. As the evening goes on, Jane is flushed and excited.

Cresta notices this. It's time to have some fun, thinks Cresta. Liven the place up. It's all gone a bit middle-aged.

"You look so lovely," whispers Cresta to Jane. "You know, when I saw you in that mobile home, I thought, what a stuck up bitch, but now we are just all together, relaxing, and I can see that you really aren't such a cow after all, are you?"

Jane simply giggles. "You are so funny, you really are, Cresta. I thought you were very stupid, so there we both are. Is all this being recorded? Yoo-hoo," she shouts over at Rupert, waving a hand in the air.

Simon rolls his eyes and draws his forefinger across his neck, signifying to Rupert that he has no intention of using this evening as footage on the show.

"Cresta and I, we are just great, aren't we?" says Jane loudly, putting her arm around the It Girl.

"We are perfection," laughs Cresta.

"Oh listen to you two lovebirds," says Philip. "Anyone would think you have the hots for one another."

Jane knows just what to do. It's as if she has scripted it. She knows it is daring, but she is full of sangria and she doesn't care.

"Oh, we do," says Jane. "We do. Don't we?"

Cresta looks at Jane. Alright you silly posh lady, thinks Cresta. Here's one for the memory bank.

And Cresta leans over and kisses her full on the lips.

There is silence around the table. Jane sits motionless on her chair. Gemma opens her eyes very wide. Alan, sipping water, chokes. He nudges Gemma. "That's my stuck up neighbour. Can you believe it?" he whispers. "My God! Young Cresta is certainly keen to make an impression. This show. It changes people."

Philip can bear it no longer. If there is any horseplay, foreplay, call it what you want, he wants to be involved in it.

"Let's all go," he whispers.

"Go where?" says Jane. "I haven't finished my crème caramel."

"Go where?" Cresta echoes.

"Back to my room you idiots. Now!"

"Oh, right," says Jane.

Philip stands up. "We are just leaving," he announces. "To change for the rest of the evening. *À bientôt*."

"What does that mean?" asks Cresta, her arm snaking around Jane's waist.

Jane can hardly believe what is happening. She feels as if she is flying, or spinning, or both. It is just too much. She is on a TV programme and has a potential lesbian encounter before her. She can hardly contain herself. Sex and fame. Her twin peak ambitions. She vaguely remembers thinking she had better text Patrick, and tell him she would be late, but the monochrome memory of her domestic life is overwhelmed by the technicolour thrill of the present. She pushes it out of her mind by looking at Cresta's tanned and full breasts which, as always, seem as if they are barely contained by her strappy top.

"I don't really know," she says in response to Cresta's question.

The three of them walk unsteadily down the corridor. Rupert starts to follow them, but Simon taps him on the shoulder.

"We're going to cut her out of the show anyway. You can't possibly film this. Just let them get on with it. What the hell."

He swings back into the dining area where Alan and Gemma look puzzled.

"What," says Alan, "… on earth are my two neighbours

about to do? This show has turned rather surreal, in my view. Let's have some more of that crème caramel."

Jane has no idea what she is about to do, and more fundamentally, how she is meant to behave. Once the door of Philip's room is closed she starts feeling a bit hot, and then a bit sick, and not really like taking her clothes off, let alone taking part in a threesome. Yet she is only too aware that this strange night will probably never be repeated in her life. Here I am, and I had better get on with it.

She puts her arms around Cresta and starts dancing, in a self-conscious manner. Philip lies back on the bed, watching the two women cavort around the room. This is an excellent result, in his mind. The only thing he regrets is that Nigel and Jocelyn aren't still in the house, to witness him being really outrageous. Or that anyone is filming this.

"Come here, girls," he says, opening his arms wide. The truth is that Philip has never been in a threesome either. However, he isn't going to let that minor issue hold him back.

Cresta knows exactly what to do to whom, with whom, and when. She sits down on the bed and starts to take her shoes off, wriggling out of her dress at the same time. In about twenty seconds she is naked apart from a chain around her waist and a pair of gold knickers. Multiple tattoos decorate her body.

Jane is a bit taken aback by the speed in which Cresta has launched into nudity. However she senses that any demurring from the events in hand might make her look like a prude. And that, thinks Jane, she must certainly not be. She starts to undo her zip at the back of her dress. As it slithers to the ground she offers silent thanks to the fact that she is not only wearing matching underwear but also went through that tortuous ordeal at the beauty salon. There isn't a single hair peeking out from her lacy undergarments. From what she can remember of a blurry porn film she once saw, these elements are important.

Chapter Thirty-Two
Gemma

In the morning of the next day, Philip is in his silk robe, eating papaya on the terrace. "Is this not the morning of the great departure?" he says, holding a slice of the fruit with a fork. He tips his head back and drops a cube of orange flesh into his mouth. Very Noel Coward, he thinks. With a dash of Casanova, if you consider last night. Indeed, Philip has thought about little else since he woke up.

Rupert dances around him with the camera.

Simon leans against the door to the terrace, jotting down thoughts on his iPad. He has no idea how he is going to cut this last episode, showing Cresta and Philip going off together, but cut it together he will. It will probably mean the end of the series, but never mind. He certainly couldn't ever face producing one of these again.

Gemma looks at him nervously.

"Er, yes, I think so," she mutters.

She is hoping very much that he is not about to talk about the night before. Philip is clearly desperate to steer the conversation that way. In his mind it had been a night of sweaty wonder and marvel, framed by golden knickers.

Two women! The only sadness was that nobody would ever be able to really know how magisterially, decisively and inventively Philip had dealt with the overwhelming erotic capital in the room. Two women! He longed to share the details with someone. Anyone. He would even tell that idiot Simon.

Aware of Gemma surveying him, he closes his eyes as he helps himself to another slice of papaya. He hopes he looks like a sexual conqueror. He hopes she is impressed. How could she not be? It had been so fantastically exciting. Four breasts for him to help himself to! And when the girls themselves started kissing, well that was a piece of fucking joy. Every man's fantasy, was it not? Even weedy old Simon would have had a hard on looking at it. At them. Philip considered their bodies. It was funny, he had to acknowledge. How certain things were... done, and certain things not done.

Jane, being that much older, had taken care of her body in a particular way. A way he was used to with women. Philip considered her body, remembering it in detail. Every part had been exercised, honed, brushed, creamed, and waxed into an overall attitude of blankness. Thin, obviously. It was a human shape, but one on its way to erasure, a sort of clean slate on which he could exert his fantasies.

With Cresta the overall carnal situation was different. He felt slightly excluded from Cresta, to be truthful, because there was so much going on. What part of Cresta was not tattooed with mystical sayings in a foreign language, or pierced with golden studs, or infiltrated with chemical boosters? Her entire frame resembled a sort of rococo work of art. All of it. Even that most particularly delicious area. Philip smiles, a gentle, amused smile. Who knew that bushy hippiedom was back in favour between a young woman's legs?

"Hi guys!"

He opens his eyes to find one of the objects of his adventures walking past him. Cresta. She is wearing a frilled turquoise one-piece swimsuit which has a little skirt brushing over her bottom, and a plunged neckline down to her navel. The strange inky lettering cavorts around her arms and collarbone. She has accessorised her outfit with translucent plastic high heels. Her hair is up and her earrings are long.

"Good morning my dear. Did you sleep well?"

"Of course. You?"

"Indeed."

"Gemma, Alan, morning."

"Hi Cresta," says Gemma. She glances at her. She is not going to mention last night, even by allusion. Yet she likes this morning's costume. Cresta's outrageous and seemingly bottomless wardrobe has lost much of its threatening power for Gemma. She almost regards the younger woman with indulgence. Why shouldn't she promote her assets?

"You look great."

"Thanks," says Cresta. "Zara. In the sale."

"Oh, thanks," says Gemma. "Not that I'm going to get one, I couldn't possibly fit into it and it would look crap on me anyway."

Cresta sits down beside Gemma. "Don't be so sure. I think you'd look great in it."

Philip looks at the two women, irked that he is not the focus. He is anxious to bring the conversation back to him, and his pivotal position in last night's cavortings. He notices that Rupert is filming the meal, and leans across the table jovially.

"I hope you're not swapping girly tips about last night, my dear," he says. Why not? He can say anything. He's not in reality. He's in televisual heaven.

"What a pity our friend Jane had to leave late last night," he continues, leering at Cresta.

She looks at him steadily.

"We are talking about swimsuits. From Zara."

"Oh do forgive me. Well, anyone might have thought you might well have been talking about... other things," says Philip loudly, nudging Alan in the ribs.

"Thanks, Philip," says Alan testily, brushing spilt orange juice from his arm.

"Oh, the things I found out last night," continues Philip desperately.

221

The two women look at him.

"Yeah, Alan," says Philip. He suddenly opens his mouth and mimes removing a hair from one of his teeth.

"Who knew history has come full circle! It's bye-bye to the Brazilian! Who could have expected it?"

Gemma looks at him, incredulous. "That man is just unbearable," she mutters to nobody in particular. "Sorry, Cresta," she says, raising her voice but only so the other woman can hear her, "you may have had fun last night but honestly I can't listen to anything more from this... this creep. And who does he think he is? Thinks he's funny but he's really not."

"What are you going on about?" says Alan. He gets up and goes over to the buffet table. He really is not in the mood to indulge this man and his ridiculous personality any more. He is already dreading bumping into him, as he surely must, when they are back in their home neighbourhood.

"Oh I don't know," says Philip, miming the action again, and turning it into a flossing motion between his front teeth. "Girls today."

Gemma has had enough. She stands up, grabs a large jug of iced water and empties it across the table all over Philip. The water cascades over his head, his shoulders, his arms. It floods his plate and drenches his knees. Thin circles of cucumber stick to his chest. Ice drops down onto the table. There is silence. Philip looks at Gemma, his eyes blazing.

"You little bitch!"

"Well, how dare you!" retorts Gemma. She is still standing. She doesn't know why this programme is changing her, but it is. She would never behave like this back in the UK. Now however, it is apparently second nature to empty the nearest glass, jug, whatever, over her nearest companion.

"How dare you. How dare you be such a... child. I really don't care what you get up to, Philip, and with whom. As long as it's not me. And I don't care whether it's in your room, or wherever. But to talk like this... with such... with disdain, you should be ashamed of yourself. You are pathetic." She sits down again.

"Disdain? Quite the opposite, my dear. Cresta is a wonderful woman, aren't you?"

Cresta laughs. "Yep."

Gemma leans across the table, hissing the words out of her mouth. She is actually shaking with rage.

"Women can do whatever the hell they like to their bodies, alright? Just keep your schoolboy prejudices to yourself. Do us all a favour. We simply don't care. Nobody cares."

"Oooh, quite the little feminist, aren't you!" is all Philip can muster by return.

Cresta stands up.

"Thanks, Gemma. You know, Philip, I agree. I've never thought this through before but everyone has a point. All the way. Get with the programme, Grandad. And live and let live, alright? Hey, Gemms, let's go for a swim. Have you got your swimsuit on under that t-shirt? Have you? Come on then, leave it to this lot to clear up."

Cresta nudges Gemma as they walk off together. "He couldn't get it up last night anyway," she says loudly over her shoulder.

Rupert crouches down, carefully framing their exit in his lens. His shoulders are shaking with laughter.

In the distance, the doorbell jangles.

Gemma slides into the cool green water and leans forward to start her breaststroke amid the rushes. She glides past the foliage and kicks her legs lazily. Cresta comes up beside her with a busy doggy-paddle.

"I am such a bloody crap swimmer, Gemma."

"Sorry about that just then, Cresta? Did you mind that I got so cross?"

"S'alright. Nah, you're fine. What a total pillock."

Gemma laughs, chokes on some water and turns easily onto her back.

The doorbell jangles again.

Sighing, Philip goes to answer it.

Gilda stands on the doorstep surveying her drenched husband.

"What on earth are you doing here?" says Philip.

This is not what Gilda had expected.

"I came to see you," she says loudly, swinging her hair. She has had long blonde extensions put in and is wearing a pink ballet dress with a frilly petticoat.

She smiles at the cameras and points to Philip.

"My husband! Why are you so wet, my sweet dove?"

"Long story. Look, I've got to get changed. Sit down there," he says, pointing to a chair in the living room.

"Rupert, Simon, my wife."

He pads away grimly.

"Hello guys!" waves Gilda to the crew. "I'm his WIFE, can you believe it?"

"We're doing our best," says Rupert under his breath.

"How, er how did you find out where we are?" asks Simon.

"Belle told me. She's working with Jane. And I think Jane was here last night, was she not?"

"What is your name, again?" Simon replies. "Gilda? And you are married to Philip, yes? Look, love, its our last day of filming." He sees her face fall and puts his arm round her.

"When Philip is changed, he'll walk you down the drive so you can get a taxi back to your hotel."

"Really? Can't I be in the show, just a little bit?"

He looks at her special outfit. He feels so sorry for her.

"Why don't you come to the cast party tomorrow night? We won't be filming but you can meet everyone," he says kindly.

Gemma is laughing so hard in the pool she is almost choking.

"Pillock. I haven't heard that word for years. But he is. Completely. Pillock number One. What on earth happened last night, then?"

"Nothing!" says Cresta.

"Really? What about Jane?"

"Ha ha! Jane, poor lamb. She was so nervous. We had a bit of a kiss and a bit of a feel, and a bit of a strip off, but that was about it. It was fun. But that was all."

"What on earth was Philip on about?"

"I've no idea! He couldn't manage it. He looked at us two girls as if he was about to turn into the fuckin' Cheshire Cat, but there was no movement in the old boy. You know, in the old boy's old boy. Sad, really."

"What the hell was all that tooth flossing about then for Christ's sake? I feel a bit bad now for getting him totally wet. He looked as if he had never known anything like it."

"I know what he was meaning with the flossing, silly man. It's because I have a lady garden in full bloom, you know? Can't be doing with those Brazilians. Very dated. Anyway, he went down on me, of course he did, but it was hardly anything. I mean, I did it to help him out. You know, like a charity fuck. You know?"

"I don't actually, but I'll take your word for it, Cresta," says Gemma, laughing again.

"Where was Jane when this… charitable action was taking place?"

"Oh I don't know. I think she might have left, yes I think she had gone by then. She was just desperate to have it away with another girl. So once she was sorted out, by yours truly, she fled. With a big smile on her face, of course."

Gemma rolls her eyes. She is fascinated by Cresta's candour and relaxed demeanour, even concerning the most intimate of actions. She glances over at the terrace, which is empty. Everyone seems to have disappeared.

"Was that a… piece of charity work by you too, Cresta?"

"You could call it that," says Cresta, good-naturedly.

"She was just so desperate. Married women often are. Shall we get out? Or are we training to swim the fuckin' Channel?"

"Yes, of course. But Cresta, tell me, why? Why do you do this?"

225

"Because I can't be arsed not to."

"Does Moo know?"

"I don't know if he knows. I don't tell him and he doesn't struggle to find out. It's just easier that way. And you know, Gemms, it's fun. And it feels good. Usually."

Cresta pulls herself out of the pool with a surprisingly muscular action and slips her feet back into the translucent heels, sitting down on a chair. Water streams off her sculpted body. Gemma looks at her, fascinated.

She swims over to the small ladder and climbs out of the pool, trotting slowly to her room for a towel, treading carefully down the corridor so as not to slip, not even noticing Gilda in the living room.

For the first time since she has been in the house she's not bothered about winning the show. Or how she looks to the cameras. She doesn't care about any of it. She cares deeply about two people she has met here, and that's enough for her. She has a warm sense of triumph within her belly. She opens the door and runs into her en-suite.

"Come here you warrior," says Alan, opening his arms.

"Oh my God you made me jump!" says Gemma. "How the hell did you get in here?"

"You left the door open. Do you know how fantastic that was this morning? Do you? You are quite amazing, and you have got more amazing the more this madness has continued."

"I know. You know I thought we had reached a sort of rock bottom with that disgusting postcard from that Brazilian... the footballer, what was his name?"

"Oh, yes, him."

"But we clearly hadn't. I feel I've learned a lot about human behaviour on this trip. More than I had bargained for. Good and bad. Alan?"

"Yes, what," he says.

"I know you don't care about this show, and nor do I, so I think I am going to vote for Cresta tonight. Will you vote for her as well?"

226

"As long as that twerp Burrell leaves I don't care. I'd like you to win but I salute your generosity. Now, I want to do something with you which I have been thinking about for a long time."

"I think I know what that is," says Gemma, smiling.

Chapter Thirty-Three
Jane

Jane lies in bed beside Patrick. She drums her fingers happily on his solid body and yawns. She was in the reality show, she was in the reality show. She knows she is in the show, and also that she won't be cut out of it. Then there was the…other stuff. She's trying not to think about that, but not because she is horrified by it. Quite the opposite. Jane is holding back the memory of being on Philip's bed with Cresta for something to savour when she is on the sun lounger. What a triumph. What an adventure. At least now she won't worry about dying without having ever gone to bed with another woman.

Alright, it didn't go on for all that long, and it was a bit awkward with Philip being there. He had just sat there in his chair, trying to bring himself to life. And failing. That was embarrassing, Jane thinks. For him. However she suspects that his performance, or lack of it, meant that he would never, ever bring the moment up when they were all back in the UK. In reality. She knows her secret is safe with him. Why do they call such programmes reality shows, wonders Jane, when they are actually fantasies? Well, it was one of her fantasies answered. She had needed to tick that box. What a night.

She thinks about Cresta's body. What the woman had done to her. With her. Splashes coming from the poolside indicate Belle and George are already up. She hopes they are having a good holiday too. It's been a great holiday for Jane, and she credits herself on achieving almost every aspect of it.

If she hadn't met Yasmin Bird, if she hadn't known Philip already from her home, all of it. It had all been down to her, bringing everything together.

She leans across and pokes her husband.

"Patrick. Patch. What is happening today?"

"Belle's parents. Remember?"

Her mood suddenly descends into irritation.

"Oh for goodness sake. No. Please say no."

"We can't, Jane. We agreed. We can't change it now."

He was right. Belle had asked if Larry and Tracey, her parents, might come and collect her a day before her duties with George were up. They had been on holiday in Majorca and had changed their flights so they could come back via Ibiza. Jane had reluctantly agreed that that would be fine. It wasn't quite the group she had intended on entertaining but they would do. She was actually looking forward to telling someone who watched television that she had made it onto the reality show. Her body warmed up just thinking about the excitement of it all.

"Patch?"

"Uh-huh?"

"Do Larry and Tracey know Philip and Alan from back home? I rather think they do."

"Of course they do. At least, they should."

"Why don't we invite them over too?"

"Who, Philip and Alan?"

"Why not?" Jane sits up in bed, suddenly excited.

"We could have the television cameras over as well, it would be amazing."

"Jane, not everything needs to be seen via a television camera. Of course we can't have those two round for dinner. They are locked into a reality show half a mile up the road."

"That's the whole point. We could invite the show itself over."

"Not in a million years darling. I'm quite happy without

any cameras. Anyway, we have already done our thing with the show. We have had quite enough of that lot. Well I have, at least."

"You are a spoilsport, you know."

"I'm not," says Patrick, suddenly turning over, pushing his hair out of his eyes. "I am a very tolerant person and I let you do whatever you like, whenever you like. You should be grateful that I'm around."

"Well maybe I wish that you were a bit more demanding," says Jane, pouting. "I'm getting up."

"Are you going back to Yoga or whatever?"

"Nah. I've had enough of Yasmin Bird," says Jane. "I thought I'd stay here for the day. Play with George and hang out with Belle until her parents arrive." So they can see we are having a happy family time, thinks Jane.

"You do know her boyfriend is coming over today too."

"What? No, no I didn't know at all. What the hell? We aren't paying her to have a fun time with her boyfriend."

"Jane, please think this through. Think what a fuss Belle could make on the Square when we all get home. Relax and just calm down."

"Alright, but honestly."

Jas turns up at around midday, standing awkwardly by the gate and speaking down the intercom to Patrick.

"Hi, oh… hi, it's Jas here. For Belle. And, er the rest of you. Hi."

The doors swing open and he walks in. He is wearing rolled up jeans and flip-flops.

"Hey."

"Hi Jas," says Belle, hugging him warmly, kissing him chastely on the cheek. "This is George."

"I know. Remember me from home? Had any more escapes since the last one?"

George laughs and hides behind Belle.

"Well I've been walking all over the island since we tried to find you, but I haven't found any more eight year olds."

230

"Do you know how to play Uno?" George says.

"I certainly do," says Jas. "I play it with my little brother all the time. I always beat him. Do you want to be thrashed?"

"Yes, I do," says George happily.

When Larry and Tracey turn up they see their daughter sitting on a towel, playing Uno beside the pool with Jas and George.

"Belle!" Tracey runs over to her.

Tracey is fully dressed for the day as befits a woman who sells make-up products across the UK. Her face is carefully adorned with shimmering powder and pink lipstick, her hair in a French plait down her back. She is wearing a simple dress with tiny straps and an even tinier skirt.

"Mum, you look a bit dressed up," says Belle, who is wearing a long white t-shirt and a pair of man's boxer shorts over her red swimsuit.

"Oh, well, you know, Ibiza and everything," says Tracey. "Hello Jane," she says, waving across the pool, "what a perfect villa this is, how lucky you are. You look like you have really caught the sun here, I do hope Belle has been helpful, I hope you have had some real relaxation time," she says in a giant list of questions and statements which are never going to be properly answered.

"Tracey," is all that Jane will say, coming over and vaguely kissing the atmosphere around Tracey's face, twice, before turning and waving to the kitchen. "Drinks?"

Larry, a large man who spends most of his time finding life hilarious and expressing this sentiment, pads off in the direction of the kitchen and the fridge.

"Patrick, a beer would be just the job, ha ha ha," says Larry. "Bet you didn't think you'd be getting the boyfriend too, but maybe a role model for George isn't a bad thing, ha ha ha," he says.

"Yes, well we weren't aware that Jas was actually in Ibiza at all when this holiday began," says Jane pointedly. "But I think he arrived later, and as things turned out, it was very good that he was, and he was able to help us with a small… a small episode earlier in the week, but anyway I found George on my own, didn't I George?"

"Oh yes, Belle texted us about that. Quite a day, from all accounts," says Tracey.

"Oh but did she say what happened then?" says Jane excitedly.

"No, what?"

Jane turns on Belle in amazement.

"Belle. Didn't you tell them about the show?"

"Er, no, no I didn't actually. Do you mean that TV stuff?"

"Yes of course I do," says Jane, exasperated. "Well," she continues, beaming at her new guests, "I have found my way onto a reality TV show, of all things. Who could have thought it? Coming your way on BBC Television very soon. Starring yours truly."

"Yes, isn't that the one I told you about?" says Tracey slowly. "You know with Philip Burrell and Alan, from the Square?"

Jane looks at her sharply, suddenly remembers that text when they were still in England.

"That's the one. I was on it! Can you believe it?!"

"Daytime," says Patrick waggishly. "On some weird channel called Channel M."

Jane glares at him.

"Yes, well never mind. It's not some minor cable thing. It's going to be repeated on the BBC, you know. It's mainstream. And I'm on it."

"So am I," pipes up George. "So is Francesco Villa."

"In a minor way," says his mother. "Very minor. I'm the one on the helicopter, yes, there's a helicopter in the show and you'll never guess but I am in it, and you know with whom?"

"Er, no," says Tracey, who is longing for a Diet Coke and hoping that Jane might stop talking about television and offer her one.

"Philip Burrell!!"

Jane breaks off into hysterical laughter, then suddenly remembers the potentially compromising state she and Philip had found themselves in last night, and calms down quickly.

"Yes, a wonderful man. Pioneering contemporary creative. I think he may well win the show, which would be great for us wouldn't it?"

"Why, exactly?" says Patrick.

Jane looks at him, annoyed. "Because, darling, it would be so good for us at home in the Square. To have a famous TV personality living there, it would be great. Might put the house prices up."

"We have one already, don't we?" says Tracey.

"Do you mean Alan Makin? Well I have news for you on THAT point too, because from the looks of it, he hit it off with a celebrity estate agent on the show. Hilarious!" '

Tracey has had something of a history with Alan and isn't too keen to have his name mentioned in any capacity. She makes a fervent, silent promise to herself that she will never watch this show.

"Jane, do you think I could have a drink perhaps?"

And they all move to the table on the terrace, where lunch has been laid.

Jane brings out a giant pan of paella. It is festooned with shrimp and slices of lemon, and packed with glistening rice, brown crispy legs of chicken and bright cherry tomatoes.

"My word!" says Larry. "I'm famished. This is wonderful."

"Did you prepare this for us?" gushes Tracey. "You are too kind."

"Well, I didn't actually. I got it from the market down the road. Sorry!"

If you think I am going to cook you food, you parents of the girl I have employed and you, the scummy boyfriend, you have another think coming, considers Jane, heaping up spoonfuls and almost throwing them onto the brightly coloured Ibizan crockery.

There is a pause as Tracey and Larry try to smile away the insult.

"Belle, could you pass these plates around?" You're still employed today, love.

Mind you, thinks Jane, if I hadn't had Belle to do all that Uno and Lego stuff with George, then I would have just missed out. All the way.

"Are your parents on holiday too?" Tracey asks Jas nicely.

"Nah. They usually go skiing in France later in the year."

"Of course," says Tracey. "I know your mum is a whizz down the slopes."

"Do they really?" asks Jane incredulously. She knows Jas and his brother live on the nearby council estate.

"Yes, why?"

"Well, I just thought... no reason really," says Jane.

"Too posh for them?"

"No, not at all! I'm just surprised, that's all."

"Well, Dad's a bit here and there on the work front, but my mum's business brings in a lot of cash these days. So many treatments, particularly in the summer. So they go away every winter."

"What does your mother do?" asks Patrick. "What sort of treatments?"

"She runs a spa. Nails, facials, eyebrows, that sort of thing. They're not the big earner, however."

"What is the spa called?" asks Jane, with a slight feeling of anxiety.

"Love Your Body," says Jas. "It's on the High Street."

"What is the big earner?" Patrick persists.

"Brazilians of course. In the summer. You know, when women get all the hair ripped off their..."

"Yes, we all know what a Brazilian is, thank you Jas," says Jane pertly. "Please remember George is here."

"Is it a Brazilian like Fernando Villa is a Brazilian?" pipes up George.

"No, it is very much not, sweetie," says Belle, laughing.

"We met Fernando Villa," says George to Jas.

"I know you did. I saw him as well, walking through town. What a legend."

"He was awesome," says George, remembering the moment as if it had been a miraculous visitation from a god.

"Love Your Body," muses Patrick. "On the High Street. Isn't that where you go, love?"

"It might be… no I don't think it is," says Jane, all at once remembering the woman in a white coat telling her about her son who was off to Ibiza. As she was in the very act of waxing her groin. So, it had all been planned. Weeks before. He was probably on the very same flight. What a little snake that girl Belle was.

"If it is, then you might have met my mum," says Jas proudly.

"Well, I don't think it is," snaps Jane. "More paella, anyone?"

After lunch, Jas and Belle slip away, walking around the pool and looking at the view over the blue hills past giant creamy bushes of blossoming oranges and pinks.

"That might be us in a few years," says Jas. "Could be."

"What?"

"Well, you know. Us. On a family holiday. With a kid. Married."

"Never," says Belle.

"Oh, thanks. Cheers for that. I'll pack my bag now," says Jas, with a languid smile.

"I don't mean as in us, us together. I mean never married."

"Don't you want to marry me?"

"Is that a proposal?"

"No. Well maybe it is. Will you marry me?"

"No. Live with you, yes. Love you forever, yes. But marry you? My parents aren't married, remember. Now I know why. Have you seen what marriage does to people?"

She gestures over to the terrace where her employers are sitting, drinking, presenting, flaunting themselves as a perfect domestic setup to the other couple in a competition hinged upon a subtle notion of wealth and happiness.

"Alright. Kiss me then," says Jas.

Chapter Thirty-Four
Cresta

There were no tears, no fond farewells. As the taxi pulled up to collect Philip from the front of the villa, Simon found himself having to direct the two cameramen in a rather awkward fashion.

"Can't show that nobody has come to wave him off," he whispers to Rupert. "Frame it so it works."

"Fair enough. But he has been a complete tit," mutters Rupert, almost to himself. He squats down and frames Philip very tightly, so that all the viewer will see·is Philip shaking Robin the driver by the hand, and leaping very quickly into the taxi.

"He'll be fine. His wife is waiting just around the corner. Nice old bird," says Simon.

Alex, the second cameraman, is already in the taxi, prepared to catch Philip's thoughts on leaving the show.

"How do you feel about leaving the show, Philip?" asks Alex.

"Absolutely top-hole old thing," says Philip, but his flushed demeanour suggests otherwise.

"No, really. If you could speak in actual English it would be good, if you don't mind."

"I feel fine, fine," says Philip angrily. "Top fucking hole."

"Cut," says Alex wearily. "Start again, Philip please."

"I mean, it was time. I'd had enough. Whole experience

237

was marvellous of course and very exciting. What is there to complain about? Nothing. Nothing. But I was getting weary. I was weary of being in the constant glare of the cameras. And you know, I didn't want to win. I don't need to win."

He leans forward to Alex and looks straight down the camera lens.

"I don't NEED to win. I have enough going on in my life already. I wanted a taste of popular culture and the television world and that's enough for me. Done it. Got the t-shirt, so to speak, not that I will ever actually wear it, but Memory Lane and all that crap. I'll go back to my studio now."

"Sadder and wiser?" says Alex.

"Not a bit of it!" says Philip. He is determined not to give that creep Simon and his own bitter rival and neighbour Alan Makin the satisfaction of seeing him rueful and depressed. Never. He would actually rather lose a thousand pounds than do that. Ten thousand.

"Sad about no prize money?"

"Ha ha ha," says Philip. "I can't wait to see my wife and friends. Let's just say I will carry on my work in my studio and I think I'll be fine." Cheeky.

"Gutted that you won't be on the front of the *Radio Times*?"

That did it. His mother's favourite periodical. The title of his childhood. Him, on the cover. It would have been so great.

"Just take me to the fucking airport."

"Cut," says Alex.

The taxi speeds out of the drive and turns a sharp right, to collect Gilda who is standing on the corner of the street.

"This is like an actual holiday, now," says Gemma, laughing.

"Can you believe that nobody went out the front of the house to see that prat leave?" says Cresta. They are all sitting out at the back, by the organic pond.

"I don't find it hard to believe at all, you know," murmurs Alan. "Well. He's old enough and ugly enough to cope. He won't care anyway. He probably won't even notice. He only notices things that boost his own colossal ego. Everything else is simply filtered out."

Gemma sips her sparkling water.

"I don't want to leave this house, you know."

"You've been saying that you couldn't wait to leave since you arrived, Gemma my dear."

"Oh I know, but then was quite different. That was all about not losing this stupid show. Not being voted out by one's peers. Now it's about just enjoying hanging with you guys."

There is a pause. Wind ruffles the water on the organic pond and makes the bullrushes sway slightly.

"Yeah, well that makes rubbish TV you know," says Cresta nicely.

"Well," says Alan grandly. "I think what I have learned more than anything over the last week, is that adults are frankly totally useless at living alongside one another. We are all alright for, say, a couple of hours. A day, maybe. But anything more? Forget it. Everyone is locked into their own agendas, whether it be donkey management or magic. Or, as with Philip, himself. No matter how bizarre our life calling may be, we are all running along our specific train tracks and we can't get off them. Children can. But we can't."

"Thus ends the First Lesson of Reality Television," says Gemma. "From the expert."

"I'm right. I know I am, from the evidence of this week. Aren't I Cresta? You're the doyenne of this genre more than me. You should know."

"Yeah, I guess so. Still, it's a laugh."

"Everything is a laugh to you."

"Yes, it is. That's my life pattern. That's my train track. A laugh, with sex thrown in."

Cresta was, as ever, quite right. Three people chatting quietly by the pool, all getting on famously, makes terrible television. Simon was obliged to lay off Alex and joined them for supper. Rupert was allowed to put his camera down and remained skulking around the kitchen, just in case something happened.

They talk about the week just passed, remembering favourite moments.

"Water. Fire. Earth. Air. You guys did it all," says Simon to them, raising his glass.

"The worst was water, no question," says Gemma. "Although fire was pretty dreadful too. Poor old Jasper. Do you remember his face when his feet were burned and he had to stand in a bucket?"

"My favourite thing was that donkey. And finding the little boy. That was so special," says Cresta. "Alan?" They both look at him.

"Now. This is the best moment. Now that nobody cares. And now that there is no jeopardy. Although I sort of miss the Adventurous Parents."

"How can you say that, Alan?" screams Gemma, laughing, throwing a bread roll at him.

"That Nigel was appalling."

"I'm going to miss having all my meals cooked for me and my room cleaned for me. I'm going to miss being called a celebrity and being driven around." Gemma pauses. "Imagine it happening to you for the rest of your life."

"Infantile," says Alan, who has long become used to being on the celebrity Z list, and has given up yearning for promotion.

"Well you are still celebrities for a night," says Simon, "and as such, I have to take your votes." He hands out the formal slips, which they all fill in privately at the table. He gathers them in, stands up. "I'll be back in a minute."

He's as good as his word. After 60 seconds, he's back on the terrace, Rupert filming him by his side.

"Cresta, will you come here please."

She gasps with pleasure, pushes her braided and beaded hair back from her shoulders and slips away from the table into the lounge where the door shuts behind her.

Gemma looks at Alan.

"Oh well. Neither of us did it." She puts her hand fondly on his thigh.

"Doesn't matter though, does it?"

"Of course not. It was all down to you anyway."

"Really?"

"Yes, really. You got a voice. You already had it, but it gained such volume here. If you hadn't thrown that jug of water over Philip, if you didn't care how other people are treated, and judged, and mocked, then this wouldn't have happened. You were the crucial element to this entire show."

"All over a Brazilian. Madness."

"Do you mean Francesco Villa or…"

"Both!"

"You were crucial in both stories."

"Was I? It didn't feel like it at times."

"Well, you wait and see until it airs."

"I am dreading that."

"You shouldn't. You are an inspiration."

They turn around to see Cresta, a crown on her head, advancing in her favourite translucent high sandals onto the terrace. Rupert crouches down, filming her as she walks to the pool.

Alex, who has been dragged out of his room, films Gemma and Alan's reactions to this. They applaud her warmly.

She gets up onto the pool, slipping out of the high sandals as she does it, carefully taking the crown from off her head and turning around slowly to reveal every element of the sequinned, high cut, zippered one-piece with strategic holes cut to show off her brown, transcribed belly.

"That must be swimsuit number 300," whispers Gemma.

Cresta turns around, delighted. She's won the money. She knew she would win this show. How she would do it, she had no idea. But she's done it. She shrugs and winks at the camera.

"Ibiza… or bust!" she says, and leaps into the organic pond.

Chapter Thirty-Five
Simon

Why they all want to come to the screening party at his house in London, Simon has no idea. He texts Kate.

I only vaguely suggested it on Twitter. Don't you think they would all want to watch it with their own friends over a drink? Why the hell do they all want to get back together again? They hated one another by the end! Do you remember how unpopular Philip Burrell made himself! Even though we thought his wife was rather sweet. Amazing.

There's no accounting for people who want to be on TV is Kate's response.

Simon puts his phone down and wanders around his living room. He has put together a 'Director's Cut' of the show, a bespoke screening to be shown before Episode One is aired this afternoon. He hopes the contestants will enjoy it; there's been a lot of pre-publicity before today. Cresta looked good on that week's *Radio Times* cover, he had to admit, although he doesn't think anyone has ever had the nerve to show so much tattooed flesh before and worn underwear cut so high. Oh well. Let the editor deal with grumpy letters. Come to think of it, the amount of cleavage Cresta is showing on the cover will probably boost sales rather than anything else. He's glad she won. It will do wonders for her career and not go to her head. He has an abiding respect for Cresta. He considers her as a person who knows her value and markets it with impressive direction.

He looks at the food and drink he has set out. It doesn't feel right to be shoving canapés and Prosecco at people in the early afternoon, but Simon knows the protocol of TV screenings. Whatever the time of day it is, you have to have bits of salmon on tiny pancakes, and fizz of course.

The bell rings. Right, thinks Simon. This is it. This is the last time I will have to share a room with these people. Or even look at them. Actually, this is the last time I will have to deal, ever, with another show in the series. If it's re-commissioned they can bloody well find someone else to deal with it, even if they have to go to bloody China to get them.

He opens the door. On the step are Jane, Patrick and George.

Oh, Christ. He'd forgotten about this lot. Who even invited them?

"Hi, hi, how lovely to see you," Simon manages to say. How did she even know this was going on, he thinks. Who asked them? Of course. Her neighbours are on the programme. And Twitter. Cheers, social media.

"Thanks so much for coming," he says. He can never remember this woman's bloody name.

"We've moved back into the Square, you know, where we live alongside Alan Makin and lovely old Philip Burrell. Are they here, are they all here? They urged me to come along, I think they said they wouldn't miss it for the world," says Jane in a rush. She was so pushy. He'd never experienced anything like it. Well, she'll be gutted when she sees how many minutes she has ended up commanding on the show, thinks Simon.

Patrick nudges his wife. "Jane, please. Calm down. I'm sure they will all be here and if not, that's just fine. It's very nice to see you again, Simon."

Simon is just grateful that Patrick has reminded him what her bloody name is again. Jane. Of course.

Jane beams at him and waves a giant bunch of lilies.

"For you."

"Oh, thank you, you shouldn't have really," begins Simon.

She puts up a hand. "No. Thanks to you. For taking the risk and for making me a star on your show."

Christ almighty, thinks Simon, taking the lilies cautiously and mentally consigning them to a bucket in the washroom, since he doesn't own a vase. Star? Low-level dread creeps around his belly as he thinks about how she has been edited in *Ibiza (or Bust)*. The few minutes she is actually on screen do not present her at her best. Weeping, then drooling over her son. Cackling at the dinner table. Gurning to the camera. She's going to sue me for misrepresentation, he thinks. If only he'd had some warning that she was going to show up. He wonders if there is time for him to edit various elements out of the Director's Cut and as swiftly, dismisses the thought. Oh to hell with it, thinks Simon. Just accept the fire. He's going to be doing a *Dispatches* next season, anyway. On global warming.

"Nice to see you, kiddo," he says to George, awkwardly ruffling his hair. He hasn't seen the child since that appalling moment in the mobile home when they all arrived and ruined the afternoon of Lego play. Poor thing. Having a mother like that and being an only child, so not even a sibling to side with.

"Yes," says George noncommittally. He has agreed to come to this adults-only event only on the understanding that he will be allowed to go over to see Jack and Sam later on. Since they moved back into their old home his visits to see his friends have been drastically reduced, and he misses them. Particularly as he knows they have just taken acquisition of Lego Tower Bridge.

"Let me just go and deal with these flowers."

They all arrive, of course. Bar Cresta.

Jane had sidled up to him, laughing. "Is Cresta coming today, do you know?" she said, and looked very relieved when Simon told her she wasn't. Simon looks at his celebrities/nonentities.

After initial cries and hugs, they eventually all settle down around the television, laughing, moving up for one another on the sofa, handing out the drinks and generally looking like a collection of old university or work friends who haven't seen each other for years, and are simply delighted to be back in the pack once more. It's all about shared experience and that bond of having been there, thinks Simon as he watches Jasper dealing out cards for Jocelyn, again. The crew have also sloped up.

"They imagine they are all still around the pool, don't they?" he mutters to Rupert.

"I know," says Rupert grimly. "What a fortnight. Brings it all back, and not in a good way."

Simon knows Cresta isn't here because she is doing a Q&A at BAFTA before the main screening of the first episode, but he keeps this information from the rest of the cast.

"Where's Cresta?" says Philip languidly.

Simon can barely look at him, but he does his best to be civil.

"I think she's unwell," he says.

Philip, who is wearing a suit made out of faux patchwork pieces sprayed with artificial glitter, smiles knowingly.

"I think that's highly unlikely, old bean," he says.

Oh, shut the hell up with your Noel Coward posturing, thinks Simon.

"Oooh that's a shame," says Gilda. She plumps herself down beside her husband and arranges layers of silver tulle around her thin knees. She is dressed today as a raindrop, apparently. Simon rather wishes she had been on the show instead of her husband.

"I loved her interview in the *Mail*. Did you see that darling?" she says to Philip.

"No."

"She's never off Twitter," says Gemma, smiling at Gilda over her glass of fizz.

It's true. Since Cresta's win on *Ibiza (or Bust)* and the attendant pre-publicity for the programme, her star has been truly shining.

"Lovely girl," says Jocelyn. "Wasn't she, Nigel?"

245

"Oh, don't call her a girl," says Nigel, "particularly in present company." He points over to Gemma who pretends she hasn't heard.

Gemma sits beside Alan. After a few minutes, she creeps her hand over to his and holds it.

"Are you okay?" he whispers to her.

"Yes, fine. I'm quite excited actually," she whispers back.

Simon senses it's time to bring everyone together, and stands up, tapping a glass as he does so.

"Celebrities, welcome. It's truly astonishing to see you all, and even more surprising to see you all still speaking to one another. Thank you for making it today." There is laughter.

"Before the show properly starts on BBC, I want to show you a little compilation I have made of some of my favourite moments. I hope you enjoy it."

As he sits down, hoping Jane has to suddenly rush to the bathroom for at least twenty minutes, the doorbell rings.

"I'll pause it," says Simon.

"I'll go!" says George, running to the door. He opens it to find, to his joy, none other than Francesco Villa standing nonchalantly on the doorstep.

"Wow!" says George. "Every time I open the door, it's like you are standing outside! Sick!"

"*Ola*," says Francesco, ruffling George's hair and stepping into the house. "How are the keepie-uppies?"

"Oh, great, great," beams George, astounded that this person has recognised him.

Francesco turns and waves to a person in a long black car outside.

"See you in an hour, yes?" he shouts to the car.

"Now, George, can I come in?"

"Wow!" says George again. He trots ahead of Francesco, opening the door to the living room with a flourish. "Only the Champions League star," he shouts.

"My goodness," says Simon, slightly flustered and thinking urgently about whether he has enough food and drink, and whether he ever informed Francesco's people about today, "to what do we owe the pleasure? Aren't you meant to be in Madrid?"

"Oh no," says Francesco easily. "I was over here doing some press. And my people found out that you were holding a little morning viewing. So I thought I'd come and join you."

"Of course, of course," says Simon, inwardly marvelling yet again at the power and precision of Francesco's 'people'. "Kate, can you get a chair for Francesco, Francesco can I offer you some Prosecco? It's only Prosecco, of course, but still…"

Francesco holds up a hand. "No, no. Water is all I drink. You know, I am a sportsman. Not a donkey handler!"

Simon laughs, remembering in the instant about Francesco's card. He wonders whether Gemma is having the same thoughts. He fervently hopes she is not.

Gemma looks across the room at Francesco. He catches her eye and offers her a mock salute across the room. She smiles briefly and looks away.

"Arse," she whispers to Alan.

"Still can't believe that he sent me that card of his, well you know."

"Did we ever find out whether it was his or not?"

"No we did not," she says firmly, and then smiles at him.

"What a mad fortnight that was. It all seemed to make sense then. It's only now that it seems so ludicrous."

"What was your favourite moment of the show?"

"Meeting you, of course."

"No, Alan, really."

"Really."

"You mean it?"

"Yep. I will never forget you, striding across the dining room on that first morning, dressed in a lovely yellow outfit, shouting at Simon for calling you a girl."

"Oh, God. I don't know why that made me so cross. I was so nervous."

"Forcing me to go and wake up bloody Philip who was stark bollock naked."

She covers her mouth, because she is laughing so loudly.

"What was your favourite moment?"

"Well, apart from meeting you, of course, because now I have to say that since you have said it first, I would say it was... I think giving Simon a bollocking after nearly drowning, with you, on that bloody raft race. Do you remember?"

He nods happily. "It wasn't all THAT bad was it?"

"Yes it bloody well was," says Gemma, giggling.

Elsewhere people are having similar conversations.

"What was your favourite moment, my darling on the show?" says Gilda to Patrick. He looks at her, momentarily editing out the indelible memory from his brain when Cresta suddenly unleashed her enhanced, spectacular breasts from their golden cage and allowed him to suck one of them.

"Seeing you on the doorstep of the house of course. And going home with you."

"Do you mean it?"

"I most certainly do," he says.

Simon looks at them all, marvelling that through the alchemy of time, things which seemed so catastrophically dreadful now seem nostalgically wonderful; the rows over rooms, the arguments about Burro the donkey, Jasper getting his feet burned, the dreadful moments when someone had to leave the show. It wasn't just time, he knows. It was also the experience of being cast out from life and being put into a microcosm of it, without any outside influence, which has bound them all together. He thinks they will be joined together for as long as they live. He knows it. They will never forget their fortnight with him in Ibiza. Is this something to be proud of? He only wishes it were.

Jane is very contented. She is sitting amid the celebrity cast of a show that she is actually part of. People will start recognising her on the bus. Plus, a huge footballing star is there alongside her. She waves over at Francesco.

"Hello! I'm the mother of George, you know, the little boy who was lost for a very very short time. He's a big fan."

"Kidnapped, you mean," says Francesco severely.

"Oh no, no," laughs Jane, "not at all."

"Oh yes," says Francesco. "I've read the press releases."

"What press releases?" says Jane. "Simon, are there press releases?"

Simon does not want to go into this now. He motions to Jane to be quiet.

"I'll speak to you about it later," he signs. "Show's about to start."

She sighs and wishes it had been different. If only she had got to know Francesco Villa before he had been unveiled and left the show. He might have hit on her as he apparently did to that silly mouse Gemma. She looks over at Gemma and smiles falsely at her.

The show begins. Within about five minutes Jane wishes she was falling through the earth never to be seen again. She's so grotesque! She looks so fat, for a start. God, she had never thought she was so fat. That belly! And she had always thought she had good legs. Why had never anyone told her that her thighs were so large? And her face, that couldn't really be her face, could it? It was so wrinkled! She looks like someone's mother. Middle-aged. Alright, she is a mother, she is George's mother but why are there so many awful shots of her, showing her with make-up running down her face, her lipstick all wrongly applied and, oh my God, thinks Jane, is that a sweat mark under her armpit? She feels sick and sad. Standing on screen next to Cresta, who somehow always manages to look beautiful – even though Jane thought she had far too much make-up on – she looks particularly drab.

"This is terrible," she whispers to Patrick. "I look like a middle-aged woman. Please can we leave?"

"It's fine darling," he whispers back. "Shush. You are a middle-aged woman."

"But Patrick I look terrible, just appalling. Can't you see?"

"You look just like you, darling. It's fine. It's reality television. I still love you. You are terrific."

She looks up at him.

"Patch, you are the best. You are. I know I run you a merry dance, but to love someone who looks so hideous…"

"Don't be a moron."

Patrick tries to concentrate on the screen but all he can think of is the real fear which he recalls gripping him when they had lost George, and his monumental relief when it was discovered that he had just gone to play with his friends. He doesn't really like thinking about that moment, much. He looks forward to this party being over and having the chance to go home, back to their own old familiar house.

Simon sits and tries to watch the shots of his cast undergoing the trials he had set them; the swimming on lilos, the walking on fire, the motorbike riding. And even the ones he hadn't set them, but they had set up for themselves; the bitching, the gossiping. The moment when Philip Burrell was pushed into the swimming pool. All said, surprisingly, he's quite proud of the peaks and troughs in this show.

"We come over quite well, you know," Alan whispers to Gemma. "Everyone looks as if they like each other."

"I will never believe another television reality show as long as I live," says Gemma. "What we are seeing on screen is so unlike how it was. However cheesy it is I have to say it. I wouldn't have met you without it, so I am deeply grateful we did it."

"Was he pushed?" says George, who is standing next to Simon's elbow. Overwhelmed by proximity to Francesco Villa, George has found sanctuary next to Simon.

"I think he might have been," whispers Simon, smiling.

"Why do people want to be on this programme?"

"I don't know, George." Simon looks at the screen, watches his candidates capering in their fish bowl. "I've been producing this show for five years and I still don't know. I think it may be because they find ordinary life just too dull. But you'll have to ask them."

George looks around at the cast who are sitting, holding hands, arms around each other, watching themselves on a giant screen with a mixture of awe and pride.

Jane has dropped her fingers from her eyes and is even smiling indulgently at the antics displayed on screen. A slowed-down sequence of Jasper performing his lemon trick makes everyone laugh.

"Do you think they would all like to have stayed in that house forever, Simon?" says George. "They all said they felt very sad when they get asked to leave. It's bad. Apart from Francesco Villa," he whispers hoarsely, "who plays in the Champions League so that's worth going back to, isn't it?"

"Yep," admits Simon.

"It's like, for everyone else apart from Francesco Villa I mean, it's like their life is heightened and made more real, than it is anyway, than it is back at home, isn't it Simon?" asks George.

Simon looks at the child as the laughter dies away.

"Yes, it is. It's bigger than reality in fact. It is like being in a fairy story."

Acknowledgements

I would like to thank my brilliant agent Cathryn Summerhayes at Curtis Brown who encouraged me to write another novel and gave me an irrestistible deadline. You are an inspiration. Everyone at Legend Press, particularly Lauren Parsons, Lucy Chamberlain and of course Tom Chalmers, thank you so much for enabling me to do it again. To Phoebe, Gabriel, Honey and Lucien. I love you, even when I'm in Hull. Pip; thanks for putting up with all of this. Finally, my gratitude to the cast and crew of Channel 4's *Celebrity Five Go To Lanzarote*. Even though I was slung off the show FIRST, I never forgot you.

Come visit us at
www.legend-press.co.uk

Follow us
@Legend_Press